CW0051743?

OBLIVION
BLACK

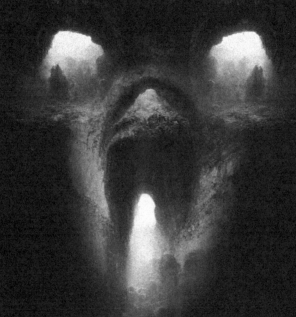

DARREN LEE FLOYD

STRATOSPHERE BOOKS

Published by

First edition published August 2020
This edition published August 2022

Cover design: Chris Nurse

Interior formatting: Mark Thomas / Coverness.com

For my gorgeous piglet Sian

"The warrior stared into the black.
He yelled his mighty war cry,
And oblivion looked back."

Traditional Athabastara song

CHAPTER 1

S am Hobson ran his fingers over the bristles on his chin and looked down at the yellow plastic telephone. He'd been staring at it for five minutes, telling himself that it wasn't going to be too bad. Hobson let out a deep sigh, scooped up the handset, and punched the number in before he chickened out. The cold plastic handset felt clammy against his ear despite the sweat running down his face. The phone rang once before it was answered. The man at the other end didn't speak; he just listened.

"I think I've found it," Hobson said in a strangled gasp.

"Think?"

"I'm sure I've found it."

The line was silent for five seconds.

"Where?"

"Alaska. It's called Black Cove."

"Give me the exact location."

Hobson did as he was told and could hear the scribble of pencil on paper on the other end. Jennings never used pens.

"I'm sending the plane. I want to see it immediately."

Hobson shook his head. He'd been awake for eighteen hours straight, but he knew it was pointless to argue.

"Okay, I'll-" The line was already dead.

*

Hobson knew better than to second-guess Joseph Jennings. He'd thought that his boss was crazy before, betting on a seemingly insane business idea only for Jennings to win big. Whether it was with the original drill bit business, which had started it all off, or the airline, Jennings had an uncanny ability to know what the next big thing was going to be. Hobson had learned to trust Jennings. He'd worked for him for a long time – just over twenty years now – having joined Jennings Tool and Bit Co. when he was seventeen. That was back when the company consisted of only ten people. His first day was burned into his mind. Hobson was surprised as he walked into a prefab building on a bit of scrubland. It was not at all what he'd expected after hearing about a business whiz kid. He'd checked the job offer letter twice just to make sure he had the right address.

Inside the office the receptionist sat behind a stack of papers, peering at her typewriter. After a moment, when she hadn't acknowledged him, he coughed and said, "Morning! I'm Sam Hobson. I'm starting work here today—or I'm supposed to be."

Just then the door shot open, and a tall, thin, handsome man with piercing green eyes barreled in.

"Who are you?" he barked at Hobson.

"I'm Sam Hobson. I'm-"

"Great! Come with me. I've got a little project for you."

The *little project* was sourcing airplanes for Jennings' new airline, and for the next six months, Hobson's feet didn't touch the ground.

Jennings had been so confident back then that Hobson found it easy to overlook his slight eccentricities, but ever since Kennedy and Khrushchev's game of chicken over Cuba in '62, Jennings had been a special kind of spooked. With all the noise from the US-Soviet standoff, no one had noticed Jennings go to ground and not appear again for two weeks, once he was certain that the clock wasn't going to chime midnight. Since then, the project that had obsessed Jennings was finding his own sanctuary so that he could escape the nuclear apocalypse that he was certain was coming. He'd taken Hobson off the government aeronautical project he'd been working on so that he could exclusively search for his sanctuary, and, as with everything Jennings did, he had a very precise set of criteria for his refuge. Ultimately, the sanctuary had to be completely self-sufficient, which meant that it needed its own water supply that would remain uncontaminated.

Hobson guessed that, from the outside, people would have a hard time seeing why he continued to work for Jennings. The pay was good—though not as good as you'd expect working for a multi-millionaire—and the hours were long. Hobson would often get back home and his wife, Fran, would be long asleep, accompanied by a half-finished glass of red on the side of his bed and a dog-eared novel on the bed. He'd groan with relief to be easing, finally, into his bed, only to have the phone ring soon after with another urgent request from Jennings, which just couldn't wait. After three months of midnight phone calls, there wasn't anyone in the bed to come home to.

He'd often wondered over the years why he'd stayed. It wasn't as if he hadn't had offers to leave, but he'd realized that it was just too exciting being in Jennings' orbit. There had been times, working for Jennings, that Hobson hadn't known what he'd be doing from one day to the next. As much as there was a big part of Hobson that wanted to get away from the craziness, he also wanted to see how it would all end.

Four years into his search for an appropriate sanctuary for Jennings coming up to four years. He'd come up with three possibilities, two of which had instantly been dismissed by his boss even though they seemed to fit his criteria down to the tee. The third place, a set of deep caves in a cliffside on the west coast of Mexico, had required a two-day off-road trek to reach. Jennings had spent six minutes there. He hadn't said a word. He'd just left, shaking his head and giving Hobson a withering look of disappointment. There was no additional feedback—that was his way, and it was understood. Hobson was expected to deliver, and he knew that he was running out of choices.

*

The mountain stood high above the Arctic Ocean. Waves lashed against its base. The rock turned with a dizzy suddenness into the surrounding water. A few hardy trees and some vegetation clung desperately to the cliff's edge, defying the elements. Clouds rolled across the ocean in a vast expanse. From a distance, the mountain had a purple hue, veined with seams of black and gray. Trees clung stubbornly to the rock face, jutting out at angles that seemed to defy gravity, their roots digging into the rock. Water ran down one of the other sides.

Hobson looked at the mountain, deep in thought. The proximity of Russia to the location concerned him. Still, it could have been worse; they could have been on the west coast. If Hobson had had any other choices, he wouldn't have brought his boss here. But he was out of options. In the distance, dark clouds obscured the endless horizon, making it difficult to tell exactly where the sky began. It was one vast dark gray, canvas of cobalt.. Hobson strained his eyes, thinking he could see a ship in the far distance.

Not far from the cliff's edge was a tower of rock that stood stubbornly against the erosion of the sea. It looked very solid, and Hobson decided he'd need to take a closer look at that if Jennings liked this place. They might be able to make use of the rock outpost if it proved to be sound. He guessed it had originally been part of the cliff but had been eroded away and now managed to survive alone in the water. The arctic wind gusting off the sea blew through the layers of Hobson's clothing. He might just as well have been standing there in his underwear.

It wasn't just the view that took your breath away. For one

sharp second, he thought about leaping off—a heart-stopping moment when he imagined himself plummeting to the rocky shore below, air rushing past, and the final impact before the waves took his body out to sea.

"Ready?"

Hobson snapped back to the moment and turned around. Standing with him on the mountain was Joseph Jennings, his thin frame covered with a charcoal gray suit and matching overcoat. In all the years that Hobson had worked for Jennings, he'd only ever seen him in this style of suit. The only thing that ever changed was the color—and that just alternated between black and gray. His black hair was slicked back from his face. His signature scent carried on the wind. It was an expensive cologne, Amethyst, but to Hobson it smelled like peppermint—a smell he always associated with Jennings.

"Yes," Hobson replied, noticing that Jennings was holding a copy of the *New York Times*. "Bobby Announces Presidential Campaign," the headline declared.

"It looks like Bobby could go all the way," said Hobson.

"He's never going to get to the White House," said Jennings with a cold certainty. "Are you sure about this place?"

"Yes, it meets all of your criteria."

"You said that about the last three locations, and they were sadly lacking."

A cold chill ran down Hobson's spine.

"This place is different."

Jennings was silent and let Hobson lead the way.

"We discovered the caverns on the second sweep of this area. They're deep within the mountain."

The two men navigated their way carefully along a damp pathway through thorny shrubs. Some large rocks had been moved aside, leaving deep troughs in the ground to show where they had once stood."I took your advice and wore some old clothes."

Hobson looked at Jennings's immaculate suit, thinking that he'd never owned a suit, which looked nearly as good.

"You'll need to put these overalls on… and this helmet."

Jennings did as he was told.

"There's a stream that runs into the entrance. It goes on for around eighteen feet. At its deepest, it gets about up to your midriff."

"And there's no other entrance?"

Hobson shook his head. "This is the only one at the moment. If we were to develop this, we'd build other entrances and redirect the stream from the current entrance location."

The path weaved its way to a cave mouth, which gaped in the middle of the mountain.

"I've rigged up some lights. They're not much, but these flashlights will help." Hobson pressed down hard on the handle of a generator and cranked it into life. Slowly, lights blinked on, casting long shadows across the rough ground. Jennings breathed in the mossy, earthy smell of the cave.

"The cave goes on for around fifty feet, and then…" Hobson walked up to a hole in the ground. Despite his nerves, he couldn't help but smile. "This is where it gets good."

He took a flare out of his backpack, lit it, and hurled it through the hole. He followed it with two more. The flares erupted with red sparks, offering crimson glimpses of the cavern below.

The flares illuminated jutting rocks, which framed a tar-black darkness. A few moments later, they heard the faint thud of the flare hitting the ground. They could just make out the red pinprick of light as it blinked out.

"Hmm," murmured Jennings, which was as close as Hobson ever heard to him expressing any emotion.

"Have you been down there yet?" Jennings asked him.

"Yes, I took a small team down there last week. The space is roughly the shape of a bottle—narrow at the top, but then opening out into a large cavern."

"How big is the cavern?"

"So far we've mapped the ground level to an area of four hundred by two hundred and seventy feet."

"Ground level?"

"Yes. We've identified three levels, and possibly a fourth. The ground level is the largest. There are catacombs and tunnels leading off all levels. We haven't begun to explore them yet. We found a spring on the ground floor."

"Have you been able to trace the source?"

"Not yet. We've identified a layer of lime in the rock, which acts as a natural water filter."

"Can we go down there?"

"Uh… well…" Jennings's request surprised Hobson. His first instinct was to say no, but Jennings wasn't a man you said no to. "Yes, we can. We've rigged up a rudimentary type of… well, I guess it would be too grand to call it an elevator, but it'll get us down to the ground level. First, we'll need to get down to the plateau just a few feet below. There are no lights set up, so we'll have to be careful."

Hobson went first. He lowered himself down and was swallowed by the inky darkness. Jennings paused. An unexpected spike of fear gripped him as he peered into the void: It looked like the waiting mouth of a hungry beast.

"Mr. Jennings?"

"Coming."

The two men swept their flashlights around. The space was as big as a good-sized hotel suite.

"The plateau goes out for around forty feet," Hobson pointed out with his flashlight beam where the ridge ended. "It falls off to another ridge around twenty feet below, and then it's a sheer drop except for a few outcrops that mark the different levels."

Hobson's voice echoed around the cavern. Jennings went up-close to the edge and shone his light into the abyss.

"Hmm," Hobson heard Jennings murmur again. "We'll have to do more structural and environmental surveys."

"Yes."

"And I want the source of the spring found."

"Right."

"So, I'll have that information by Friday?"

Hobson had to stifle a groan. That gave him three days.

"The sea can provide one source of energy," Jennings mused.

"As should some well-placed solar panels around the top of the mountain, and perhaps a wind farm on that outcrop we saw on the way in. The mountain acts as a natural shield, and we can also incorporate additional shielding," added Hobson.

"Hmm."

Jennings walked around the plateau, deep in thought. He stopped suddenly and whipped his head around. "What?"

"Pardon me?"

"What did you say?"

"I didn't say anything."

Jennings was silent. He stood stock-still but rotated his head.

"Wait, what's that?" said Jennings, pointing his flashlight at the rock face in front of him. Hobson walked up to the rock. Painted on the rock, he saw what at first glance looked like a furnace, but when he looked closer, details began to emerge. Set deep into the mass of red flames were two dark globes, which could have been eyes. On either side of the flames were two appendages, which were either hands or claws. The flaming creature was towering over some stick figures, which seemed to be holding something up towards the creature—perhaps offering something in sacrifice or attempting to ward it off. The creature looked as though it was getting ready to attack.

"That's incredible!" said Hobson. "Cave paintings! I hadn't

noticed them. I wonder how long they've been here. I wonder if there are any more."

"Can you hear that?"

"What?"

"The... whispers."

Jennings jabbed a finger at the paintings. "What's that *behind* the paintings?"

Hobson looked at where Jennings was pointing. The only thing he could see was a fissure in the rock.

"What is *that*?" Jennings hissed, his eyes wide with fear and wonder.

"I... I can't see anything."

A shudder rustled through Jennings's body. "No, no, of course. It's just shadows. I thought I saw... just shadows. I've seen enough."

They walked towards the makeshift elevator. Hobson looked behind him and saw Jennings staring back at the cave paintings.

Jennings heard the paintings whisper.

"We found something else. Something else that seems to suggest that we weren't the first people here."

"Other people? When?"

"Let me show you."

A set of pulleys had been set up with a large weight and a large counterweight at the base of the cavern. Hobson and Jennings approached a crate made of wire and wood.

Jennings paused and looked it up and down.

"It looks flimsy, but it'll easily take our weight," said Hobson.

"Right."

Jennings walked in, missing the fact that Hobson had his fingers crossed.

"I'll warn you: It won't be a smooth journey to the bottom."

Jennings nodded. Hobson untied the rope, and they plummeted until the counterweight kicked in to control their descent. Hobson thought he might lose his lunch, but Jennings looked fine. They sank deeper and deeper. Eventually, the crate shuddered to the bottom of the cavern.

Jennings looked at his surroundings, sweeping his flashlight in a circle. The space seemed to go on forever.

"I need to show you something," Hobson grinned.

They padded through the ground level, Hobson nodding his flashlight back and forth to illuminate the way. As the two walked deeper into the cavern, a green light began to slowly illuminate their surroundings. The two men entered the sub-cavern from which the light came, Hobson leading the way. The ceiling and walls were ringed with crystals, and stalagmites like jagged teeth. The crystals seemed to pulsate with green light.

"A cave of diamonds," said Jennings, and Hobson saw him smile for the first time in a long while. "What's causing the green glow?"

"We think it's some kind of phosphorescence. The crystals or diamonds themselves are made mostly of apatite and another element that we haven't been able to identify yet. The other noteworthy thing is that this is the first of the chambers where we have found evidence of previous human habitation and maybe a continuation of the images from the cave paintings."

Illuminated by the green glow was what appeared to be a collection of rotting scarecrows made from twigs, mud, and mangy animal skins. The scene mirrored what had been depicted in the cave painting. Three stick figures had been made from twigs and bark tied together with vines and other vegetation. Judging from the twigs and vegetation scattered around, there had been more figures, but they'd slowly decayed and fallen apart. They formed a ring around a large central figure, which could have been mistaken for a bonfire had it not been for the rotting animal skins it was dressed in. It had a central body of branches, which rose vertically from the ground, with branches tied across it for arms. It dwarfed the other figures. Set in front of the giant figure were two stones with a third, stained a deep crimson, laid across them. Both men stared at the stain.

"With the altar and the figures, the Smithsonian has speculated that this could've been a place of worship."

Jennings stared at the stick figures.

The only sound in the cavern was the slow drip of water in the distance. The ground was uneven, with small rocks scattered throughout. Jennings shone his flashlight at the walls, which were jagged and wallpapered with moss.

"The conditions are right for at least moss to grow down here?"

Hobson nodded.

"And if moss can grow down here, it's a good sign that we could cultivate limited crops."

"We think there may have been a group of American Indians who lived here. The paintings you saw earlier seem to predate them though. I went through an intermediary and contacted three experts in early North American history at the Smithsonian. The story was that it was a collection of artifacts acquired for a private collection and your name was never mentioned."

Jennings nodded.

" The experts at the Smithsonian believe it was the Athabastara tribe who lived here. We found some other paintings, which I'll show you later. They date from later than the paintings you saw. They make reference to a tunnel called the Bridge of Souls."

"Bridge of Souls?"

"The experts aren't sure that's the exact translation. The entrance to the Bridge of Souls has a red ring around it—maybe that's how it got its name; we're not sure yet." Hobson coughed. Now was as good a time as ever to mention the one fly in the ointment. "Uh, I was thinking… The proximity of the cavern to… uh …"

"To Russia?" Another smile. "No, that doesn't concern me. Alaska isn't even a secondary strike target for the Soviets."

How does he know?

Hobson waited a few moments before asking the vital question. If this place didn't make Jennings happy, he didn't know what he'd do.

"So, is this …"

"Have I ever told you about my mother?"

Hobson's eyebrows furrowed and he slowly shook his head.

"She was a young girl living in Dresden when they bombed it. She said you couldn't hear the bombs until it was too late, but that, just before it would blow up, there would be a terrifying silence. It was a terrible time... a terrible time. She had to dodge around the dead and dying. She was barely more than a child, but she found a way to survive. During the heaviest bombardment, she was running blind, in a panic, like anyone would, like an animal. When she was running scared, a floor beneath her collapsed—Lord knows how far down—into a basement. Everyone else around her was dead, but that accident saved her life. She was buried down there for two days as the bombings continued. She managed to scavenge food amongst the debris, not knowing whether another bomb would bring down more of the house to crush her. But she survived down there, buried. She told me time and time again how she had to hide in basements of burning buildings to stay alive. She burrowed down—deep, deep down. That's the only way she survived the bombs. It was the only way she could feel safe."

Jennings stared at the crimson stain on the stone altar. "Yes," he said, a ghost of a smile on his lips. "Yes, I think this will do fine."

CHAPTER 2

———

D anny Keins pulled the laces tight on his sneakers and lunged forward to stretch his calf muscles. He hated having to stretch—he would have preferred to just get going—but it was a necessary evil to stop injuries. He always found things to do before going for a run, things to put away, stuff to watch. There were two routes that he could take: One would just help him 'spin his wheels' while the other was a lot harder. Today, Danny was in the mood for some punishment

Finally, he stopped putting it off. There was nothing that needed to be done in his apartment that he couldn't leave until he got back. He had run the course hundreds of times but there were still turns that surprised him. He had to be alert because, more than once, he'd stumbled when his mind had been elsewhere. His route was flat for the first two miles, where he ran alongside the barrier. He found himself glancing over the side and was both thrilled and terrified by the sight. These two miles served as a warmup, leading to a series of inclines, pushing him farther and higher. He felt the strain on his thighs and his breathing became deeper and more labored. Danny pushed himself. It felt good to be sweating and to be in the moment, the endorphins washing away any jaded feelings.

Danny thought about what Connie had asked him: Was there really something in here with them? Could it be possible?

He hit an incline and felt the kick as he began to climb, but he concentrated on putting one foot in front of another, taking in deep lungful's of air. As he ran, he tried to take in his surroundings: the smooth ridges and the rough jutting rocks. Danny kept close to the walls. He checked his watch. He was a bit ahead of his pace from two days earlier. He reached the final incline, threw himself at it, and instantly felt the drag. "Come on! Come on!" he growled to himself through clenched teeth. He could feel the sweat streaming down his face and his heart pounding in his chest. Only one more minute, two at most. Not far to go. His thighs were screaming. And then he was at the top.

Danny carried on running when he reached the plateau but took the time to look up. There were tinted lights built into the metal. Now they were shining a blue light across the shiny surface, giving the impression of a clear, sunny day. Occasionally a projected cloud floated across to complete the illusion. All that spoiled the picture were a few spots of rust that had begun to show.

The blue felt both comforting and oppressive at the same

time. Danny knew what lay beyond the metal sky. He put his palms in the small of his back, bent backwards, and took four deep breaths before beginning the descent back to his apartment, careful to keep his knees flexible to disperse the impact throughout his legs. It was a grind, but Danny felt great and couldn't help reflecting on where he'd been just one year ago.

*

MAY 13, 2019

Something dark was on the horizon.

He couldn't breathe.

There was somewhere he was trying to reach, but he wasn't going to get there in time.

There was something coming to get him.

Noise, interference, someone calling to him.

"Danny? Are you okay?"

No, I'm not okay. There's something…

Something was chasing after him.

He stumbled and nearly fell.

However hard he ran, he was never going to get there in time.

The nameless dread thing caught up with him and…

*

"Oh, fuck…"

The fear was replaced by the relief of waking up. The sheets were damp from his sweat, his lips caked with salt. He reached to his left to get a glass of water.

"Was it the usual?" Jane asked.

Danny nodded "That's the third time this week."

"Anything you want to tell me?" she asked.

He ran his fingers through his hair. *Fuck, yeah: Tomorrow's board meeting, the ongoing conspiracy to elbow me out of my own company... where to start …?*

"Is it anything to do with the board meeting tomorrow?"

Danny sat bolt upright as though he'd just been shocked. "How do you know about that?"

Jane laughed. "You've left reports around the apartment, and I've lost count of the number of times I've walked past you frowning at your laptop." She ran her fingers across his cheek, and he flinched. She took her hand away. "You don't have to go through this alone. I…"

"Do you want a coffee?"

She stared at him. "Fine."

Jane lied back down and turned onto her side.

Danny put a dressing gown on and padded to the kitchen.

You don't have to go through this alone.

Danny glanced back at the bedroom. He imagined going back in, touching her bare shoulder, looking into her eyes, and telling her the truth.

I'm scared. I'm utterly terrified. They could take it all away from me; if that happens, what's left of me? What's the point of me? What am I then?

An image of his father came to mind, with his default

expression of anger and disappointment. *"Stop your crying or I'll give you something to cry about!" He was right. For Christ's sake, man up! You didn't build this company by being like this. Man up!*

Danny straightened his back and headed for the kitchen, his head full of interference.

*

Danny frowned as he read the report in *The Wall Street Journal*. The days of subsidies were long-gone, and now it seemed that the government was actively legislating against the renewable energy sector. He'd heard gossip about this for months and the language being used was far from encouraging. Now that this was being reported in mainstream media, it was almost certainly true. The human race seemed to be hell-bent on destroying itself and the planet, and it wasn't doing too much for Danny's company's balance sheet. He knew that, in the board meeting today, Randall Bateman, the chief financial officer, would use it as a cudgel to hit him over the head with. He knew that members of the board had been making a power play behind the scenes to try to oust him. *Bastard.*

With only an hour till the board meeting, Danny just could not get his shit together. He rubbed the corners of his eyes. Jane wasn't speaking to him, and he had a horrible feeling that this might be the straw for their relationship but, like many things, he pushed it to the back of his mind to deal with later.

Why can't I speak to her? What am I afraid of?

*

Danny was rapidly losing the will to live. Three espressos had done nothing to get rid of his general feeling of weariness and only heightened his anxiety. Now he was standing in front of the board.

"Is that the way you see the business going, Daniel?"

Danny was silent. Then, just as Randall Bateman was about to speak, he smiled. "If you'd really read the report—and especially cross-referenced the details of upcoming legislation, which, for some reason, are buried in the appendices—you'd know we're continuing to target emerging markets, especially in China and Asia. Renewables, as normal, but with an added emphasis on recycled food waste, which is where we've had our biggest margins over the last five years." He watched with satisfaction at Randall's growing dismay.

Danny had lived to fight another day. He looked every board member in the eye as they left the room and gave them all a firm handshake. He waited until everyone had left before he walked slowly to the nearest executive toilet and threw up the three espressos into the bowl.

The thing that had kept him going throughout the meeting was the prospect of lunch with his best friend, Matthew Hampton. They'd met as students in Caltech. While Danny had carried on to the highly successful renewable energy business, Matthew had gone into filmmaking and was now a much-courted film director. He was currently working on something to do with robots, but Danny's attention always switched off about a minute after Matthew began to talk about it. Danny didn't know which of them earned more money. He'd never asked because he wouldn't have been able to stand it if it had been Matthew.

Whenever Danny was half an hour late, Matthew would always manage to be later. Danny looked down at the menu for the fourth time. He wanted the burger, but would probably go for the chicken salad. He felt on a high after his tussle with the board and now, in the hot California afternoon, waiting for his friend, he couldn't believe the anguish he'd gone through. Whenever the mist descended on him, he tried to remember this feeling. Maybe it would work next time.

"Yeah, sorry I'm late!"

Danny put the menu down and got up to give Matthew a hug.

Matthew was out-of-breath and sweating lightly. "I was just heading out the door when someone from costumes wanted a word, which turned into several. Anyway…" He scanned the menu as a waiter approached. "Two beers, please. Coors Light."

Danny could have said no to Matthew's order, but didn't.

"I've got some news for you."

"Oh, yeah?" Danny tried to sound nonchalant, but it had been the first thing on his mind: the only thing, if he was honest.

Matthew lowered his voice. "I've had a call from the committee; they want to meet you."

"That's awesome!" They clinked their bottles together in a toast.

"You're not in yet."

"Right, so what's next?"

Matthew sat back in his chair, smiled, and raised his eyebrows.

"Ah, come on, don't be a dick."

"Okay, 'cause it's you… you get to actually go to the Sanctuary and meet the committee. An interview. Then they make their decision: You're in, or you're out. It's as straightforward as that."

"What? So the money's not enough? They want me to jump through hoops?"

"It's not about money, bro; it's about *exclusivity*."

Exclusivity. There it was: the word that got him hooked.

*

He'd first heard about the Sanctuary a year ago. He had been at a party and was about to head home when he'd heard a whispered conversation in a low-lit alcove: "Going to the Sanctuary this weekend?" He'd glanced at the speaker in time to see her make a gesture to her companion to shut up. He'd paused momentarily, then dismissed it. The Sanctuary was probably just another club that would be the place to be seen at for a few weeks until the next new place opened. Over the following few months, he began to hear more mentions of the Sanctuary. He'd be in a club—in the *real* VIP area, behind the commoners' VIP area—and would overhear one or two conversations where the Sanctuary was mentioned. He'd see glances exchanged between the elite. It was definitely the new thing to be in the know about … and to make sure it was known you were in the know about.

Danny had once heard a story about a billionaire who'd

arranged to have a painting by Munch stolen to add to his private collection. The theft had gone off without a hitch. It made news globally. The police mounted a major hunt for the painting, but everyone had gone to ground. The heist had been well-planned, and there was enough money sloshing about to buy everyone's silence. The billionaire eventually gave it back anonymously: What was the point of having it if you couldn't show it to anyone or brag about it?

Eventually, over the next six months, Danny was able to piece together the story of the Sanctuary. The final piece came when the name of the legendary billionaire madman Joseph Jennings was mentioned in the same breath as the Sanctuary.

It hadn't taken him long to realize that, of his immediate circle of friends, Matthew was the most likely to have connections—and it wasn't just connections that Matthew had. That was two months ago: an eternity to a man not used to waiting for something he wanted. He sat, ground his teeth, and waited. He tried not to think about it. However, even during intense moments—fucking someone or looking at property— Danny was thinking about the Sanctuary.

"I suppose you're already a member?" Danny had asked Matthew when he'd brought up the subject at a private party.

Matthew had laughed. "Of course."

Danny wanted to punch him in the face. He thought about those people in the Sanctuary, in their exclusive club with him on the outside. The bullied, unpopular eight-year-old from Kansas screamed and wanted in.

*

"When is it?" he asked Matthew.

"Tuesday."

"Shit."

"Is that a problem?"

"No, not a problem."

In fact, it was a *big fucking problem*. Yet, after a frantic few day of rescheduling, Danny found himself, one overcast afternoon, standing in a parking lot the size of a baseball field by a rundown mall.

"Jesus! How do people live like this?" he said, looking at the mall and thrusting his hands into his pockets.

He waited for ten minutes before an anonymous black sedan pulled up. The back door opened and he got in. He was the only person in the back. The windows were tinted so he couldn't see out. Danny was uncomfortable in his own company and the ride seemed to last forever, involving a short play-journey with a car waiting at the other side. After a bumpy ride, the car stopped and the door opened. In front of him were two pairs of thickset, broad shoulders, squeezed into smart black suits.

"Please come with us, Mr. Keins."

Danny was only too happy to get out of the car. He looked around at the mountain top in front of him and realized that he didn't have a clue where he was. One of the suits gestured for him to go with them.

For a moment, they just stood in front of a giant rock.

"What now? Are we gonna …?" There was a grinding noise

and the rock divided to reveal a steel door. The door slid open and the two suits ushered him in.

Danny found himself in an antechamber where there was another steel door with a number pad to one side. One of the suits tapped in a six-digit number and the door opened to reveal three men in even more expensive suits. An African-American man in steel-rimmed glasses took a step forward, shook Danny's hand, and gave him a wide smile. "Mr. Keins, glad to meet you. Welcome to the Sanctuary."

Danny followed the three men as they walked around the rim of the cavern beyond. This was obviously meant to impress him, and it worked. He couldn't begin to guess how deep it was, but if you fell down there, you weren't going to be doing the electric boogaloo anytime soon. He thought he could glimpse water—maybe a pool at the bottom? Was that the edge of a farm? The details did nothing to distract him from his nerves.

As he followed them, he saw apartments built into the rock, and walkways and steps, but it was hard to take in the size or the geography of the place. Danny was taken into a plush, modern, air-conditioned meeting room. Had he not known better, he would have assumed he'd walked into one of the many meeting rooms he often found himself in at his office. The only difference was that this room had a slightly sweeter fragrance in the air, one he couldn't quite place—jasmine, perhaps? Danny had tried to anticipate the sort of questions he may be asked but was immediately wrong-footed when it seemed to be more than a mere sales pitch. He'd almost begun to relax when the first question came out of nowhere.

"We understand that your father died young?"

Danny floundered, which what they wanted. They'd done their research on him. From that question on, he was in battle mode.

"Weren't you on the brink of bankruptcy ten years ago?" Every question was a jab.

"That's none of your business! What's that got to do with anything?"

Danny left the room feeling bruised.

CHAPTER 3

T hree Advils washed down with two cups of strong black coffee had failed to make a dent in Robert Jayston's headache. He couldn't remember having a hangover this bad, not even in the bad old days, and he hadn't even touched a drop. He was now sixteen days without a drink—good to his word to Cherie—and he felt like shit. He tried to think about the money he was earning from this job, which normally improved his mood, but not even that chipped the corners off.

He was known in the profession by his surname and Jayston's specialty was surveying and reinforcing old mines, extending their life and the lives of those who worked in them. Everyone agreed that he had a talent for the work, but they also agreed that he had a short fuse. He would get frustrated when people couldn't see what he was getting at. *Why didn't people understand?* The last time this happened, he'd put his fist through a partition wall, broken three of his fingers, and had to take six weeks off while his hand healed. He was working on his temper. Sometimes he was more successful than others.

That incident—and his drinking—had meant that he'd left his previous job by mutual agreement with his employer; it had been a bit more mutual on his employer's part. He had been on welfare for the last two months. This contract had come through at the right time, via an old work colleague.

Too many days had started with a hangover, which couldn't be ignored, despite the continued high quality of his work. His stretch of unemployment had left him on thin ice with Cherie, but the money they were offering with this current contract was enough to not only blow away all their debts, but also start building the college fund they had talked about for their kid. Why *couldn't* they have the things that everyone else had? Getting the job had involved so much cloak-and-dagger that, had it not paid so well, Jayston would have walked away. He had received a letter with no sender's address on it, and no postmark, telling him to expect a phone call on a certain day. The letter stated that he would receive the call to tell him where the interview would be. If he missed the phone call, he was out of the process. At times, it had felt more like a kidnapping than an interview process. But he had gotten through the interviews and was amazed that his previous employer had vouched for him. No bad feelings, indeed. When Sam Hobson had rung him to tell him that he'd gotten the job, he'd put down the phone and almost burst into tears.

The future looked bright. He'd been given a second chance. Thank you, Jesus, Mary, and Joseph! He just had to get through the next few months, do the grind, and get the job done. It wasn't such a sacrifice, not really.

He'd had to sign a confidentiality contract, of course. Not a word could be spoken to anyone outside of the project about anything he did or saw: If he did, a whole storm of shit would be unleashed upon him. Jayston could understand the request for secrecy—that was the reason the pay was so good—but a nine- to fourteen-month contract working in Alaska wasn't going to be to everyone's taste. He'd been asked to put together his own crew and knew a few people who would come onboard if he asked.

Jayston had worked with John "Joe" Halliday in his last job and knew that he would be looking for a new job. He and Joe went way back. Jayston remembered walking in on day one of his very first job and wanting to throw up as soon as he stepped into the mine. The acidic burn at the back of his throat warned of a technicolor yawn to come. He had to take a moment, close his eyes, and focus to get the nausea to subside. There had been a dozen men looking around the tunnel.

"What support and bolting do you think this section of mine needs?"

Confidence is the key.

"It needs split set friction rock stabilizers with split set rock bolts." He had looked the boss man straight in the eye when he'd said it.

The boss man —a big fat fuck of a man, who hooked his thumbs into his already-straining belt—looked impressed, right up to the point that a beanpole-thin blond guy in the corner spoke. Jayston hadn't taken any notice of him until that point. He looked like a hard sneeze would knock him on his ass.

"I don't agree. We need something more heavy-duty. You can see the fissure cracks in the rock. We need some mine roof bolting and split shift bolting with support meshing."

The boss man took a step back and beamed with a big shit-eating grin on his face. "It appears we have ourselves a disagreement." And he let them fight it out amongst themselves until it looked as though they would actually come blows. Eventually, the boss man stood between them.

"Boys, we need to keep our heads cool. You've both got some good ideas. We're going to use a combination of them."

Both men remained as far away from each other as they could manage. Mercifully for Jayston, the contract was only eight weeks long, and he breathed a sigh of relief to see the back of the beanpole, Joe Halliday. Jayston went home to Cherie but didn't have to wait long for the phone to ring with the next offer of work. He walked into another contact and almost straight into Joe Halliday.

"Jesus Christ, not you again!"

"The feeling is mutual."

Their second job was working on a drainage system in a coal mine in Peterborough, New Hampshire, and they had to work closely together.

"Wait! What's that?" quickly became Joe's catchphrase. At first, Jayston thought that Joe was too jumpy, too quick to panic, but as the contract progressed, he began to trust the other man's cautious instincts. When the contract finished, he even managed to slap Joe on the back. "It's been good to work with you," he said, and he pretty much meant it. That didn't stop him shouting out "Fuck!" when they both walked into the same room, at the same time, on the next job.

"It seems like someone wants us to be together," said Joe in his usual deadpan fashion.

Much to the other workers' bemusement, they both broke out laughing so hard that Jayston blew snot bubbles out of his nostrils. When Jayston finally stopped laughing, Joe allowed himself a wry smile. Even though their paths continued to cross over the years, it would have been a stretch for Jayston to have called Joe a friend, but they worked well together, and Joe had mellowed over the years. He'd been the first person Jayston had called when he'd got this contract, and recruited him to the team. .

The third member of Survey Team Number Three was Larry Paines, a twenty-two-year-old graduate. Jayston had worked with him in his last job and liked his energy and enthusiasm. The important thing about Larry was that when you asked him to do something, he did it—which was all-too-scarce these days. He also liked Larry for his sparky humor, which—although it needed to be reined in from time to time—kept him smiling. A few weeks ago, Larry had taken to calling Jayston "skipper."

Larry was often the butt of the other two men's good-humored jokes, and he seemed to take the gags with a casual shrug and smile: "See, I thought I understood, but I don't."

*

So here he was with Joe and Larry deep in a cavern in Alaska. Jayston smiled and massaged his temples, trying to get ease away the last vestiges of the headache.

"I've got a bastard behind the eyes." Jayston said.

"No change there, then," said Joe.

"Yeah, yeah, yeah. Fuck you very much." Jayston laughed; he could take playful insults as well as he dish them out.

"When you first told me how much this was paying, I was ready for a lot of things…" Larry said.

"It's simple: Our boss doesn't want chickenshits like you blabbing about what's going on here," said Joe.

"Our boss Joseph Jennings?"

Jayston grinned. "You don't know it's Jennings. And even if you did, you're getting paid enough to keep that big mouth of yours shut."

"Understood. What's on the schedule today, skipper?"

"We're checking Tunnel Sixteen—nothing complicated, just a basic survey job to see where it goes and if it can be used for anything. I'm thinking maybe ventilation at this point. It may be a pain in the ass to do anything more with that with the tunnel, but hey, I've been wrong before, just not that often." He smiled. "Come on, boys, let's get to work."

"Yeah, Tunnel Sixteen: The Bridge of Souls— "

"The Bridge Assholes?" Larry laughed until he had to bend over to catch his breath, and the others couldn't help but join in. But then their laughter was drowned out by a deep rumble.

They all looked around.

"What was that?"

"Probably some work going on somewhere else in the cavern."

"Yeah, right."

They peered into the tunnel.

"Come on, let's get this done."

"So do you buy the story, Joe?" Larry asked.

"About this being an old diamond mine? Nah, that's pure bullshit. I've worked in a lot of mines, and this ain't no mine. Those rooms at the top? They're a top luxury fit—*big bucks*. Have you seen all that agricultural stuff? If I didn't know better, I'd say they were setting up farms …"

"What the fuck is this all about, then?"

Joe looked around before he spoke, which made Jayston smile.

"Lord only knows. One thing's certain: Jennings is crazier than a shithouse rat."

The three men laughed.

"Come on, boys, we're not being paid for the yakety-yak. Let's see what this tunnel has got for us."

Another team were surveying Tunnel Thirteen, one of many tunnels that led off the ground level. Some led to dead-ends, others snaked back in on themselves, and others opened into smaller chambers. The three members of Survey Team Number Three walked into Tunnel Sixteen, and before long, had to stoop to get through. All had miners' hats with lamps attached to battery packs, and powerful flashlights. As they walked along the tunnel, Joe called out measurements and Larry wrote them down. They carried a spool and laid down a string of lights that were connected to the central generator. The three of them got into a rhythm and managed to cover a lot of ground. The tunnel opened up, and they were able to stand upright again.

After an hour, they reached a point where the tunnel split into two. They stopped to drink some water and look around.

"We're going to run out of the lighting rig soon, skipper. Are we heading back?"

Jayston looked back at where they'd come from and at the paths leading from the junction. If he mapped out a bit farther, his team would be way ahead of the others. Surely that would get him noticed—and being noticed by Jennings would be a good thing.

"No, let's press on a little farther, boys. We'll check out where one of these paths goes, and then we'll head back."

"How far do you think the tunnels go?" asked Joe.

"Dunno. This mountain is riddled with them. Some of them probably go on for miles. Who knows where they lead? But it's our job to find out." He clapped Larry on the back, but Larry was staring down the right-hand path.

"Are there rats down here?"

"No, no rats, but maybe some of their flying cousins. Why?"

"Bats, that's probably it. It's just… yeah, bats. I thought I saw something down there," he said, sounding as if he was trying to convince himself.

"Come on, let's get moving."

"Which path, Joe?"

"Let's take the left. We don't want to spook Larry."

"Fuck you," said Larry with a wide grin.

With their headlamps to guide them, they made their way down the tunnel.

"This tunnel feels cooler," said Jayston as he took off his gloves and ran his hands over the tunnel walls. "The walls are bone-dry, so no evidence of any underlying ground water here. Odd. There's still signs of some of the plant life around. Never really seen anything like this before." He pointed his flashlight to the patches of scrubby plants growing out of the jagged, snarled-up rock wall spiderwebbed with cracks. Jayston ran his fingers over them: They had a tough, bristly feel, like tumbleweeds. *Gotta be tough to survive down here,* he thought. "We know that there's a substantial underground spring, and I would've guessed it extended out to here. You getting this down, Larry?"

"Yes, skipper."

The men slowly edged their way along the tunnel. A light whisper of a breeze whistled through the tunnel and over the men.

"Could this tunnel lead all the way into the open?" asked Joe.

"I don't see how. It's more likely to circle back to one of the other caverns. I've taken a look at the primary surveys and the only entrance is the one we came in by. There's talk of creating another entrance, but nothing's been done so far. There could be some air breach from another, intersecting tunnel, but that's what we're here to find out."

The men laid down markers as they continued. Jayston found fissures in the rock where he inserted a Rohde & Schwarz ultrasonic anemometer to check for airflow. He wedged the yellow plastic casing into the rock and called the results out to Larry to record.

Larry's headlamp began to flicker and then went out entirely. Larry took off his hat and hit it a few times.

For a split-second, Jayston wanted to slap him. *Larry, you dumb fuck, you forgot to put new batteries in.* An incandescent flame of fury wrong-footed him. *Holy shit, where did that come from?* He managed to swallow his anger.

"Son of a bitch! I only put new batteries in it this morning," said Larry.

"Let's just carry on. You've still got your flashlight."

They edged down the tunnel and Jayston felt a sudden spike of fear, akin to an animal being backed into a corner. For a split-second he nearly spun around and ran in the opposite direction in blind terror, but he took some deep breaths and managed to calm down.

"You okay, skipper?"

"Yeah, fine, just... you know... breakfast. Shouldn't have eaten it so quickly. Anyone got any Pepto-Bismol?" he asked lamely.

"Jesus! What's that smell?" asked Larry.

"What were you saying about breakfast?" asked Joe. They all laughed. "No, but seriously, what the fuck is that?"

One summer, Jayston had worked for a delivery service—in reality, two cousins with two vans—and for a seemingly endless two weeks, he'd helped one of the cousins to deliver meat. This involved offloading headless pig carcasses to restaurants. He never thought he'd get the ripe, sharp smell of the pigs' carcasses out of his nostrils. The smell in the cave, somehow, reminded him of those two weeks with the dead pigs. This, too, had the sharp, stinging, rotting smell.

"It's sulfur. You get that all the time underground," said Jayston. He got some mumbles from the other two. *They know I'm bullshitting them.*

The three men walked in silence for a few moments until Jayston heard a crunch under his feet. He shone the flashlight down. There were scattered pieces of scuffed yellow plastic. The flashlight picked out the word Schwarz; it was the ultrasonic anemometer. He knew he'd lodged it in firmly. It was a heavy-duty piece of kit. Even if it had fallen out, there was no way…

"It must have dropped out," he said, trying silence his doubts.

"How did it get here? This isn't where we left it."

"How the fuck should I know?" he snapped, and just at that moment his flashlight began to flicker. "Fucking thing!" Jayston slammed his palm against the flashlight, which only made the flickering worse—but it did distract them from the matter of the debris on the floor. After one last splutter, the flashlight died.

"Skipper, I'm getting the fear. Let's get back."

"Oh for…" Jayston bit his lip. "Okay, okay, just another minute and we'll leave."

They'd just begun to walk when Joe's flashlight spluttered out, leaving the team with one fully working flashlight and Joe's flashlight — which began to flicker.

"Fuck! Don't you fucking dare!" yelled Joe. It gave two more flickers and then died.

"No!" Larry yelled.

"Right, calm down, boys, calm down. We've still got my headlamp and your torch Larry We can make our way back to the junction, and from there, we've got the lights."

From deep within the tunnels came a grinding noise, which tapered off into a sigh.

"What the fuck was that?" shouted Joe.

"Calm down, for fuck's sake! That was nothing. Just the sound of the rocks settling. Come on, let's get out of here."

They made their way back along the tunnel. It all looked the same.

"It wasn't this far, was it?" asked Larry.

"Calm down, it's not much farther," said Jayston, just as the last remaining flashlight was beginning to flicker.

"No! No! No!" Larry yelled.

"I said calm the fuck down, Larry!" shouted Joe. "You panicking like a little fucking girl isn't going to get us anywhere."

"Boys, we're not far. The junction has to be just ahead of us," said Jayston.

They picked up the pace as Larry's flashlight spluttered and finally died, leaving the three men in the dark. Joe could hear Larry breathing.

"Fuck! What the fuck was that?" said Joe, clutching his chest.

"Skipper?"

"Look, we're fine, we can't be more than fifty-"

"Skipper?"

"What?"

"I think… I saw something…" said Larry slowly.

"Something? Something like what?"

"It…" Larry took a deep breath. "It looked like some kind of huge bear."

"Don't be so fucking stupid. There's no bears down here," said Jayston.

"I said it *looked* like a bear."

"Jesus! What are you trying to do—give me a heart attack? Calm down. Just calm down. Feel the sides of the passage and edge forward slowly."

All that could be heard was their labored breathing. The seconds ticked away like hours.

"How are you doing, Larry?" asked Joe. "Larry?"

"Larry?" Jayston joined in. "Where the hell's Larry gone, Joe?"

"I don't know... maybe he's found a shortcut?"

"Larry!"

"Larry!" they both shouted down the passage.

"Fuck! Fuck! Right. We'll get out and send people back to find him. Come on, we've got to get out."

They carried on shuffling until a loud thud filled the tunnel. The sound of his heart beating sounded like a bass drum in Jayston's ears. "What the fuck was that? Joe? Joe? Shit, shit, shit!"

Jayston stood alone in the darkness. Somewhere in the distance, he heard the dripping of water. His breathing sounded thunderous in his ears.

Stay calm, stay calm.

He reached his hands out against the rock wall. The icy stone felt comforting. He felt his way across the wall like a blind man and tried to move faster. He couldn't see any light; he may as well have had his eyes closed.

"Hello? Hello?"

The hairs on his arm stood up, and time seemed to stand still for a moment. Robert Jayston's final thought, the second before the dark swallowed him, was that if he got back home, he was going to buy his wife a steak and some flowers.

*

"How long have they been missing?"

"Nine days."

"Has there been any sign of them at all?"

"Nothing. We've sent two teams of five up. The Bridge of Souls is a maze; anything could have happened to them." Hobson ran his hand through his hair.

Jennings thought for a moment. "Call the search off."

"What? You can't call the search off! These are men's lives! You can't just leave them!"

"What would you have me do?" Jennings asked calmly. "We've already sent two teams to look, and nothing. Would you have me send even more men, farther in, and have them lost as well?"

Hobson ground his teeth. "There must be something we can do."

"We've done everything we can. What have their families been told?"

"It was only," Hobson checked his clipboard, "Robert Jayston who had dependents: a wife and a young daughter. The other two had extended families: parents and siblings."

"Make sure they're provided for."

The two men stood looking at the entrance to Tunnel Sixteen.

*

Four hours later, Hobson stood alone in the cavern. He'd spent that time ringing the families and now, more than anything, he wanted a drink. The cover story was that there had been a rock fall and that the bodies were buried under rock. As Hobson had suspected, being told that they'd be "looked after" had provided little comfort. There had been tears and swearing, and all three calls had ended with the phone being slammed down after a barrage of accusations, leaving him numb and holding a dead phone. Boy, did he want a drink.

Hobson's head whipped around to the left as he saw

something dart into one of the tunnels.

What was that?

He looked around and squinted into the darkness. Was… was something moving?

"Hello?"

He jumped at the slight echo his voice created.

Hobson ran his hands over his face. This place did strange things to you. You ended up jumping at your own shadow. Was there something down here? He hadn't even seen or heard the bats that some of the contractors had suggested were indigenous. Other than shadows, he had seen nothing. He'd heard some strange noises, but so far down in the earth, that was bound to happen. No, nothing odd—except, even before the survey team had gone missing, he hadn't wanted to go near the Bridge of Souls. Hobson couldn't explain why; the place just felt *wrong*. Even just staring into the entrance made him feel nauseous, as if he'd eaten something that had turned rotten. The thought of the Bridge of Souls and that nauseous feeling prompted him to take a swig of his coffee, which was now lukewarm. He must have been up for fourteen hours. Everything was getting a little hazy around the edges, and he felt a bit punchy. No wonder he was seeing things.

CHAPTER 4

———

The senator for Delaware looked at her letter of resignation. The letters flashed on her screen— innocent and oddly abstract, but life-changing. She took a deep breath, popped two Tums in her mouth, and ground them between her teeth. Connie O'Hagan was crunching these like they were M&Ms. They didn't do much to knock back her indigestion.

Calm... calm... calm...

She looked around her office. It looked no different from any other day. Same as it ever was. Where had she heard that before? She looked out of her window. She had moved heaven and earth to get an office overlooking the park. Weeks had gone by when she hadn't even noticed the park; in fact, some days, she drew the blinds to block out the view.

How could I do that?

Connie pushed her chair back and took in the sight of the

park. It was a gorgeous spring day, and there seemed to be a collective relief amongst everyone that, at last, the mornings were getting lighter and the evenings longer.

Connie was in her late forties, a handsome, slim woman with white streaks in her hair, which was almost constantly swept back into a bun. The advance of age had only started to trace its lines around her eyes and lips, but on a good day, she could kid herself that it gave her character.

As she looked out at the park, she noticed the people walking around carefree and felt a sharp stab of envy and hatred. They were walking in the sun without a care in the world—hand-in-hand, laughing, eating ice cream cones—completely unaware and happy in their own lives.

Calm… calm… calm…

The cursor at the end of the resignation letter blinked at her. She brought her fingers up to her mouth and chewed her nails. Connie had chewed them raw over the last few days.

She should never have let Chuck talk her into it. Who was she kidding? She should never have closed her good eye to how rotten the whole deal was: Shit stank, and it was your own fault if you got it all over your shoes. She knew it was a bad deal, but she'd let the dollar signs blind her.

Chuck would always turn up with a bottle of Wild Turkey and be able to make two glasses appear seemingly from nowhere. He'd make the same comment— "Nasty shit for nasty times!"—and would laugh a clogged-up Marlboro laugh, punctuated by a phlegmy cough. Connie always joined him in the drink and the laugh.

Even wearing an expensive Italian suit and a good wig, he still looked like a bag of potatoes—just a better-dressed one. She'd known Charles 'Chuck' Hagel since school. Back then, he'd had bad skin, even worse breath, and been unable to make eye contact. She would never have remembered him, but strangely, their paths had crossed fleetingly over the years. He'd always made a point of reintroducing himself and reminding her about their shared humble beginnings. Chuck would always shake her hand a little too long and keep eye contact a few more seconds than necessary—long enough to make her skin crawl—but he was well-connected and a useful man to know.

He'd rung her office and, when her assistant had mentioned his name, Connie had sighed and rolled her eyes. His offer of a *no-strings-attached*, fail-safe investment offer had come at the right time, but nothing is ever really no-strings-attached. Before she knew it, Chuck was asking her to speak to a few of her senate colleagues to give preferential treatment to their deal over others that were on the table. Next, she was using her influence to talk to a few people just to "oil the wheels," which didn't come cheap. In return for the favors she requested, she found herself voting for bills she wouldn't otherwise have lit a fire with and offering bribes at a local level. One of the legislators was strong-arming her for more money than she had, and she suspected he was already in touch with the press. It had all started to unravel when a reporter began to pick up on her changed voting habits. Now Chuck wasn't returning her calls. And here she was, looking at the flashing cursor of doom at the end of her letter of resignation, wondering what she would wear for the press conference when she made the announcement.

Connie ran her hand over her face and read her letter again. She'd be lucky if she could get away with *just* resigning. There was a real chance that she'd do time for this. She stared at the bottom draw of her desk and blamed it for not having a bottle of whiskey in it. For good luck, she gave it a kick and scuffed her leather Christian Louboutin shoes. Everything was coming up Connie.

CNN burbled, muted, in the corner. Tensions were mounting between India and Pakistan—but weren't they always? Maybe that was the answer. Maybe India and Pakistan were finally going to have the dust-up that they'd promised for years and would blow everyone else up in the process. Then she wouldn't have to worry about Chuck, about oil wells, resignations, or jail time. Everything would be in ashes. For the first time in a long time, she thought about the Sanctuary. Might it be time to take a trip? Maybe disappearing for a day or two—hell, a week or two—would be great.

Connie was sick to death of the cursor blinking. She didn't have to send the letter quite yet—though the day of reckoning was coming soon. She saved the document and closed the computer.

"I'm stepping out for a few minutes to get some air," she told her assistant. In her attempt to get some air, the first thing she did was to buy a pack of Camels. Connie hadn't smoked in over ten years and the first inhalation smacked her right between the eyes. She felt a pleasant dizziness and nearly had to sit down. The second drag kept her steady. She walked in the park, smoking and thinking.

Calm... calm... calm... This too will pass. There will come a point in the not-too-distant future when this will be resolved.

This was all true, but she was the only person who could resolve it. Her big fear had been that the news would break about her and Lloyd leading *very* separate lives. That type of thing really hurt your political career, but not to the extent that this deal with Chuck would.

Calm... calm... calm... Think, Connie. There must be a way out of this.

She needed to buy some time. Then the answer came to her in a flash. She would go gunning for Chuck, take the fight to him—she had plenty of dirt to do it. It might not work—*might not? Probably wouldn't*—but at least she'd go out swinging and it would buy her some time. It brought to mind the scene in *Raging Bull* when Jake La Motta was on the ropes, his legs turned to jelly.

You never got me down, Ray. You never got me down.

Fuck it! She was not going down without a fight.

Instantly, she felt better and decided she was going to get herself an ice cream cone—just like the young people did.

*

Doctor Theresa O'Brien fell against the door and nearly collapsed into the room. She resisted the urge to switch the light on, knowing that it probably wouldn't work anyway. She was happy to have the door slam behind her, a welcome relief from the noise of the world outside. Theresa slumped against a pile of dirty laundry and looked at her watch, straining to bring the numbers into focus. She was sixteen, no, seventeen hours into her shift and had a half-hour break—although she reckoned it would probably be closer to fifteen minutes.

Theresa sat down heavily on a pile of bed sheets.

"Oh, man!" she said, and nearly fell asleep right then. If she were lucky, she might be able to smoke a cigarette or have a quick sandwich, but probably not both. She decided to get her priorities right and opted for the cigarette. She groaned as she pushed herself up so she could check the door before lighting up. She took a battered paperback out of the back of her trousers.

The first drag of the cigarette brought a second "Oh, man!" from her, which was quickly followed by "That's nice!" for good measure. She was into the last stretch. Only another four hours to go—hopefully. These were a blessed few moments. She dared to kick off her shoes.

Jesus, my feet stink.

She took another drag and leaned back, just as the door opened.

Fuck!

She quickly stubbed the cigarette out under the bed sheets.

A man in a smart, expensive-looking suit walked into the room. He had startling green eyes, a crooked nose, and an amused, detached air about him. A few white strands of hair were combed across his bald pate. He looked a bit like a well-dressed vulture and carried a folder under his arm.

"No reason to put out the cigarette. I'm a friend."

I'll be the judge of that. Fuck it. She lit another cigarette.

"I'm sorry to interrupt your break. I'll be quick. We want you to come and work for us."

She blew cigarette smoke into the room and watched it whirl. "Odd, isn't it? I'm a doctor. I make people better. I know these are slowly killing me, but I carry on smoking. And pretty much every doctor I know smokes. What does that say about the human race?"

"I represent the Brighter Futures Group, and we require the services of a doctor on an ongoing basis. We know that you've been putting out feelers."

"Yes. And?"

"Well, we know you have particular interests—or should I say *I* know you have particular interests—concerning the fate of Joseph Jennings."

"How do—"

He held his hand up, killing her question. "I also know you're close to burnout." It was a statement, not a question.

Two hours ago—although it felt like a lifetime ago—she'd been dealing with a road accident victim who'd been brought in. He just had a few bruises from the collision, but from the general state of him, it looked as though he lived on the streets. This was an opportunity for her to patch him up and get him into a better state than before the accident. She'd been checking his feet when she felt something tapping her head. Before she'd had a chance to look up, she felt something trickling down her face. "Oh, Christ!" she had moaned, before looking up. Another hour had passed before she'd been able to shower. "I've got to get out of here," she had said under her breath as she dried herself off.

"How did you find me?"

"We have our ways. We've been sourcing people from these high-pressure medical institutes… seeking out the talented overworked-and-underpaid staff. We'd very much like you to consider our offer." He handed her the folder that had been underneath his arm.

"Everything's there, including a business card with my cell number if you have any questions. If we could have your reply before the end of the week?"

"No pressure, then."

"Well, considerably less than you're currently under." His appearance softened with a smile. "This is your chance to join a very select group. We look forward to hearing from you," he said, then slid out of the room.

Theresa lit another cigarette and scanned the documents, her eyebrows raised.

It's got to be the Sanctuary! Oh my God!

She checked her watch and groaned—five minutes late.

She put the paperback away. It wasn't as if she hadn't read it a thousand times before. The cover was so creased that you could barely make out the title: *The Life and Death of Joseph Jennings*.

*

Sarah Turner smiled and tried not to look nervous.

Just getting to this point had been a nightmare. The call for the interview had come through just as her washing machine had broken down and was flooding her kitchen. She had been soaking up the water with old gray—once white—towels when her mobile had rung.

"Yes?" she barked down the phone.

There was a pause, and just as she was about to hang up, a voice said, "Mrs. Turner?"

"*Ms.* Turner, but yes. Who's this?"

"My name is Michael Redman. I'm the senior recruiter for the Brighter Futures Group."

Senior recruiter? Well, ain't that just swell for you! Brighter Futures Group? By Christ, this had better not be a sales call, or I swear to God I will…

When the penny dropped, Sarah had to stop herself from swearing. "Is this about the administrator role?"

"The *senior* administrator role."

Always with the senior *with this one.* "Great, how can I help you?" She looked down and realized that her fingers were crossed so tightly that they'd turned red.

"We'd like to invite you for an interview."

"Brilliant!" She wanted to punch the air, but managed to rein it in.

"Tomorrow at the Holiday Inn on Main Street, at eleven."

"Uh, tomorrow…" She hesitated as a spike of terror stabbed at her heart.

"Very well. Thank you for—"

"Tomorrow at eleven. Yes, that'll be fine."

There was a heart-stopping silence at the other end of the line. "Are you sure?"

"Yes, no problem. That's fine. Tomorrow at eleven. The Holiday Inn on Main Street."

She took down the details of where to meet and then began the horse-trading of who would look after Alice, her eight-year-old daughter. This would almost certainly mean begging her ex, through gritted teeth, to take her. Then there was the question of how to get a day off from her current dead-end job on short notice and without arousing suspicion. Sarah didn't want to be dishonest and have a sick day. Instead, she rang up and said she had to take an urgent day off, giving the all-purpose excuse of "personal reasons."

This was her opportunity to get back on top.

Sarah walked out of the two-hour interview exhausted, not really caring whether she had got the job—and expecting that she hadn't. She had faced an interview panel of three people: two men and a woman. They had raked over her résumé. They had obviously done their background research, leaving her no place to hide, so she'd had to do some dancing and weaving just to stand a chance. She was happy—relieved, in fact—to get out of the Holiday Inn. She managed to get home and drink half a glass of red wine before falling asleep on her sofa.

Sarah forgot about the senior administrator role—and the stupid money they were offering—and just carried on battling with life. She was amazed when she got a call, nearly a fortnight later, for a second interview, preceded by the usual psychometric tests.

This time she had to schlep out to Baltimore to a nondescript office, which Sarah guessed was a short-term let. This time she was faced by a different set of people, but the same ratio of men to women. If anything, the interview was harder this time around and, ten minutes in, she felt herself break into a cold sweat. Sarah decided that this time she was going to get a few jabs in herself. When they asked the inevitable "Do you have any questions for us?" she was ready.

"Yes. Who's this job actually working for? I've done a bit of research on the Brighter Futures Group. It's a phantom, the second cousin of Harvey the Rabbit. The only information I could find out was that it's a 'leading national organization,' but that could mean anything from NASA to the mob."

"It's certainly not the mob," the woman said with a little laugh, which made Sarah want to punch her.

"So, what is it?"

"A leading national organization. Do you have any further questions for us?"

"No." Sarah was certain she'd fucked it up this time, and she didn't care.

She was opening an overdue bill and giving a nervous glance at what she thought was a leak from her newly repaired washing machine when the phone rang.

"Mrs. Turner?"

Oh, God, who is this and how much do they want? "*Ms. Turner. How can I help you?*"

"This is Michael Redman."

Michael Redman? Why is that name familiar?

"The senior recruiter at the Brighter Futures Group."

"Oh, hello."

"Hello. The interview panel was very impressed with you."

They were?

"We'd like to invite you to a third and final interview, but it's in an unusual location. You may need to allow two days for it."

Oh, God, what have I signed up for? Never mind! I might not get the job.

This time she did have to take the day off sick. She found herself at a cold, wind-swept, private airfield at 5:30 a.m., dressed in her best—her only—business suit. She was joined by two other people, who were shivering in their finest attire: a bearded, slim man, and a grumpy, blonde woman. Sarah couldn't blame the woman for looking grumpy; she wasn't happy about being up at this time. They all exchanged half-hearted smiles.

From a hangar, an unmarked private jet taxied towards

them, stopped, and the door opened. A heavily built, suited man with a shaved head stood at the top of the steps and gestured for them to come aboard. Hesitantly they all filed in.

Sarah had expected the private jet to be more opulent; the truth was that it had seen better days. There were twelve seats in all, and the stuffing was coming out of a few of them, and the walls were scuffed.

"The flight will be approximately one hour and thirty minutes, followed by a fifty-minute car journey at the other end." Those were the only words that the thickset man said for the entire journey.

They all buckled up and were in the air within five minutes. The noise of the engines precluded any conversation, so the three interviewees either looked out of the window or looked down at the threadbare carpet.

They landed in a location that Sarah found hard to distinguish from the one where they'd taken off. They were ushered without a word into a large people carrier, before setting off on their twisting and bumpy journey. Sarah had never been a great traveler, and the only thing that stopped her throwing up was being able to prize open the window slightly to get some fresh air. When the car stopped, she was so relieved to get out that she'd almost forgotten about the interview to come.

Sarah found herself on a windy, snow-dusted mountain. She looked at her fellow interviewees; they seemed to be as bewildered as she was.

"Before we go any further, there are two things I'm going to need you to do," said the muscle, handing them a two-page document and what looked like a piece of cloth.

"What's this?"

"It's a non-disclosure form. Regardless of the outcome of this interview, it's to confirm that you won't discuss anything you see today. Take time to read it, as we do aggressively police it."

"Okay," said Sarah. *Holy shit!* "And what's this?" she said, holding up the cloth.

"It's a blindfold. When you've read and signed the disclosure form, put the blindfold on, and you will be led to where the interview will take place."

Sarah laughed. "You're joking?"

The expression on his face made it very clear that he wasn't.
Jesus, this had better be worth it.

She read the document—it took her ten minutes. It was pretty full-on. She signed it and put the blindfold on.

I can't believe I'm doing this.

After a few moments, she felt an arm on hers.

"Follow me. I'll lead you," said an unfamiliar female voice.

She let herself be led.

It felt as if they'd been walking for three minutes before they stopped. She heard some tapping on a keyboard, a "whoosh", and then they went inside somewhere. A voice said, "You may take the blindfold off." She obeyed and saw the other two do the same. She blinked at the light and found herself at a junction with corridors leading off in four directions. There was a door in front of her.

"If you'll come with me."

Sarah turned around and saw the first smile of the day from a red-haired lady. The interviewees were taken off in three separate directions. The red-haired lady led Sarah along a circular walkway. She looked over the barrier and her queasiness from earlier returned.

Where the fuck am I?

She could barely see the bottom of the drop. There were apartments built into the rock, and she could make out three bridges crisscrossing the space.

Am I going to be working for a James Bond villain? Maybe not Bond. Maybe...

The lady politely-but-firmly guided Sarah away and into a meeting room. There was a vast black table and at the nearest end was a slim man. He walked forward and shook Sarah's hand.

"Afternoon! It's good to finally meet you. My name is Michael Redman."

"Great, it's good to put a face to the name." *This must be good news, being met by the senior recruiter.*

There were two other people in the room: a ginger-haired woman and an African-American man. Neither introduced themselves; they just nodded at her.

After the previous two interviews, Sarah didn't think there was anything else they could go over, but they surprised her by bringing up aspects of her life and career that she'd forgotten about. Then came the knotty problem of why she had left her previous job.

"I'm going to be completely honest as I don't think there's any point lying. It was politics. I made the wrong alliances and I paid the price."

"We were told something different."

"Oh, yes?"

"We were told you weren't up to the job. That when it came to the crunch, you didn't have the requisite skills."

Holy shit! Sarah didn't know if she meant the interview panel, or her previous employers: the motherfuckers who had bullied her, sidelined her, and then gradually nudged her out. She could feel a tide of anger rising inside.

"Look, I'm going to make an educated guess here. You contacted my former employers back before the first interview?"

"Why would we do that?"

Sarah shrugged. "Dunno, but I'm thinking that if, you really believed that, then I wouldn't have gotten a phone call in the first place."

Silence.

"As I'm on a roll, I'm going to make another educated guess. I think this place is the Sanctuary, the bunker created by Joseph Jennings back in the 60s, and—if the rumors are true—refurbed as *the* exclusive destination for people who don't want to be disturbed." She saw a slight twitch in the left side of Redman's face and had to suppress a smile. "Why would you hold that information back until this late stage in the process?" She shook her head slightly. "You've seen where I've worked. You've no doubt talked to *all* of my past employers. You know I can do this job; *I* know I can do this job. You have everything you need to make your decision, so give me the job or don't."

She looked each of them in turn in the eye, and none of them could return her gaze.

Well, that's me fucked.

Redman cleared his throat. "Well, thanks for coming in, Mrs. Turner. We'll be in touch."

They rang the next day and offered her the job.

*

Theresa looked out at the wet, gray afternoon and tried to decide what to do with her life. She tried not to look at the letter, smoothing it out on the table and drinking some of the coffee she really should have put more milk in. However hard she tried not to look at the letter, her eyes kept getting dragged back to it.

Dear Dr O'Brien.

Thank you for applying for the role of Senior Trauma Consultant. We regret to inform you—

Yes, I bet you deeply regret it.

She knew she'd aced the practical exam, and the third interview, in front of the medical board, had been all smiles and nodding heads, so how had that translated into "We regret to inform you"?

At least now that she was single, she wouldn't have to put up with that flash of pity in his eyes after this latest setback. Theresa could cope with anything else, but she was starting to doubt exactly how much more she could take.

She was tired.

It wasn't fair. What did she have to do? They seemed to have some hidden checklist, and whatever was on it, she didn't tick the right boxes. When was it going to be her turn?

"Have you made your decision?"

Theresa almost spilled her coffee. The well-dressed vulture guy seemed to have appeared out of thin air.

"Jesus! How did you- No, never mind."

And there was that vaguely amused look on his face. "Well? Have you made up your mind?"

"In all honesty, I'd forgotten all about it."

"That's fine. I admire honesty."

I somehow don't think you do.

"What's the letter say?"

"Nothing." She folded it up and put it in her pocket.

"You still haven't answered my question."

She'd lied. She hadn't forgotten; it had been at the back of her mind since the offer had been made, and she had decided. She'd decided to turn it down. Her fingers felt the paper of the letter in her pocket. *We regret to inform you...* it whispered.

"I've decided to accept your offer."

The vulture man smiled.

*

It was with a mixture of fear and excitement that Sarah entered the Sanctuary on her first day of work. It almost washed away her guilt at having to ask Alice's grandmother to look after her for the next three months. No families or children were allowed in the Sanctuary, and it was understood that it was a three-month live-in position with a month off. There had been tears from Alice. "But why do you have to go away, Mom?" she had said, her incomprehension showing through wet, puffy, red eyes. No amount of promises or explanations from Sarah could dry her daughter's tears.

Sarah hoped that some sort of understanding could be reached after she'd worked there long enough. She'd even looked at the possibility of moving to Arrow's Reach, the nearest town, but that was a bridge she'd cross when she came to it. For now, she had to concentrate on the job.

After getting through the seemingly endless sets of doors, she stood at the main vantage point, which afforded her the best view of the cavern. Its vastness was breathtaking. She looked down onto the ground floor piazza, where people were walking around at a leisurely pace, some dressed in bathrobes. She noticed the layers of different levels and the two elevators that connected them all. She looked up and saw what looked like another mini-level, but with just one set of badly lit stairs leading to it. It stood out to Sarah because it contrasted so much with the rest of the Sanctuary. The top of the cavern seemed to be open to the elements, but after staring longer, Sarah realized that they'd somehow managed to artificially create a blue sky, even down to the occasional cloud floating by. It almost looked metallic.

Welcome to the Sanctuary!" He put his hand out and plastered on his most charming smile.

"Thanks." She shook his hand. Did he see her go to wipe it on her pants?

"We hope you have a long and happy career with Brighter Futures Group. You'll see me around, and if there's anything I can do for you… *anything*… don't be afraid to ask."

She just nodded and thanked him again.

"Well, I'll leave you to it." He had moved to walk away, then turned back in a manner designed to look casual and said, "Oh, it would be useful if in the next few days, you could check if there are any artifacts from the original inhabitants that haven't been declared. It's not a big thing, just an interest of mine." He looked her straight in the eyes. "I'd appreciate it if you could look into it." He smiled. "So… I'll leave that with you." and with that, he walked off.

*

Rodger was running. He ducked into Portland Place and looked over his shoulder. They were still chasing him, but he was pretty sure he could lose them down Redcar Avenue. He had lost his mate Rich somewhere while they had tried to make their escape.

It had been Rich's idea to rip off the corner shop, but Rodger didn't think the two men chasing him would really care about whose idea it had been. His lungs felt as if they were going to bust, but he couldn't afford to get caught. He was out on parole. If they caught him, the best he could expect was to be turned over to the police, and that would mean he wouldn't see the outside of Erlstroke prison for a *long* time. They would probably give him a beating and *then* turn him over to the police, so Rodger pushed on with fear propelling him. He sped around a corner, sweat flying in a sweep off his face, and ran up the high street, dodging the office workers on their lunch break. As he approached Saint Nick's Market, he glanced behind him. He'd lost one of them, but the other was catching up with him.

"Fuck!" Sweat was turning his Umbro top a dark green. The only chance he had to lose his pursuer was in the rats' warren of alleyways around the market. He slowed down, pulled his hood over his head, shoved his hands in his pockets and joined the people who were looking around the stalls. He glanced up to see his pursuer running past, elbowing his way through the shoppers to the other side of the market. When Rodger was sure that he wasn't coming back, he turned back onto the high street, chuckling to himself as he rolled himself a celebratory cigarette.

Rodger headed out of the center of Bristol towards Clifton and the house he was squatting in.

After fighting his way through the overgrown garden, he looked around before shifting the piece of timber and plywood out of the doorway, put there to bar entry to the door. The nails had been left in place to give the impression that the door was securely boarded-up.

The pungent smell of marijuana wafted out as soon as he removed the plywood. A huge smile spread across Rodger's face as he anticipated a very pleasant afternoon in a haze of smoke, telling stories of his daring raid and extraordinary escape.

The air was knocked out of him as he was slammed against the wall of the squat.

"What the fuck do you think you're playing at?"

Rodger tried to swing a punch at his assailant but only managed to weakly push back.

"Oh, Jesus, Mazza, you scared the shit out of me."

Mazza was the oldest resident of the squat. His face had deep lines and a permanent red tinge—Rodger couldn't decide whether it was from drink, being out in the sun, or a combination of both. Mazza's hair was gray, short, and spiked on top, with a rat-tail hanging down the back of his neck. His arms were sleeved in tattoos, some self-inked.

"You've really fucked yourself this time, boyo."

That was the problem with Mazza: the big fucking chip on his shoulder.

"Yeah, what makes you say that?"

"Do you know who you and R2D2 tried to rip off? The Samson brothers."

"Oh, shit." Rodger felt as if a bucket of cold water had been thrown over him.

"Yep."

"What am I going to do?"

"You're going to fuck off sharpish, boyo. That's what you're going to do. The Samson brothers are going to be looking for you, and they're going to find you. So I'm packing up and getting out. Well done, you fucked it up for everyone. You'd better find a rock and hide underneath it, but I doubt that'll save you. They've already fucked Rich up pretty bad. He'll be supping most of his meals through a straw from now on. You don't just have to get out of Dodge, you have to get as far away as you fucking can."

Rodge needs to get out of Dodge.

Rodger rammed the few clothes he had in a rucksack and got out of the squat as quickly as he could.

Walking through the streets of Bristol, Rodger couldn't help but feel twitchy. He constantly checked over his shoulder. As he walked and smoked a cigarette he'd rolled earlier, he formed a plan. He'd been thinking of getting out of Bristol for a while and had stashed some cash away from a few deals. Leaving now meant that he had to move some plans forward, and it required a groveling phone call to his estranged brother in America. His hands were shaking as he dialed the number.

Please pick up.

"'Allo?" a gruff voice answered.

"Ken, it's Rodge…"

Ten minutes later, after a lot of apologizing for past misdeeds and slights, he'd bagged himself a stay in Anchorage with his brother. He stopped off at a set of lockers to pick up his passport, visited an ATM, and then caught a bus to Bristol Airport. As Rodger flew over the city, he tried to summon a feeling of remorse for leaving the place he'd called his home for twenty-plus years, but he felt nothing.

Twenty-two hours and one stopover later, his taxi pulled up outside his brother's house. He'd only stopped briefly outside the airport to buy a chunky lighter with the Harley-Davidson logo on it and roll himself a cigarette; he lit another as he looked up at his brother's home: a large, detached house that resembled a log cabin.

He's done well for himself.

"You're here, then," said his brother, hardly happy to see him.

Rodger was so tired he could barely stand up. After he'd slept for fourteen hours, he sat down to breakfast and coffee. Ken's wife, Sandra, sat and silently stared at Rodger.

"So you've just come for a holiday?" Ken asked him.

"Something like that," Rodger said, looking down at his ham and eggs.

"How long you staying?" the wife asked.

Fucking hell, you're really making me feel welcome.

"Uh, I dunno. Maybe a couple of weeks."

"A couple of weeks," his sister-in-law repeated.

Ken and his Sandra exchanged a look that made Rodger think it may not have been such a bad thing to have stayed in Bristol and squared up to the Samson brothers. The next day he started to look for a job and a cheap—very cheap—apartment.

A week later, and Rodger was being made to feel about as welcome in the house as a dead possum underneath the floorboards. He was spending his time in Henry's, the local bar. He hadn't had any luck finding employment—possibly not helped by the fact he wasn't quite legit when it came to work. Although it wasn't critical yet, Rodger was aware that his cash was dwindling, and the joyous in-laws had begun to make noises about charging rent. He was becoming better-known in the bar, though, and felt comfortable making some discreet inquiries amongst the regulars about work.

"I know of a job," a truck driver told Rodger after he'd had his lips loosened by a couple of Budweisers.

"What's it doing?"

"Sorta farmer, sorta gardener. It's well-paid and accommodation is thrown in for free."

"Sorta farmer? I could do that. I've done it in the past. What's the catch?"

The truck driver shifted on his stool, accidentally let out a fart, and laughed.

"Well, here's the thing. It's not your usual gardening job. For one thing, it's underground."

"Eh?"

"Yeah, long story. Usually with this place there's loads of hoops you have to jump through, but I've heard that they're desperate for someone and it's a six-month contract."

"How did you get to know about it?"

"I'm a friendly guy," he said, taking a big glug of his Bud. "I take a lot of supplies to this... place, and I get talking to people. I know they've been struggling to find someone without attachments who's willing to take on a six-month contract. I think you'd fit the bill."

"Great!"

"Of course, if I make the introduction, I'd have to have something to make it worth my while."

"How much?"

The truck driver stared at Rodger and licked his lips. Rodger could almost see the cogs turning in his head, wondering how much to pitch his figure at.

"Two hundred dollars."

"Fuck off!"

The truck driver took another swig of his Bud.

"Okay, okay, I'll cut you some slack. One hundred and fifty—but just because I like you."

"Yeah, yeah, yeah. Okay, I'll pay. But if this is a con, I swear to God—"

"It ain't no con. Meet me outside here at 5:40 a.m. tomorrow with the cash."

Next morning, Rodger was still wiping the sleep out of his eyes when the truck driver arrived to pick him up. Three hours later he was outside the Sanctuary. An hour later he was being interviewed by the head of HR and was told he had the job. He rang his brother to tell him he wouldn't be back. That was the last time Rodger saw daylight for six months.

*

Theresa O'Brien had originally taken the job in the ER at Detroit Mercy Hospital out of a strong desire to do something good, to make a difference in the most deprived areas. Her then-boyfriend hadn't shared her sense of civic duty. Towards the end of the relationship, whenever they were in the apartment together—and usually drunk—they were only able to communicate with each other by shouting and slamming doors. The last horrific two weeks had been like a war between them. After one particularly ferocious argument, he had managed to inflict a deep wound.

"You're damaged goods," he'd said. "There's a flaw in you. It's not big, but it's there, and one day something is going to turn that flaw into a crack that's going to break you apart." And with that, her boyfriend had picked up his bags and left.

A flaw? What the fuck did he mean by that? If there is ever money lying around in the apartment, it inevitably ends up in his pocket, so if there's anyone with a flaw…

She had to face the silent judgment of an empty apartment.

Theresa didn't have much time to reflect on his words except in the few seconds before she fell asleep.

There's a flaw in you.

CHAPTER 5

Rodger didn't know what they wanted to talk to him about, but he had a feeling it wasn't going to be good.

It had been a normal day. He had doused them the week before to make sure that they were dead. Rodger liked to burn them, too, just to show the little bastards who was boss. He had felt really satisfied up until the point that Tom, his supervisor, said, "Can I have a word with you once you've finished that?"

He didn't know what he'd done wrong, but he suspected the other farmers were jealous—especially Tom, who wanted him out so he could become head farmer.

The fucker. Well, if that's what he wants, he's fucking welcome to it. I don't give a fuck.

The problem was he did—as his clenched fists proved as he walked into the office with Tom. He loved it in the Sanctuary. He'd never felt as at home anywhere else, and he was good at his job—*really* good, actually. Rodger had done some gardening before but had exaggerated his experience in the interview.

However, as soon as he began to work on the farm, he found that he just got it. He seemed to be able to make things grow when other people couldn't, and the plots he managed were always the most productive. The other farmers nudged him for his secret. What did he do to the soil? Did he bring in his own chemicals? The only secret was that he loved his job. Rodger loved the process of cultivating the crops, seeing the cause-and-effect of his work, and the benefits that care brought. Three months into working on the farm, the head farmer quit, and Rodger and Tom found themselves filling in. Leave had been curtailed—which was no skin off Rodger's nose as, whenever he'd gone out, he'd just found himself getting drunk in Arrow's Reach and killing time 'til he could get back to the farm. Rodger volunteered to let Tom have his leave.

"Take a seat. This won't take long."

Yeah, I bet it won't, you snake. I should pick the chair up and smack it across your fucking head.

"Alright, Rodge?"

"Yeah, fine, Tom. You?"

"Yeah, good." He coughed. "The thing is…"

Here we go…

"The thing is we need a full-time head farmer, and I was wondering if you'd be interested in the role?"

"I … what?"

"Would you be interested in being head farmer?"

"But I thought …"

Tom shrugged and smiled. "I could do without the ass-ache,

to be fair, and I think after this contract comes to an end, I'll hang up my mole-man gloves. I miss seeing the sun."

Rodger nodded.

"So, what do you think?"

Rodger didn't know what to say. "This has been okayed with…?" Rodger tilted his head upwards.

"Them upstairs? Yeah, the hours you've put in and the work you've done haven't gone unnoticed. So, what do you reckon?"

"Uh, what? The job?" Rodger laughed. "Yeah, of course."

"Great! It's a pay raise—a big pay raise, to be honest. Not that you give a shit, I suspect. There'll be a three-month probation period, but again…" Tom shrugged once more. "Congratulations, head farmer!" He put his hand out and Rodger shook it. He walked out of the room happy but dazed.

*

Theresa felt at home from the moment she walked into the Sanctuary.

This is it. This is the turning point.

She hadn't immediately taken up the offer from the recruiter at Brighter Futures s Group; in fact, she'd forgotten all about it. She'd put it in the pocket of her green scrub trousers together with the rest of the detritus of her day. Two days later, while in the ER looking for a bandage for a meth addict who'd come in with a head injury, she suddenly had to shake herself awake. She realized that she'd just put her head on a pillar and had fallen asleep standing up. She couldn't have been asleep for more than a few seconds but, upon waking, her current situation came into sharp focus, sending her into deep despair. She shook her head to try to shake out the fog. Theresa put her hand in her pocket and pulled out the Brighter Futures Group card, which had miraculously survived a wash. She stared at the number on the card in the sickly light and, in that moment, resolved to give it a call. She then found the bandages and went in search of her eighth coffee of the night.

Less than a month later she was walking into the Sanctuary. Two days after she'd rung, she'd had an interview and had been offered the job as auxiliary doctor. Because she had so much untaken leave, she didn't have to give her two months' notice. Then there was a frenzied round of giving her landlord notice and boxing up what few possessions she had. She would be working three months on and three months off. The three months off was paid leave, and Brighter Futures Group even provided a choice of apartments—one in Arrow's Reach—if she wanted one.

Since accepting the job in the ER, Theresa hadn't had time to stop, and so, when she walked into the cool, air-conditioned climate of the Sanctuary, she felt as if she could breathe again. She was shown around the site, including the infirmary, which was cleaner and better-equipped than the ER she'd worked in, where she met Arnold Schriver, the primary physician, who was tall with curly, thinning hair, and glasses. He smiled at her and shook her hand warmly.

"I hear you've come from Detroit Mercy?"

"Yep."

He whistled through his teeth. "That must have been a tough gig."

She smiled. "It had its moments. You?"

"Ah," he said, running a hand through his hair, "long story— similar to yours but in a more senior position in the Bronx. They like to recruit medics from intense ERs. They figure— probably rightly—that you can handle anything that can be thrown at you."

"And what do you get thrown at you here?"

He lowered his voice. "This is a sweet gig, to be honest," he laughed. "The worst thing I've had to deal with has been a sprained ankle. Most of the time it's topping up prescriptions, and there's not even very much of that. Like I said, it's pretty sweet. Anyway, you'll want to see your apartment. You're in for a treat! I look forward to working with you." He shook her hand again and she was shown out.

The next stop on the tour of the Sanctuary was her apartment. Schriver was right; it was a treat. It was more luxurious than any of the apartments she'd ever rented. She looked at the bed and couldn't wait to collapse into it. She thought that, as soon as her head touched the pillow, she would sleep for forty-eight hours. It felt like a weight being lifted off her shoulders to think that, when she woke up, she wouldn't have the stress of going into the ER for an eighteen-hour-plus shift. Theresa wanted to savor the feeling of release and walked out to look around at the vast space of the Sanctuary. She was amazed how, this far underground, deep inside a mountain, it could be so light.

She looked up at the "sky." It was blue and light. She'd heard the light changed according to the time of the day and the seasons to keep the residents' circadian rhythms in order. She understood that the steel roof was painted with some kind of high-spec green paint, and there was some setup with mirrors that reflected natural light into the Sanctuary.

As she took in the view a voice seemed to whisper in her head.

Find it.

She turned around and standing behind her was a tall man who looked to be in his seventies. He had piercing green eyes, high cheekbones, with the few remaining white hairs combed across his head.

"I was wondering if I could have a word."

CHAPTER 6

THE PRIVATE JOURNAL OF JOSEPH JENNINGS—
NOVEMBER 3, 1968

*H*obson might actually have done something right for once! Ha! This looks like it could be the place. I have concerns, of course. I do wonder about the structure. Hobson assures me that this can be overcome, but it remains to be seen. He continues to come to me with trivial details. Hasn't the man got a brain in his head? What do I pay him for if not to sort these details out? It'll be worth it if we can get this to my specifications.

Hobson has also discovered something of a curiosity—a cave painting. It seems primitive but retains a certain power. I seem to be drawn to it and ask myself questions: What kind of creature does it depict? It is undoubtedly a creature. Did the people before us worship it? Did they make blood sacrifices to it? I have a feeling that they did. I've seen paintings by the great masters, but this simple, faded cave painting—probably done with berry juice *and coal—is the most fascinating piece of art I have ever seen. At last, I have found my sanctuary from the coming apocalypse. It is coming and I must be prepared. I have seen it, as clearly as I can see this pen and paper now: fire raining down on the earth. I find that I must explore my new sanctuary more. I suspect—in fact, I believe—that we are not alone there. Something was there before us and may still linger. I must find out what lies in the shadows.*

This place whispers to me…

*

Hobson stood on the ground floor of the Sanctuary and looked up. He couldn't help but feel satisfied, and he allowed himself a smile. It was hard to believe that it was just two years ago when he'd been standing on the ledge, looking down into the inky darkness. Since then, they'd done a lot of work burrowing into the cavern and reinforcing the sides. They'd worked on a spiral design which opened the cavern out at the ground level. They would easily fit in everything that had been requested and still have a vast amount of room for any future development: Jennings was nothing if not mercurial when it came to his whims. Not all of the Sanctuary had been developed yet, but enough had that, if the shit hit the fan tomorrow, the apocalypse could be waited out in a certain degree of comfort.

The ground floor was the size of a football pitch, but it had an irregular, kidney bean shape. The ground had been leveled and poured over with concrete. Three farms had been set up shortly after they'd started converting the cavern. Nutrient-rich earth had been brought in at great expense along with hydroponic lights. A full-time gardener had been employed to ensure that the farms would be producing viable foodstuffs as quickly as possible. Although the farms had only been finished a month ago, they were already producing sweetcorn and potatoes. The farms were sandwiched between the natural springs, which were helping to irrigate the ground. Some basic apartments had been carved into the ground floor. Between the ground floor and Jennings's apartment some storage units had been built into the walls. Food and medical supplies were stockpiled there and could be accessed via ladders attached to the walls. The distance from Jennings's apartment to the ground level was eight hundred feet, and so a set of steps had been built into the rock, which spiraled around the cavern. A rudimentary elevator had been built to transport tools and workers to the ground level. Any produce from the gardens could also be lifted to where it was needed. A plumbing system had been set up to supply water to the apartments. Each apartment was fitted with central heating, which was powered by solar power cells set up on top. Work was ongoing to build a wind farm on the outcrop and a hydroelectric plant to harness energy from the Arctic Ocean.

Hobson had walked around the perimeter many times. He knew there were many tunnels and catacombs that snaked out from the ground floor and into the mountain. About a quarter of these hadn't been fully explored, including the Bridge of Souls—also known as Tunnel Sixteen—which had been declared out-of-bounds and blocked off. The Bridge of Souls was situated on the very outskirts of the Sanctuary's perimeter, at the farthest point to the north. Survey Team Three, led by Robert Jayston, had never been found, and now, eight months on, Hobson doubted if they ever would be. When Survey Team Three failed to return from the Bridge of Souls, Hobson had told those who had asked that they had finished their work and had left the site. Only two people had asked—which was as much a relief as it was depressing.

Suddenly, out of the corner of his eye, Hobson thought he saw something dart into one of the tunnels.

What was that? He looked around, squinting into the darkness. *Was... was something moving?*

"Hello?" he said, jumping at the slight echo his voice created. Hobson ran his hands over his face. This place did strange things to you. You ended up jumping at your own shadow. But was there something down here?

He'd been down in the cavern—now renamed the Sanctuary by Jennings—more than anyone, including his boss, and he'd not seen any evidence to suggest that there was anything other than the people they saw fit to bring down. He hadn't seen or heard the bats that some of the contractors had suggested were indigenous. Other than shadows, he had seen nothing. After being down here so long, you started to forget that there was anything thing else, that there was a world outside. At the height of construction, there had been forty people working to convert Black Cove into the Sanctuary.

Jennings had expressly asked that his apartment be built on

the plateau. He'd drawn up the plans for the apartment himself. It was built around the cave paintings that they'd found, and the cave paintings were to remain uncovered. The majority of the work done in the Sanctuary had been to reinforce the structure of the cavern, and significant work had been done on Jennings's apartment and the ground level. Most of the ground level was being used as storage for food and other necessities. It was a bit basic and, if he were being charitable, Hobson would describe the ground level as a warehouse. In amongst the necessities, such as food and medical supplies, some of the digging equipment was still lying around. It wasn't pretty.

After a painstaking survey, the source of the water had been traced to a spring even farther down within the mountain. The porous rock did a good job of purifying the water. Hobson couldn't have asked for a better solution. The power had been a harder job to complete, and Hobson hadn't told Jennings that it wasn't yet completely finished. The fledgling solar panels had been working to seventy per cent of their potential at best, and the wind and hydro farms had taken a lot of work to set up for not a great deal of return. But Hobson was confident that these were all problems that could be ironed out. Every day saw an improvement. He just wondered if they would be quick enough for his boss.

The outcrop tower of rock had been the focus of Hobson's attention when it came to self-sufficient power. However, just getting over there was a project in itself. On more than one occasion, Hobson had felt like the Sanctuary itself was fighting against him, that it didn't want to be changed, that it wanted to be left alone. The first crew had nearly capsized getting over to the outcrop. The second crew had got there without any trouble but had found that pretty much all their equipment had malfunctioned in some way. Eventually, Hobson had managed to get the hydroelectric plant working on the outcrop, but only by throwing a lot of men, time, and money at it. The outcrop had been identified as the best location to harness gusts blasting in from the Arctic Ocean, but for various reasons, the plant was only operating at sixty per cent of its capacity. Hobson finally had to step back from the problems with the outcrop to manage the work being done elsewhere on the Sanctuary, which had been reliant for the most part on the petrol-powered generator. Hobson estimated that if the shit hit the fan and they had to go into lockdown, there would be enough power to keep the place going for two months, with perhaps an additional month on a rationed power supply. Not that Jennings seemed overly concerned.

The entrance had been built up and reinforced with a series of thick steel doors, which had been bolted into the rock of the mountain. Hobson had suggested having a viewing deck built at the very top of the Sanctuary, with one-way, reinforced glass, from where they could look across at the Arctic Ocean. Hobson imagined just how stunning it would be—even better if you were warm and looking at it with a Scotch in your hand, ice clinking in the class, taking in the full vista of the ocean, regardless of the state of the world. When Hobson had managed to grab some time with his boss, he had outlined his idea. Jennings had responded with an infuriating non-committal, "Hmmm, yes, we'll see," which could mean anything. This is what Jennings always said when he didn't want to make a commitment in case it all went wrong. He liked to have a get-out. Hobson thought it was worth pursuing, so had plans drawn up. Now all he had to do was find time to put them under Jennings's nose. He ran his hand over his face.

Jesus, I could do with a cup of coffee.

Something like a growl echoed around the cavern, and Hobson decided it was time to get out, way out. He wanted-—he needed—to smell the ocean and feel the sun on his face, even if it was just for an hour.

*

The Private Journal of Joseph Jennings— June 3, 1969

I couldn't possibly have guessed, all these years. How could I have known? I didn't know until I came down here that I was just a shell. I didn't know until I came here that I was just play-acting at being Joseph Jennings. Ha! Whoever is he? Whenever people mentioned Joseph Jennings or addressed me by that name, I would look around, searching for him. I didn't recognize him. They couldn't be talking about me, could they? Joseph Jennings was alien, something other, nothing to do with me. How could he be? It wasn't until I burrowed into the ground that I found my true destiny. All this time. All these wasted years. I've spent all these years with distractions, building and buying, and all to fill this hole in my center: the deep hole in this shell they call Joseph Jennings. Shoveling more and more dirt in to fill the hole. Trying to fill it. But nothing can fill this deep, deep emptiness. I didn't know true emptiness until I came here. I've looked into the Bridge of Souls and seen the emptiness, the void. The deep dark Oblivion Black. I fear it, but I want it. The Sanctuary was always here. I knew it was here; I just had to find it. Maybe I'm home. Maybe I can finally be safe. In the darkness, it waits for me. It's been waiting for me for a long, long time. I hear Oblivion Black calling. And now nothing else matters.

CHAPTER 7

They quite clearly didn't need him—or possibly want him—as a member, and because of that, Danny wanted it even more. He'd left with no idea if he'd got in or not. He really wanted to tell them to shove their attitude and their sanctuary up their ass, but then, as the weeks went by and he heard nothing, his anger began to dissipate, and he started to wonder. He'd been close to ringing Matthew when the call eventually came.

"They've made their decision. You free this afternoon?"

He wasn't. "Yeah."

From then until the meeting, Danny began to cultivate the nonchalant attitude he was going to present when Matthew told him he hadn't got in. The last time he could remember time dragging like this was when he was waiting to hear if he'd got the loan for his first start-up. For once, he couldn't get to the bar quick enough for the meeting. Every minute that Matthew was late, Danny's fists clenched a little bit more; when he finally turned up, it took every inch of self-control not to scream at him for an answer.

Before he'd even sat down, Matthew said, "You're in."

"Shit! Really? Awesome! When can I go?"

"Anytime you want, but I have to go with you the first time. I've got to act as your chaperone."

"Fuck off!"

Matthew smiled.

Danny quickly cleared his diary for that weekend and, after some questions back and forth, arranged the hire of a private jet to take them to the Sanctuary.

When they arrived, there was some administrative work to complete, including taking Danny's fingerprints for a lock scan, which he hadn't noticed the first time around. They were welcomed at the door by a professional-looking woman in a smart dress, with her blond hair tied back and a broad smile.

"Hi, I'm Amanda. I'll be showing you around and taking you to your exclusive luxury apartment. Yours is number 43, which has just had a complete refurb."

For this privilege, Danny had paid a substantial non-refundable deposit, in addition to locking himself into a minimum two-year contract. As soon as they got into the Sanctuary, Amanda gave him the guided tour. It didn't take long before Danny was unable to work out where he was in relation to the original meeting room where he'd had his interrogation. His eye was caught by an apartment that was set apart from the others; in fact, there seemed to be no way of getting to it. It sat high-up in the Sanctuary, positioned on a podium made of metal that looked a lot older than that used to construct the other buildings. There were no lights on it and the windows were blacked-out. Danny would certainly have missed it had it not been for the steps that had been carved into the rock walls and spiraled the length of the Sanctuary. They looked to be the same age as the apartment. The railing that ran parallel to the steps was rusted and there were parts missing, and it looked like the exterior of the apartment had been patched up with other building material. The same care and attention hadn't been paid to it as had been lavished on the rest of the Sanctuary. It seemed to skulk in shadows at the corner of the cavern. Uneven steps snaked all the way up to the apartment, but the last stretch had been sectioned off with a heavy-duty padlocked chain.

"What's that?" Did he see Amanda flinch?

"Oh, that's just our tech center. It deals predominantly with our Internet. I'm not techy, I'm afraid, so I can't tell you much more," she said a little too casually. "I'll take you down to the lower ground level so you can see the communal area." Danny looked up at the orphaned room before being ushered into the elevator. The journey to the lower ground level took two minutes; they slid past the plush rooms built into the rock, heard the elevator sign to a casual stop, and stepped out.

"Most of the communal area was created as part of the ten-million-dollar refit ten years ago. Three of the hydroponic farms are based here—as you can see—giving you a taste of the outside, should you need it."

Despite himself, Danny was impressed with the farms. They were a hive of activity. One of the farmers was weeding, while another pushed a wheelbarrow across the length of the ground, and a third sprayed the crops. Danny didn't think he'd seen crops look so healthy above ground. Eight hydroponic lamps ringed the farm, nodding over the ground like huge sunflowers.

"If you didn't know it, you'd never guess that we're quite some distance underground. There were many things put in place during the refit in addition to an upgrade of the existing infrastructure. For example, the renewable energy resource was expanded so that we could comfortably meet the energy needs, even if we were at full occupancy."

Danny made a mental note to investigate the renewable infrastructure rig they had set up. He'd be very surprised if his company hadn't supplied some of the kit. The Sanctuary would have put the order through using a dummy company, but he'd be able to trace it back.

"What else was put in place during the refit?" Danny didn't really want to know; he was just bored. Amanda seemed delighted that he'd asked.

"Well, we put in place a more robust security system and a fully functioning hospital with a thirty-bed capacity and a full-time staff of six. We also installed an additional elevator and reinforced two stairwells to make sure that all six levels are completely connected."

"In addition to that disused set of steps."

"Indeed." She wasn't biting. "As of three years ago, the

Sanctuary is completely self-sufficient with the addition of the top wind farm—which you may have seen when you arrived?"

"No."

"No problem, you can see it later if you're interested. This has been backed up with an off-coast hydro farm. The lion's share of our energy needs comes from the wind farm on the outside, but there's also a backup of solar power cells. Every six weeks we have a four-day lockdown to test the system—and we've passed every time. We've also got a fish farm…

"There's an internal checklist of what we need to do," Amanda seemed to have read his mind, "should any global emergency occur. Over the years, we've established the targets we need to reach, and all those can be measured in four days."

The communal piazza was horseshoe-shaped and looked out at the fish farm, which incorporated a mini waterfall and rock pool. The sound of flowing water could be heard from any of the bars, cafés, or restaurants in the horseshoe. People were sitting at tables around the piazza eating, drinking, and chatting. Some were dressed in white toweling robes. There was certainly a relaxed atmosphere in the area.

"As you'll be aware, the Sanctuary is only available to young senior executives; children and families aren't allowed."

"Suits me fine."

Amanda smiled. "We have three cinema-quality screens available in this area." She gestured towards three tubes suspended above them.

Even as she smiled, Danny's mind couldn't help but pick at what was happening with his company.

What did Randall mean by that comment on Friday? He thought I didn't see that look, but I did. Jesus. What's going to be waiting for me when I get back? What if...

Danny had hoped that this trip would give him a moment's respite from the stomach-twisting anxiety that rose every time he thought about work.

I wonder what Jane would think of this place. She'd probably hate it, roll her eyes, and say it was full of rich douchebags. She'd probably be right.

"You'll have to try the fish from the fish farm. I'll guarantee you'll never have tasted better. On the first floor is one of our gyms and spas. The Sanctuary has a total of three, which contain jacuzzis and steam rooms—everything you'd expect from an exclusive premium destination, of course."

"Of course." *I'm going to ring Jane when I get out of here. Make things up to her. I've been a dick.*

What Danny did enjoy, as they walked around the area, was seeing faces he knew, and being acknowledged with a vague nod and a slight smile. Danny tuned out from what Amanda was saying. It didn't matter anyway; he preferred to discover things for himself. Eventually, he was taken to his apartment, and it was perhaps here that his boredom with the Sanctuary first began to set in. The apartment itself was huge. The decor, facilities, and detailing would not have looked out-of-place in a high-end five-star hotel. The setting was unique, of course, but other than that he'd seen it all before.

Now that he had it, he no longer wanted it.

*

Danny met up with Matthew for a drink in Hobson's bar on the second floor. It was good to be spotted there. Danny liked to think that he was recognized. The bar was very swish, with lots of black slate and low lighting. The beer was cold and tasted expensive. It reminded Danny of a bar in Tokyo—or was it Boston?

"Can I show you something amazing?" Matthew asked.

"Be my guest," said Danny with a smile.

They looked out across the vast expanse of the Arctic Ocean, framed by gleaming steel. They could see the sea undulating, but the crashing waves were obscured by the mountain.

Matthew had brought them to the fourth-floor viewing deck. They sat with their drinks, the only people taking in the vista.

"It's odd, isn't it? Being able to see the ocean but not being able to hear it. It's one of the few original features they kept from Jennings's fit."

"Yeah, I thought they might be some mentions of Jennings, but I've seen nothing. I'm a bit disappointed."

"Well, I guess they want to sweep Jennings under the carpet after all that hoopla a few years ago about the journals and those conspiracy nuts. This is the Sanctuary 2.0. It's like when you go to Vegas and see little mention of Sinatra, Elvis, and certainly no mention of the mob."

Matthew leaned over and pressed his fingers against the glass. "I don't know how they did it. It just looks like a normal glass window, but apparently, it's reinforced and many, many inches thick, as robust as the rest of the Sanctuary." Matthew blew onto the glass, leaving no trace.

"Shall we get out of here?" asked Danny.

"But we've only been here…" Matthew checked his watch. "Shit! It's not even been three hours."

"Yeah, but you know…" Danny looked around at the empty space they found themselves in and got an involuntary shudder. He had an overriding urge to get as far away from the Sanctuary as he could.

"If you're sure you want to go."

Danny looked around then looked back at Matthew. "Yeah, let's go."

*

Mentally, Danny put the Sanctuary on the shelf alongside the signed Roger Clemens Red Sox pitcher's mitt from 1989 and the Andy Warhol he'd bought at auction and rarely noticed.

He did visit it once more with Matthew, whose turn it was to charter the private jet.

Danny stood shivering on the tarmac, despite his thick, padded Rab Batura jacket, while Matthew went back for the shades he'd left on the jet.

"I've got an SUV booked. We don't have to freeze our asses off here." After they'd both gotten espressoed up, they climbed in, put the heating up to its highest setting, and set off.

"So, what was all that James Bond bullshit about when I first came here? All those different cars and stuff. Did they do that to you when you first came here?"

"No, they were just fucking with you!" Matthew laughed. The more pissed Danny looked, the harder Matthew laughed until he had to pull over until the laughter subsided.

"Well, actually, there was a bit of that cloak-and-dagger stuff, but no way as full-on as what you went through."

When Danny popped his head around the door of his apartment, it was pristine. Not a flake of dust appeared to have fallen since he'd last been there six or seven months ago. He spent the rest of his time getting drunk in the bar with Matthew. As much as he was bored with the place, leaving it meant getting back to his real life. The pursuit of the Sanctuary had temporarily kept his anxiety at bay but, now it was done, Danny could feel the familiar dread creeping back. He searched his pocket for some Vicodin. He'd still not rung Jane, and found himself in a self-perpetuating wheel of guilt: The longer he left it, the harder it got to bring her number up and ring it, and every time he didn't the guilt and self-loathing increased. In his heart of hearts, he knew why he kept putting it off.

What if she says no? What if she doesn't want me anymore?

Before too long, it was time to leave.

He hadn't taken much in on the drive over. A year later, as he drove at breakneck speed across a dust track in Alaska, he wished he'd paid more attention.

*

Martin O'Shea, the Chief Financial and Operating Officer for Brighter Futures Group stood beside a ditch. In the ditch was a car, with smoke billowing out into the cold November night. He looked back at the car and the girl in the passenger seat. She had her head on the dashboard, and you could be forgiven for thinking she was asleep, were it not for the blood.

O'Shea had managed to wipe his own blood out of his eyes long enough to ring the number on the card that he kept in the back of his wallet. It seemed only a matter of minutes before a black, unmarked sedan pulled up.

Rodchenko climbed out of the sedan and surveyed the scene.

"Do you think? Do you think?" said O'Shea, gesturing towards the girl before breaking into sobs.

Rodchenko had to stop himself recoiling from the smell of whisky on O'Shea's breath. "Don't worry about it. I'll get it cleaned up. I'll sort it out. The important thing is that we get you away from here," he said, ushering O'Shea into the waiting car.

"How can I ever thank you?" O'Shea asked before getting in.

Rodchenko smiled. "I'll be in touch."

CHAPTER 8

With one eye on the road, Danny checked his phone. Still no signal. He was beginning to think that chugging those two extra Vicodins was a mistake as his heart felt as if it was going to burst through his chest. At the last turnpike, he'd thought he was going to skid off the road, but somehow he'd managed to stay in control. "Fuck!" he shouted, as his pickup hit a bump and his phone flew off the passenger seat. He felt every bump driving on these roads at nearly eighty. He looked around at his surroundings, some of which looked vaguely familiar. Not for the first time, he cursed himself for not paying more attention when he'd last driven here. He checked the satnav—it was blinking at him but still not finding any satellites. He felt like punching it. He brought the pickup truck to a skidding halt.

"Right, right. Come on, Danny. Don't panic. Focus!" He looked back at the provisions he'd packed. Actually, packed was too grand a word for it: He'd thrown a collection of food and water in the back in a panic, plus there was the reassuring rattle of pills in his jacket pocket. He took a deep breath, checked his crumpled map, and took another look around. He was sure he was going in the right direction. He could see a tangle of trees, one of which seemed to have been struck by lightning: It was burned and scorched. There had been a mention of something like that in the directions, and Danny thought he remembered seeing that the last time he'd been here.

Am I just making it up?

He gunned the car back into life and shot forward. He had been driving for about ten minutes when he began to relax. He'd recognized three landmarks in rapid succession. He could also see windmills on the horizon. What had the woman who showed him around—what was her name?—said about being self-sufficient? The surroundings were now very familiar.

"Oh, thank God for that!" Danny said, leaning back into his seat. He switched the radio on for the first time in hours. He'd been worried about what he might hear.

"A last-minute meeting between the two sides has broken down in disarray. The president of the United States is working in conjunction with…"

Danny put his foot down. Ten minutes down the path, a felled tree blocked the way.

Shit! Must have come down in a storm.

It was only when he stopped and got out that he realized it was the only tree around. Four people—three men and a woman—appeared from behind some rocks. Danny spun around and tried to get back into his pickup but one of the

OBLIVION BLACK

men was quicker and got between him and the door. One of the others, with a shaved head and carrying a tire jack, walked towards Danny.

"Whoa! Whoa! Calm down! Where you going in such a rush? We don't mean you any harm."

"That tire jack says otherwise."

The man looked at it, smiled, and moved next to the pickup. "Yeah, well, this is, uh, just in case we get a flat. I'll introduce the gang. I'm Greg, that's Tania and Dale, and you've already met Dwain." Greg gestured to the man standing between Danny and the pickup. "And you are?"

"Danny."

"Great. Now we're all friends. There's just one thing I want."

Danny absently put his hand in his pocket, found his keys, and put the sharpest between his fingers. He wasn't much of a fighter, so he'd have to fight dirty and hopefully surprise would give him the upper hand. It's all he had.

A low rumbling noise like thunder rolled around the plain.

"How do you get into the Sanctuary?"

"What's the Sanctuary?"

"Don't fuck with us."

"I don't know what you're talking about." Danny's fingers clenched around his keys.

"Ever since the trouble kicked off, you fucking Ivy League rich kids have been running here scared. All our families have lived around here for years. You owe us. Now be a good rich kid and get us into the Sanctuary."

"I know as much as you do."

"I said don't fuck with us!" Greg swung the tire jack round and slammed it into the side of Danny's pickup.

The sound of an explosion boomed across the plain and a plume of smoke bellowed in the east. Danny took his opportunity and threw his weight against the man standing in front of the truck door. Greg fell backwards, and Danny leaped into the seat, slamming the door behind him. He fumbled with his keys and dropped them on the floor.

"Fuck!"

Danny scrambled for the keys, scooped them up, and managed to get them in the ignition in time to see Greg slam the tire jack into the truck again. The truck rocked with the impact as Danny tried to turn the key in the ignition. His hand was shaking too hard. Greg smashed the tire jack into the windscreen. It splintered but didn't shatter. He brought his arm back again as Danny managed to turn the key and gun the truck into action. He floored the gas and the truck shot forward. Greg leaped at the truck and clung onto the hood. Danny swerved sharply to the right, to try and avoid the fallen tree and to shake off Greg, who flew off to the side. The left tire mounted the tree. Danny ground his teeth as the engine screamed in agony. The wheels spun but the truck went nowhere. Clouds of dark smoke bellowed out of the back. Danny pressed on the gas so hard that he thought his foot might go through the floor. With a final scream from the engine the pickup lurched forward and cleared the tree. Danny looked in his rearview mirror and saw Greg get unsteadily to his feet.

I can't be far away. It can't be more than twenty minutes, surely.

However fast he drove, the windmills in the distance never seemed to get any closer.

Danny could feel a cold sweat beginning to break out and the steering wheel becoming slippery.

The tablets rattled in his pocket.

Time to take things a little easier?

It was then that he noticed a large granite bolder, which looked out-of-place in the middle of a field. Just beyond that was a hill, which Danny thought he recognized as the housing the doorway he'd used to enter the Sanctuary.

It has to be the doorway! Please, God…

In his rearview mirror was a battered 1980s Chevy, gaining on him rapidly. Danny's truck wasn't speedy.

Shit!

It was going to be close. Danny thought he was going to push the gas pedal through the floor. "Come on! Come on!"

The truck shuddered as he hit a pothole. Everything leaped into the air. In a heart-stopping moment, the car swerved randomly, but Danny managed to get it under control. The Chevy had gained ground. Danny gunned it, but the other car was catching up. It couldn't have been more than seven hundred yards behind.

Danny slammed on the breaks, grabbed the instructions

to get into the Sanctuary, slung a bag over his shoulder, and made a break across the field. The truck's engine was still running, and he heard the tear of metal against metal as the Chevy shunted into the back of it. Danny slipped, falling in some mud, but scrambled up again and ran for the hill. He was running so fast that he collided with the it. Recovering, he ran his hands around until he found the hidden door. He pulled the papers out of his back pocket and followed the instructions on how to unlock the door. Danny punched in the key code and there was a rush of air as the door opened. He glanced behind him and then ran towards a further door, which was operated by a retina and finger print scan. Danny turned around as he thought he heard something. There was an echo of another distant explosion. He quickly put his palm on the scanner and his eyes up to the retina reader. He heard a whirring noise and a click as the door opened.

"Oh, thank fu—!" The air was knocked out of him as someone barreled into his back. Danny shot through the door and fell to the floor. He managed to get up in time to dodge a punch. The room he found himself in was dimly lit. There was one last door to go.

Shit! What had he been told? With no time to check his instructions, and not for the first time that day, he wished he'd paid more attention at the induction.

He could vaguely see a hatch at the far end of the room, which he felt sure led directly to the Sanctuary.

Danny wasn't lucky enough to miss the second punch,

which landed hard against his nose. A flash of pain, a crunch, and he felt the warm flow of blood on his face. He collapsed and saw Greg charging towards him. Danny managed to kick out and—more by luck than judgment—connected between his legs. Danny pushed himself up and stamped on the hatch. After some initial resistance, it opened. There was a small set of steps down into darkness. Danny made to go down just as Greg tackled him. They fought at the top of the hatch. Greg took a swing at Danny, who managed to dodge the blow, but they both lost their balance and tumbled through. After what seemed an age, Danny felt himself smack against something hard. He saw a flash of red and passed out.

CHAPTER 9

Danny touched his sore head and then scrambled for some Vicodin.

Jesus, it must have been a great party. It feels as if a cat has crawled into my head, had a shit, and died.

Gradually, he opened his eyes to see a beautiful smile. It belonged to the red-headed woman who was leaning over him.

"Don't move, Mr. Keins. You've had a bit of a bump; at worst you've got a very mild concussion. You're going to be okay and so is your friend."

"Friend? Where am I?"

"Yes, the man you were with. He's fine. He was dazed, but he's been taken care of. Oh, and to answer your question, you're safe. You're in the Sanctuary."

Friend? What friend?

Danny rubbed his head and almost grasped who she meant, but he was doing so through a pounding headache.

"Who…"

"I'm Dr. Theresa O'Brien. I'm the auxiliary doctor here. We're just waiting for Dr. Schriver, the primary physician, to arrive."

"Can I get up?"

"Sit up and tell me how you feel."

Danny sat up and a sharp splinter of pain shot through his head.

"Yeah, I'm feeling fine."

"Okay, but take it easy."

"How's it been?"

Theresa looked around the empty infirmary.

"Very quiet. Haven't had much to do, to be honest."

Danny swung his legs off the bed and felt temporarily dizzy. He steadied himself.

"No, I meant the situation between India and Pakistan."

"Uh… yeah. It's not got any better, which is why we're currently on lockdown. I'm sure it'll work itself out." Theresa didn't look as if she believed it herself. "If you're feeling okay, you could check into your apartment?"

The Vicodin.

"Where's my jacket?" he felt a stab of panic.

Theresa looked around and took the crumpled brown corduroy jacket off a hook. "Here you go."

Danny grabbed it off her a little too eagerly. His hand instantly went to feel the reassuring outline of the container.

Oh, thank fuck for that.

He rubbed the back of his head.

What did she mean, "friend"? Did she mean that guy I fought with? Did he make it in?

Danny walked through the Sanctuary in a daze. He ran his hand over his face, which was still sore. He noticed a distracted-looking female staff member behind an information booth. In normal circumstances, he would probably have tried to hit on her—she was just his type—but he was still fuzzy and wanted some information.

"Excuse me."

Her perfect smile snapped into place.

"Hi, how can I help you?"

"Uh, yeah, I'm wondering if my friend's checked in?"

"Yeah, sure, what's his name?"

For a second the name escaped him.

"Matthew! Matthew Hampton!"

"I'll check."

Jesus, how great would it be to kick back with Matthew now and have a beer. How weird is this?

"No, I'm afraid not." Danny's face must have dropped because she quickly added, "But the system's being updated all the time, so maybe he's not been logged in. Check again in a few days." Perfect smile in place.

"Okay, thanks."

It was only when he got inside his apartment that a wave of exhaustion hit him. He fell to his bed and was asleep within seconds.

When he woke up, he was feeling ten times better. He

stretched and heard a pleasurable set of clicks and found himself feeling far more optimistic. He switched his phone on and was surprised to see he had a signal, although it was weak. He was sure that a last-minute deal must have been brokered— or soon would be—to end the emergency.

Shit, the truck!

He'd even left it running.

It's never going to be there when I get back. Is it insured? Does it really matter? But it'll irritate me.

There was a lot of unfinished business to take care of. The board had made an offer for his share, which, quite frankly, was insulting. But Danny was looking forward to the game of hardball to come.

Now that the immediate excitement was over, he realized he was starving. He looked in the well-stocked cupboards for something to eat. His eyes scanned the expensive produce and lit up when he saw a packet at the back: Pop Tarts! He fished them out and within minutes was yelping at the molten filling.

He made a cup of coffee and switched on the TV, but just got static. He then realized that since signing the contract, he'd never actually checked whether everything worked. He showered, dressed, and left his apartment.

Standing on the walkway outside his apartment, he got a sharp spike of fear. He looked around and up. How could somewhere so vast feel as if it was closing in on you? What he needed was a drink with a friend.

The Sanctuary was eerily quiet—that is, until the elevator

reached the communal area on the ground floor. Large screens were suspended from the roof into the piazza. Around sixty of the inhabitants were standing, grim-faced, watching. Two of the six screens showed nothing but static, which echoed around the cavern. The other four were a babble of panic and stampeding people. Danny could make out the occasional word.

"What's happening?" Danny asked.

"It's all going to shit," someone next to him croaked.

One of the screens showed a disheveled reporter. There were dark rings under his eyes, he had three or four days' stubble, his shirt was undone at the top, and his tie was askew. He had a finger in his right ear.

"What was that, Jenny? What was that? Say that again," he said, with his brow furrowed and his teeth bared. Danny wasn't quite sure if the reporter knew he was live. "Hello? Hello?" A wave of interference momentarily ran through the picture.

When the picture stabilized, the reporter seemed to have regained some composure and was looking directly into the camera as chaos was erupting behind him.

He straightened his tie. "This is Ralph Harding reporting live from Islamabad." And then, under his breath, "But not for long." He coughed. "There has been wide-scale looting in the streets and people are… people are panicking. If the latest reports are to be believed, all efforts to resolve the Kashmir territory dispute have—"

He was cut off as people around him began to scream and point up in the air. The reporter shielded his eyes and looked upwards. His eyes opened wide. "Oh, God! Oh, God!" he screamed. The screen froze in a digitized picture of the reporter's horror before it too went to static.

"This can't mean…?" Danny stared up at the screen, then turned to look at one of the few screens that was still transmitting a picture.

"Failure… panic… imminent strike… desperate last-second effort…"

"Holy shit," said Danny quietly to himself. He saw people come together and start to hug each other. One of screens seemed to come into sharp focus as the reporter began to say, "There are… there are reports that… oh, God!… nuclear missiles have been launched… please, God!" The reporter began to cry. The screen went blank, then turned to static. The other screens became a muddle of pixels before crashing into static. The sound of static echoed around the otherwise silent cavern.

He saw other inhabitants shambling along with the same shocked look on their faces that, presumably, he had.

Danny went to the window looking out at the ocean where he and Matthew had sat not so long ago. The ocean looked the same but of course everything had changed.

Oh God, where is Jane? Why isn't she here with me?

His face flushed hot with shame when he thought about the casual way he'd treated her. Danny pressed his feet against the edge of the window, pushing himself further into the clammy embrace of the sofa. He wanted to cry with frustration at all the choices he should have made, but all he felt was a numb incomprehension at the enormity of what had happened.

In a trance, Danny found himself walking to Hobson's Bar. The bar was unusually quiet, apart from people muttering their orders to the equally stunned bar staff. Danny ordered a double Bombay Sapphire and tonic and knocked it back in one gulp, which made his eyes water. This didn't stop him following it with another, and then another, which was joined by two Vicodins from his rapidly dwindling stash to help knock the edge off the day. The volume of conversation rose as more drink was consumed. As Danny felt his limbs begin to loosen up, his head swiveled around to the person next to him.

She was smoking a cigar. She tapped it, and the ash fell to the floor.

"I gave up smoking eight years ago," she said, taking a large glug of the triple Glenfiddich in front of her, "and drinking about the same time. Well, that's not strictly true, but I don't think anyone's keeping score."

"Don't I know you?"

"Yeah, probably. I'm the senator—well, I guess the *former* senator for Delaware. Connie O'Hagan, at your service."

Danny shook her outstretched hand. "O'Hagan?"

"Yes, I'm from good old fighting Irish stock."

"I thought you'd have a bunker of your own, senator?

"Yeah, I do, but I couldn't get to it in time. I've always kept this place as an insurance policy."

"How bad do you think it is?"

Connie looked at her whisky. "You saw the footage. What do you think?"

"Yeah, but surely the government has some kind of back up?"

"Well, this happened very quickly. There's been a lot of cutbacks recently, but before I burrowed down here with the rest of us rats, I heard that they were putting everything into trying to prevent what we just saw. I knew we were fucked. There was just something about it this time, something in the air. I knew they weren't going to be able to pull back. Not this time." She waved the glass around. "That's why I'm here. It seems like it's turning into quite a party." The bar was peppered with laughter.

"Sorryz," said a drunk, thickset man with arm around an equally drunk, blond-haired woman, as they bumped into Danny and Connie. "Let me buy you a drink to say sorryz," he slurred.

"No, I'm fine, but thanks," said Danny, smiling.

"Ah, what the fuck! It's a free bar anywayz. My name's Stue— short for I am *stewed*! And this lucky lady is… uh… sorryz, little darling, I've forgotten your name."

"I am Michella," she said, aiming a playful punch at Stue and missing.

"Now, if you don't mind, me and… Michella are going to find a booth and get better acquainted," he said with an exaggerated wink. Michella didn't seem to mind. She laughed as they disappeared.

"And why not?" said Connie. "The world's fucked, so it's all we've got left."

"Do you really think that?"

Connie shrugged. The glass slipped from her hand and smashed. No one seemed bothered, so Danny ordered them both another drink and quickly downed his. In the dark corners of the bar, couples had started to pair up; some had started to have sex.

Is Connie right? Is this all we've got left: drinking and fucking?

*

Danny rolled over and looked at the woman beside him and groaned. He had a vague memory of what had happened. He remembered Connie had bailed fairly early. Many others had joined her, leaving only the hardcore to party the rest of the night. As Danny slid out of bed, he realized with a hazy dread that there was nowhere to run. The woman rolled over, opened her eyes, looked at Danny, and frowned.

"Uh… morning," she muttered, as she clutched the bedsheet to her.

"Quite the night," Danny said lamely.

"Yeah!"

Somehow, she'd managed to retrieve and get into her underwear, put her blouse on, and was zipping up her jeans. Danny didn't know what to do. It seemed ridiculous to look away after spending the night together, but to be fair, he couldn't remember much about what they had done.

"Er… can I fix you breakfast?"

"Why, aren't you the gentleman!" She laughed. "No, but thanks for the offer, hon." She went to leave, but before she did, she turned and said, "You honestly don't remember me, do you?"

"Uh, yeah, I do, We," he squeezed his eyes, "met in the bar last night and…"

"I mean before that?"

"Uh?"

"I showed you around when you first came to the Sanctuary? My name's Amanda."

"Oh, yeah."

She smiled and left.

Danny made himself a coffee and tried not to think about taking a Vicodin. Instead, he made his way to the fourth-floor viewing deck which looked out across the Arctic Ocean. It looked calm and gave no clue as to what was actually going on outside.

When will I get to be outside again? Months? Years? Never?

Somewhere out there, amongst whatever was happening, was Matthew. Danny had never checked back in to see if Matthew had made it to the Sanctuary. He had a sickening feeling that he hadn't and that he'd never see his best friend—someone he'd known for nearly twenty years—ever again. He tried to bring to mind the last time he'd seen Matthew, but couldn't. Looking across at the rolling ocean, he wanted to feel something—to feel sad, to cry—but he felt nothing.

Danny walked back to his apartment. His fellow inhabitants

were emerging blinking into the artificial daylight of the Sanctuary.

"Hello? Hello?" The cavern amplified his voice and bounced it around. He checked his watch. It was 11:49 a.m., so *just* morning. Danny's apartment overlooked the piazza. He looked over the railing and saw that a podium had been set up. Behind it stood a woman in her mid-fifties. Danny thought he recognized her from somewhere. She leaned forward and spoke into the microphone.

"Hello, I'm Sarah Turner, senior administrator for the Sanctuary. I thought it was important that I update you on what's happened. Let's start with some positives. The Sanctuary is fully operational, completely to spec and beyond. We are completely self-sufficient and working beyond our parameters. I-"

"What's happening outside?" someone shouted. A flash of annoyance showed on Turner's face.

"We don't know. That's the truth. We're trying to make contact, but so far all we've got is static. As soon as I know anything, you'll know. We're also waiting for the results of the external radiation tests. As soon as I know anything, I'll publish them on our internal network, which you can access via the laptops in your apartments. In the meantime, you're safe. We have supplies to last many, many years."

But how many years?

"But how many years?"

"Shit!" Danny grasped his chest and spun around to see

Connie with a massive devilish grin on her face. "How long have you been there?"

"Long enough. Enjoy yourself last night?"

"You know I did. What did you do?"

"I went for a walk around this place. I still haven't really had a good look around. I walked for two hours without doubling back on myself. There are still some passages that no one's explored. Who knows how far into the mountain they go!"

"How do you know all this?"

"I read it. It's all there on the laptops if you look and check the maps of the place. They may as well put 'Here be dragons,' Tell me, do you think there's anything apart from us down here?"

"What do you mean? Like bats?"

"Yeah... maybe."

"Why do you ask?"

"No reason... it's just, when I was walking around last night... I guess even with all the work that's been done here, it's still a windy old cavern, and there's bound to be odd noises." She sounded as if she was trying to convince herself. "You going for some breakfast?"

Danny's days then fell into a pattern of drinking, watching old films, and the occasional bout of sex with an obliging stranger—and, despite not remembering her the first time around, Amanda was still interested. The days drifted into weeks, and the weeks melted into months. When Danny thought about the declining amount of Vicodin he had left, he would break out into a cold sweat, so he tried not to think about it, but he tried to ration the pills. Most of this time for Danny was spent drunk, which seemed to be how most people were spending their time. He often met up with Connie in the morning for a strong coffee and breakfast, and Connie sometimes joined him in the evening to watch a film, especially if it was a western.

*

Connie was sitting on a comfortable sofa, looking out at the Arctic Ocean framed by the viewing deck. She wondered how it had come to this. Once upon a time, the future had stretched on ahead with hope and opportunities. Now she was sitting here, in this hole, while the rest of humanity rotted. As she cradled a Glenfiddich, her mind went back, as it often did, to the happiest time in her life—but, of course, at the time she hadn't realized that it was.

She had just been made a partner at her law firm.

"That's great! About fucking time!" her husband Lloyd has said on the phone. "Right, then, I'm taking my favorite legal eagle for steak, fries, and beers at Renarldo's."

"Last of the big spenders," she'd teased. Renarldo's was their favorite restaurant, and she didn't know what they did to the steak—dipped it in crack, maybe—but it was the best she'd ever had.

All was great and it was a Friday night. Yet she couldn't help but worry. She was late, and she was never late. Connie knew she'd better check. Thirty minutes after walking out of the toilet, she was still staring at the little green plus sign on the pregnancy test.

"Calm… calm… calm," she said aloud to try to slow her racing heart. "Let's take this one step at a time.

"You're sure?" Lloyd asked for the fourth time.

"As sure as I can be. I can get a second opinion, but…"

"Right, then." Lloyd pushed himself back in his chair, his expression changing constantly between a smile and a frown.

"So…?"

"So what?"

"What do you think?"

"Brilliant! Brilliant! I'm going to be a dad!"

"Oh, thank God! I thought…"

"What?"

"Never mind. I'm just glad you're happy about this."

"Of course, I am! Why wouldn't I be? The only thing is…" He took a sip of his beer. "What will this mean for your partnership?"

"Shit, I hadn't thought of that." Connie rotated the glass of water in front of her. "They'll be fine. They'll be fine."

"Are you sure? 'Cause doesn't your firm have a bad rep with this type of thing?"

"It's precisely because of that that they're trying to change things. It'll be fine, I'm sure it will."

"So, when are you going to going to tell them?"

She laughed and took a sip of water. "Give me a week or two

just to let this sink in and then I'll tell them. Okay, sweetheart? But we're all good?"

"We're all good."

Three months later, she was clutching the toy rabbit that Lloyd had given her and staring out of the hospital window. When he had first got it for her, she'd wanted to throw it back in his face. However, over the last few days, she'd found herself clutching the rabbit when the pain that the medication couldn't mask got to be too much. She glanced at the clock—11:30 a.m.—then at the door, and right on time, in came Lloyd, looking ill.

He smiled at her and dropped some magazines he'd bought for her onto the bedside cabinet. "How you doing, sweetheart?"

She just nodded at him. He was wearing aftershave—his good aftershave.

Why is Lloyd wearing his good aftershave to the hospital? Where is he going afterwards?

This was the routine they seemed to have fallen into over the last few days.

After she'd batted off his questions about how she was feeling—*how the fuck do you* think *I'm feeling?*—he'd try to fill the silence with small talk and avoid looking at the clock on the wall. She wanted him to be there, but the instant he was in the room she wanted him to get out. She also knew what he wanted her to say, the reassurance, but her whole being felt too bruised to throw him that bone.

"I'm going back to work next week," she said.

"Are you sure? Are you up to it? What did the doctor say?"

"The doctor said I was okay to return if I took it easy.

"Well, as long as you're sure. It'll probably do you good, help keep you busy."

She nodded.

He checked the clock on the wall. "I've got to…"

She nodded again and he left.

Things had never been quite right between them again. She found herself wishing she'd brought the rabbit into the Sanctuary with her.

"What you thinking about? You look like you're miles away."

Connie turned and saw Danny. "Oh, nothing. Just watching the ocean. What've you been up to?"

"I've been trying to patch through to the outside," Danny told her.

"I didn't know you could do that. I'm impressed."

"Well, don't be too impressed. I haven't managed to get anything. If they know anything, they aren't telling us."

"I've been doing more exploring," said Connie.

"Still? I'd have thought you'd have seen it all by now."

"No, the official map is only half of it. There are miles and miles of caverns. I've been drawing up my own map."

"Here be dragons?"

"Yes, here be dragons. Remember when I asked you if you thought there was something down here with us?"

"Bats?"

Connie laughed. "I don't think it's bats down here with us. It's something else."

"What?"

"I don't know, but when I'm in the tunnels... I hear a whisper, or I see a shadow, and I know I'm not on my own. You know these caverns have been here for thousands of years. Jennings only rediscovered this place and gave it a brush up. Who knows what was here before us, or is still here?"

"I don't know about that!" Danny said with a laugh. "I haven't... although I haven't explored as much as you... I haven't..."

"Shit, just forget it. I was only yanking your chain."

Danny looked doubtful.

"Have you thought about the supplies?" Connie asked.

"What do mean?"

"They can't keep it going like this. It's not just a rich man's playground anymore. Sooner or later, we're all going to have to earn our keep."

"How long do you think we're going to be down here?"

Connie shrugged. "I think we're in for the long haul. Things are going to get pretty fucked up above-ground. We've got to make the best of it down here. This might be all we've got."

"But there'll be survivors above ground. They'll be putting things back together," said Danny.

"If there are, we haven't heard from them yet. This might be all we have. This might be it."

"How long do you think the supplies are going to last?"

"They said they would last many years."

"Did you ever stop to wonder how true that was or what it actually meant?" asked Danny, as a short, sharp stab of fear knifed his guts.

"I don't know," Connie said and smiled at Danny. "But it's a question that has to be asked."

*

Danny couldn't get the question out of his head, so the next day he found himself going to one the farms on the ground level. He wandered around and realized that he was more nervous than he'd been in a long time. He walked along the plots until he found the head farmer, a rope-thin man with his hair cropped close to his skull. His skin was stretched tight, showing every knot and muscle, and his eyes were set deep in his head. His ears and nose were pierced, and there was a smattering of tattoos on his arms. He was rolling a cigarette as he sat on a battered camp chair with a steaming mug of tea at his ankle.

"Hi, are you Rodger, the head farmer?"

"Who's asking?"

"Eh?"

He lit the cigarette with a Harley Davison lighter and took a deep drag while baring his teeth. "Yes, I'm Rodger. And what can I do for you?" he said, with a look of amusement on his face.

"Is that an English accent?"

"Yes, Bristol."

"Right." but Danny only had a vague idea where that was, somewhere near London?

"How did you end up here?"

"It's a long story, which I might tell you one day. What can I do for you?"

"I was just wondering… is it possible to help out on the farm?"

"Sure, what can you do?"

I can set up a renewable energy network and screw every last nickel out of a deal.

"Uh, well, anything you need doing."

"Mucking out animals?"

"If that's what needs to be done."

"It certainly does. We've got eight cows, two dozen chickens, and six pigs. That's a lot of shit." He looked at Danny. "Be here at six."

"In the morning?"

Rodger laughed. "Yeah, in the morning. Is that a problem?"

"No, six is fine."

"Great." Rodger stood up, put his hand out, and shook Danny's hand. "Right, then, see you at six o'clock tomorrow morning. Be prepared to get dirty." He relit his self-rolled cigarette, drank the last of his tea, threw the dregs on the soil, and walked off.

Arriving at the piazza, Danny saw Connie sitting down, having a coffee. "Mind if I join you?" he asked.

"It would be my pleasure," she replied.

Danny sat down and ordered a coffee.

"Danny?" Connie appeared to be searching for the right words. "Have you heard any... any odd noises down here?"

"Depends on what you define as 'odd.' Why d'you ask?"

"No reason... it's just... when I was walking around last night, I could've sworn that..." She looked around. "I could've sworn that there was something else there."

"What did you hear?"

"Not sure. Have you ever had that thing happen to you where you know someone's watching you from a window—you just know—and you look up and there they are, chewing gum and gawping?"

"Yeah, occasionally. What, did you look up and see someone looking down?"

"No, not exactly. It felt as if there was something around and," Connie looked across at Danny, "it felt as if there was something in my head."

Danny burst out laughing.

"Alright, alright!" Connie smiled. "Yeah, I know, the only bats flying around here are in my head. Come on, you can buy me breakfast for laughing at a lady." She got up and walked off. Danny joined her, but as he got up, he thought he could hear a sound from the far edge of the cavern. It sounded like a chicken leg being torn off a carcass.

Here be dragons.

Danny stretched and looked up. Above him, on the next level, was a tall man with the remaining white strands of his hair combed across his head. He had piercing, catlike eyes. His arms were clasped behind his back, and he was looking around with an amused smile on his lips. He reminded Danny of a king surveying his kingdom.

"Who's Nosferatu?" asked Connie, looking up.

"I dunno. I was wondering that myself. I've seen him around the place. I'm pretty sure he's not strictly a resident. Dunno why—I think it's the way he carries himself. I've seen him talking to Sarah Turner."

"So he's something to do with the committee?"

"I dunno. I don't think he is, but he's certainly got some kind of sway here," said Danny, looking up again, but the man had disappeared into the shadows.

*

For the first few seconds that morning, Danny didn't know where he was. Then, as he stared at the alarm clock blinking 5:30 a.m., it all came back. It would be so easy just to turn over and go back to sleep, but he'd made a commitment, so he dragged himself out of bed. The Sanctuary was even more eerie than usual. Most of the lights were off, leaving only the low lights to pick out the way. Without the general burble of people talking and going about their business, the only noise filling the Sanctuary was a low electrical hum, which Danny had never noticed before. It sounded as if the Sanctuary was snoring. He decided not to take the elevator and, instead, walked down to the farm. Rodger looked surprised to see him. There were more than a dozen people already working.

Danny had never seen them before.

"Right, then, lots of work to do. Weeding would be a good start. Weeding never ends. There'll be weeds around long after we're gone. Over there. I'll be your boss man."

"My what?"

"Your boss."

It had been a long time since Danny had had a boss.

"This is where we dump the weeds."

"Why?"

Rodger stared at him. "Cause I told you to."

"Wouldn't it be much better…?"

"No. No, it wouldn't."

*

Walking back from the farm, Danny bumped into Dr. O'Brien.

"How are things?" Danny asked.

"Quiet, thankfully. The main doctor didn't make it in, so I'm the main medic. I'm getting used to that—so far, all I've had to contend with is a few sore heads." They both laughed.

"I've been helping out in the farm."

"Yeah?" The doctor smiled, and Danny felt a flush of pride at being able to tell her.

"It's thirsty work. I don't suppose you'd like to join me for a drink?" Danny couldn't help but flinch at such an obvious line, but it made the doctor laugh.

"I can't right now—my shift's about to start—but I'll be free in four hours, if you want to swing by."

"Yeah, that would be great."

"See you then." Danny felt euphoric as he parted company with the doctor. He planted his hands into the pockets of his hoodie and looked up at the sky. Today it looked really fake—like blue-painted steel—and he suddenly didn't feel so happy.

Danny's mood was lifted by his date. He and Theresa sat in the bar, and for a moment, Danny almost forgot they were in the Sanctuary.

"How did you get this gig?" he asked.

"Long story."

"Aren't they all?"

"Yeah, well, I was working in the ER in Detroit"

Danny whistled.

"It was full-on. There's a natural burnout for that job of around eighteen months."

"How long did you stay?"

"Just over three years." Theresa laughed, but quickly took a gulp of her drink. "I think I was reaching the end of my tether when I was headhunted for this place. It seemed like a sweet gig after being at the front line for so long, and the money was *a lot* better—not that that means anything anymore, I suppose."

"How long have you been down here?"

"Before the lockdown, we'd do three months on with two months off paid leave."

"That's good. You've been working here for, what, two years?"

"Nearly three."

"In that time, have you ever seen anything… I mean, is

there any evidence of anything… living here?"

"What, like bats?"

Danny laughed. *Always with the bats—you're a regular Bela Lugosi.* "No, something bigger, like… a bear or something?"

"A bear or something?" Theresa laughed. "No, why?"

"Oh, it's something Connie said that's been playing on my mind. Don't worry. Forget about it."

They had another drink before Danny asked, "Fancy a nightcap at my apartment?"

They stumbled into his apartment, lips locked, teeth playfully biting, and tongues probing. They were giggling drunk and clawing at each other's clothes. He slammed her up against the wall. She smiled, and he clumsily pawed at her breasts like an overeager teenager. She responded by running her hand over the bulge in his jeans and tugging at his zip. More by luck than design, they fell onto the bed together.

Next morning, Danny woke up, turned over, and looked at Theresa. Her hair was tousled in a tussle around her face. Her mouth was open slightly. He watched her breathing; as she exhaled, there was the quiet rumbling of a faint snore. Danny smiled and felt more contented than he could remember being for a long time.

CHAPTER 10

R odchenko sat in a café and looked down at the battered journal as he had done many times over the years. There were two passages in that urgent spider scrawl that he came back to time and time again. They were near the end of the journal, where the handwriting was all-but-illegible. The first was:

I have cut out distractions. Cut them out like a tumor. I have had to make sacrifices. The Queen of Shadows demands sacrifice. I have to find the Totem.

He'd repeated it over and over again, and slowly, it had wormed its way into Rodchenko's brain. *I have to find the Totem.*

The other passage was:

I have had to make sacrifices, and the Queen of Shadows demands sacrifice.

The words whispered in his mind… *demands sacrifice.*

*

5TH OCTOBER 2020

Sarah Turner looked at the sheer amount of work she had to do and had to bite down the panic. She looked over the stock supply.

I'm going to have to introduce a rationing on alcohol, a drinks allowance. They're not going to like that, the entitled fuckers.

Her palms began to sweat, she pushed back into her chair, and she turned her eyes upwards looking for inspiration, but all she saw were the metal pipes for the air conditioning.

Is this all worth it?

Alice. Up until the lockdown she'd had a picture of Alice on her desk. Afterwards, she couldn't bear to look at it. She'd put the picture in her desk drawer and tried not to think about it. But last thing at night, first thing in the morning, or occasionally when she reached into the drawer, she'd get a glimpse of one of Alice's glittering blue eyes. She didn't need to see the whole photo. Sarah knew every freckle and the massive smile on her face that showed the chip in her front tooth.

Sarah had left Alice in the care of her grandmother. Sarah was supposed to be gone for three months; that was nearly a year ago.

Oh, God! Wherever you are, Alice, please be safe, please be safe…

There was a knock at the door. Sarah checked her diary and groaned. *Shit! Is it that time of the week already?*

"Come in!"

Stanley Miller walked in. He was the Sanctuary's External Communications Manager, which meant that he scanned all the airwaves and the net for any activity, looking for some sign that the people in the Sanctuary weren't the only people left alive on the planet. The depressing answer was that there was never even a squeak, just static.

"Take a seat, Stan."

He blinked at her from behind his thick glasses. He always reminded Sarah of an owl. When she'd first met him, she'd remarked on his first name.

"Yes, my parents were big Laurel and Hardy fans," he'd replied with no hint of a smile, but plenty of blinking, which reminded her more of Ollie than Stan.

"How's it going?"

"I've been monitoring…" he said, talking over Sarah's first question. Stan wasn't the most socially comfortable individual. "Um, yeah, sure, I've been fine. Yes, so I've been monitoring the web, and I've done some digging into some directories to see if there's been any activity recently."

"And has there been?"

"Uh, no."

Jesus, it's the same thing every week. What's the point? "So, no activity at all?"

"No, but I did notice something interesting."

"Oh, yes?"

"Well, there are fewer sites online now. I suspect that servers are failing, causing the sites to crash and go offline. If it continues at this rate, the world wide web will be completely offline in three months." Stan blinked.

Sarah had to temper her annoyance. *Great!* "Well, thanks, Stan, I do enjoy our little chats."

"Thank you, Senior Administrator! Oh, I was asked to tell you that the entrance in the piazza that you asked to be looked at is still requiring repair work."

"Who told you?"

"Michael Dunning."

"Right, fine. Thank you."

Sarah added a line on her already-overcrowded 'To Do' list to ask for a fake wall to be placed over the entrance until the work could be completed.

*

"I suppose you're staying, then?"

Danny looked up. He'd been working up a sweat mucking out the pigs. The smell was disgusting, but he'd gotten used to it after a while. He found that he slept better after a day working on the farm. The same went for showering after work; somehow, he felt cleaner if he'd been working beforehand.

"Eh?" he said.

"Looks like you're sticking around," said Rodger.

"Yeah." Danny wiped the sweat off his forehead, smiled, and stuck his pitchfork into the next mound to be cleared. "Looks like I'm sticking around."

"Better give you the official tour, then."

"I feel honored."

"You should be. Come on, Hollywood, follow me."

Danny did as he was told.

"Well, the first stop in the tour is the livestock farm, which, judging by how you smell, you're already familiar with."

"Fuck off," said Danny, smiling.

"Yeah, well, the livestock farm was set up when Brighter Futures Group did the refit. Originally, Joseph Jennings had set up farms to grow fruit and veg. The mad old bastard had all the soil shipped in." Rodger shook his head. "He also set up the fish farm. Anyway, that was fine when it was just him and a couple of others, but when they decided to make this a resort for rich assholes like you, that wasn't going to cut it."

"Cheers."

"You're welcome."

They walked to another farm at the southern end of the cavern, not far from the Cave of Diamonds. Danny hadn't worked on that farm yet, although he'd seen it before. He was surprised at how large it was. Space had been dug into the cavern walls to extend the stretch of ground. Huge hydroponics gazed out over the lush fruit, and the farm was divided into open ground, polytunnels, and greenhouses.

"So, this year we're growing vegetables on one arable farm and on the second farm we're growing fruit. The fruit farm's more intensive. It needs more of the hydroponic lights and nutrients. It takes more out of the soil."

"I didn't think you needed to rotate crops anymore. Aren't there chemicals that can sort that out?"

"Only to an extent—plus they make the crops taste like shit. So we maximize what we can. There's never an inch of soil left fallow. You just have to be clever about the resources you use. Right, then, that's the tour. You can have more of a nose around this farm if you want, but you'll be working on it soon enough."

"That's fine."

"Any questions?"

Danny shook his head.

"Great! Welcome to the team! Now you can make me a cup of tea—strong, leave the bag in, two sugars, and milk."

CHAPTER 11

J ennings stared at the cave painting.

There were echoes around the cavern. If you looked at it long enough, you saw other colors. It wasn't just black and red. Was there movement? There was movement, he was sure. Shapes and figures weaved and danced. If you stared at it long enough, you could see it shimmer...

Hobson coughed again. He'd been standing in the doorway to the apartment for the last five minutes. Hobson had the latest figures for how the work was going, but he thought that Jennings was losing interest in what he had to say.

The Sanctuary had been further burrowed into, reinforced, fortified, and insulated from the outside world. The renewable energy was now up to eighty per cent efficiency and was due to nudge past that in the next couple of days. Hobson wasn't sure that it was a priority with his boss anymore. He seemed to have a new obsession. Jennings had made sure that his apartment had been completed. If you closed the door, you'd have been forgiven for thinking it was a modern downtown Manhattan apartment. It had air conditioning, plush carpets, and modern prints on the walls, which made the uncovered cave painting in the middle of the room look like an open wound. Jennings had a steel chair pulled up in front of it. In his right hand was a glass of milk. He was staring at the cave painting.

He coughed again and this time Jennings slowly turned his chair around. Hobson smelled the peppermint tang of his cologne.

"Yes?"

"I just thought you'd like to know that the work has been completed. We've managed to get the self-sufficient energy up to eighty per cent, and I'm confident that we could go for a test-run lockdown in the next two weeks."

Jennings stared at Hobson. Hobson waited for a reply. When the silence stretched on, he continued, "Which means, well, that the lion's share of the Sanctuary has been completed."

"Okay." Jennings began to turn his chair back around.

Hobson clenched then unclenched his fists and dropped his head. *Jesus fucking Christ! Is that it? After all this work? After all these years? Okay?* He turned to leave then spun back to face Jennings.

"No, it's not okay, for Christ's sake! I expect more than 'okay' for all-"

Jennings stood up. "You expect? What do you expect? You've been well-paid."

Hobson opened then closed his mouth. "It's not *all* about the money."

"Isn't it?" A ghost of a smirk played across Jennings's lips, and his features seemed to take on a reptilian look, which made Hobson's skin crawl.

"The-"

"Shut up!" Jennings hissed. "Can you hear it?" He circled around the apartment. "Can you hear that? Where's that coming from?"

"What?"

"Shh! It's coming from outside!" Jennings dashed outside the apartment and almost collided with the rail around the edge of the foundations. The apartment was built on the ledge that Jennings and Hobson had dropped onto the first time they'd been down together. A tapered platform had been built underneath it to give it a foundation, and the walls were tethered to the sides of the rock. There was a set of elevators and some stairs that led to the rest of the Sanctuary. A guard rail had been built around the edge. Jennings ran to it, and for one heart-stopping moment, Hobson thought he was going to fall over the rail, but he stopped and was silent. At the same moment, Hobson found himself wondering if it would be such a terrible thing if his boss *were* to fall over the edge.

"Can you hear it?"

Hobson went to the edge and looked down at the seemingly infinite cavern.

He wasn't used to it being so quiet. All the workmen had

left. Spotlights highlighted different features: The hydroponic farm and the fish farm could be seen beyond the barrier. But Hobson knew that all the work they'd done was just keeping the savagery at bay—it had not been tamed by it.

"Can you hear it? Is it down there? I've…" Jennings paused and looked at Hobson furtively. "I've seen things. They can't just be shadows. No, they can't," he whispered. "I've seen things. I've *heard* things… when I'm here and when I'm down there."

This was news to Hobson. He hadn't realized that Jennings had actually been down to the Sanctuary ground level.

Jennings continued, "I know it's around here. I know Oblivion Black."

"Mr. Jennings, I'm-"

"Shut up! Can you hear it?"

Then Hobson heard it. *Oh, shit!*

The sound of a low growl echoed around the cavern.

"Holy shit! What was fuck was *that*?"

"It's Oblivion Black."

For a fleeting moment, Hobson thought he saw something, but then it joined with the shadows and disappeared.

CHAPTER 12

A voice whispered to Rodchenko. As the days had become weeks and the weeks had become months, the whisper had become a shout. Without Rodchenko realizing it, the words had soaked into his brain—just as they had done with Jennings. In his few quiet moments, the voice hummed in his ears like tinnitus, whispering to him. *Find the Totem.*

Rodchenko was at a company party, sipping on a glass of tonic and pretending it had gin in it. He found these things tedious. He would have preferred not to have to interact with the cattle, but these events were essential for finding out what was happening. He moved around the room, shaking hands with people and chatting. Occasionally, he would discreetly ask a question, but only when he was sure that he would get a definitive answer—something that happened rarely because Jennings disappearance, everything associated with him was considered toxic or viewed as an embarrassment.

Rodchenko sidled over to a group where a rising young executive called Barry Cullen was holding court. *He isn't going to rise much further if he likes a drink this much and lets his lips get this loose.* Rodchenko settled at the back of the group, fixed his smile in place, and sipped his tonic.

"It's the only thing they can do. Probably fill the entrance with concrete," said Cullen.

"Sorry, what are you talking about?" said Rodchenko.

Cullen paused and looked at Rodchenko, whose smile widened.

Yes, you're right to have fear in your eyes.

"Uh, that thing up in Alaska that Jennings built, the bunker. The board is just going to write it off and try and forget about it."

"Right," said Rodchenko, trying not to show his alarm. *That's not going to happen.*

*

Senior Logistics Manager Jonathan Sheppard frowned when he heard the knock at his door. He looked at his diary. There was no meeting due. Before he could say anything, the door opened and Rodchenko walked in. Sheppard groaned; he had known this day would come. "It's you," he said.

"And a good morning to you too, Jon!"

No one calls me Jon. "What do you want?"

"How's Arron doing?"

Ouch! That's right, just remind me about my son—as if I

could forget. "Yes, he's doing better, and yes… I do appreciate…"

Rodchenko waved the thanks aside. "Don't worry about that. There's something you can do for me, Joe, now that you ask. It's the Sanctuary."

"Oh, Jesus! Look, we've decided…"

Rodchenko closed his eyes and put his hand up. Sheppard stopped talking.

"I've got another idea. You're going to suggest selling it off. It's better to get something for it rather than nothing."

Sheppard stroked his chin. "That might be something I can sell to the board. How would I get hold of you?"

"Don't worry, I'll call you."

A week later, the call was put straight through.

"The board is setting up a project team to investigate selling options," Sheppard told Rodchenko. "But they've only got six months to find a credible buyer, or the Sanctuary will be mothballed. That's the best I could…"

But the line was already dead.

*

Greg Wysneck led his life in the shadows. He'd literally fallen into the Sanctuary with that douchebag rich kid and had taken an upturn. The rich kid had been knocked unconscious by the fall, whereas Greg had just been dazed. After what could not have been more than thirty seconds, a round metal door at the far end had opened and three people—a woman and two men—had rushed into the antechamber carrying a green medical bag and a stretcher. The woman and one of the men were in white coats, so in the haze, Greg had thought they were medics. He touched his head; his fingers were wet with blood.

"You okay, sir?" the non-medic asked. Greg felt fine, but best to act a bit out of it.

Greg groaned and held his head. "Uhh… what? Where is this? Is my buddy alright?"

"Yeah, your pal's going to be fine. My name's Ed. I'm going to make sure you're okay. I'll just be a moment, then I'll come and help you." Ed went around the antechamber and made sure all the entrances were closed.

Greg allowed Ed to put his arm around him and shoulder his weight. He watched as the unconscious douchebag rich kid was put on a stretcher and carried away. Ed helped Greg follow him through into the Sanctuary.

Greg hadn't known what to expect in the Sanctuary, but he certainly hadn't expected it to be so huge. The atmosphere within the Sanctuary was one of organized chaos: people were rushing around and those who were residents looked more dazed than him. They entered a roomy elevator and were taken to a medical center. As a medic came over to attend him, Greg saw the douchebag being spirited away. Greg's head was bandaged, a light was shone in his eyes, and he was asked a few questions.

"You're fine," the medic told him. "You've just got a bit of a graze on your head, and you may get a headache. Here's some painkillers, just in case."

Greg put the blister pack in his pocket.

"You're okay to go," the medic said.

But go where?

Greg thanked him and walked into the Sanctuary. He'd found that the trick was to look as though you knew where you were going, so he strode meaningfully forward. At no point since he'd arrived in the Sanctuary had anyone asked his name.

The Sanctuary and Joseph Jennings had always been part of Greg's life, but only in the same way that the President of the United States and the White House were. He was sure they were real—people talked about them, though he'd never actually seen them with his own eyes.

He'd lived in nearby Arrow's Reach, a beautiful town with a beautiful name, which in reality was simply a satellite town to the Sanctuary. His grandfather had moved up from Boston to work for mad old Jennings and had met—and knocked up—a local girl. Why he'd settled in Arrow's Reach still confused and angered Greg. He'd obviously made enough money from the looney-tune bastard to just pick up the odd job here and there and still live high on the hog.

Greg's dad had just turned eighteen when a group of douchebag venture capitalists—but well-paying douchebags— bought the Sanctuary and began what would turn into a twenty-year renovation. This had kept his dad in a well-paying job that ended with him receiving a generous severance package, which meant that, together with his inheritance, Greg's dad never had to work again.

Then there was Greg.

It had been received wisdom in Arrow's Reach that the Sanctuary would provide jobs—it always had and it always would. But in the end, the truth was very different. The renovation had ended, and with it so had the jobs. It was hoped that some of the visitors to the Sanctuary might visit Arrow's Reach to splash the cash, but all that materialized was the occasional drunken night when some of the drivers and lower-paid help would rock into town for a good time.

Arrow's Reach: There was nothing to do, and the only thing of interest was the occasional Bigfoot sighting in the forest on the outskirts of the town. The sightings were either a hoax to stir up a bit of interest in the town or the result of weed-induced hallucinations, but they gave the locals something to laugh about in the Traveler's Rest bar. Greg had never actually been into the forest; in fact, he didn't know anyone who had. There was just something… *not quite right* about the place.

He spent most of his days playing pool and drinking Samuel Adams in the Traveler's Rest, one of the few bars in town that he hadn't been barred from. He would sit in his own juice, unless he was joined by others wishing to vent their spleen. There was a sad truth that had to be faced: Greg Wysneck had been born just too damn late to be invited to the party. Where was his slice of the pie, eh? When did Greg get his taste? He was owed it. It was his right.

Greg and his contemporaries had to be content with the crumbs from the king's table. Well, he wasn't content. Not a bit of it. Not at all. When things had started to get squirrelly in

India, Greg saw his chance. More and more of the rich entitled bastards had been seen driving to the Sanctuary. One night, after a few beers at the Traveler's Rest, he'd come up with a plan—or maybe it had been one of the others; things had gotten a bit hazy after the drinking. The plan was to hijack one of the douchebags on the way to the Sanctuary, gain access, and rip those Ivy League fucks off. Things hadn't quite gone according to plan, but here he was.

This could finally work out for me.

He could still rip the rich fucks off and keep all the money himself. Greg was no expert, but he was sure that it was going to blow over, and, by then, he'd have a nice big fat stash. Yes, but he had to be smart about it. He had to work out the layout of the place, find the easiest exit and, if possible, a place to lay low. The Sanctuary had been built in a circular, spiral arrangement. It resembled a wine bottle, getting wider as the cavern extended downward. It contained a piazza with bars and restaurants, and three working farms. Greg looked down at the communal area below him as he walked. People were wandering around, seemingly not knowing where to go or what to do.

He looked up. There seemed to be three or four more levels above him, and the top had been made to look like a blue sky, which, under the right circumstances, Greg thought would be pretty calming.

The floor Greg was currently on seemed to be for services. In addition to the medical section, there seemed to be a repair shop and he'd heard there was some kind of communications center around, although who they were communicating with, Greg didn't know. He found a staircase and walked up to the next level to see what was there. He tried his best to keep calm, expecting to be grabbed by security at any point. When the rich dick he'd tumbled in with woke up, he'd certainly blow the whistle on him, so Greg had to either work quickly or go to ground. He wandered around the level for almost an hour, noticing where people were going and trying to ignore the first pangs of hunger that were making his stomach growl.

He reached a stretch of numbered doors, the first being 324. The numbers decreased as he walked further around. He stopped and stood with his back to one of the doors, looked around, and tried pushing with the back of his heel to see if it was unlocked. No luck. The first four doors were locked but he hit gold with number 319. It fell open silently and Greg slipped inside.

"Holy shit!" He was amazed by the opulence. The most high-class place he'd ever stayed was the MGM in Vegas for a pal's wedding, and this made the good old MGM room look like a crack den. He quickly closed the door behind him to search through the drawers, and realized that he'd landed on his feet. According to the documents, the room belonged to a Walter Krezneg. There was even a photo of Walter, and in a bad light, he actually looked a bit like Greg. They were both bald and had a jowly, slightly hangdog expression. By the look of the apartment, Walter hadn't checked in yet. There was a spare keycard on a table in the center of the room. Greg put the keycard into his pocket and helped himself to a large whisky to calm his nerves. A second helped to knock the edge off the day. He managed to stop himself having a third. He didn't want to wake up being dragged out by guards with an angry Walter Krezneg looking on.

Except, the thing was, Walter didn't turn up. Not that day, not the next, and when the lockdown happened, Greg effectively *became* Walter. He'd never had such a great standard of living. Greg loved the Sanctuary. There was only one fly in the ointment: Danny. When Greg had made his introductions up on the road, he hadn't really paid attention, and so now he asked a few well-placed questions to find out the douchebag rich kid's name, which he'd forgotten. The Sanctuary was big, but it wasn't *that* big. He'd seen Danny around, and sooner or later, Danny was going to see him. Something had to be done, because Greg couldn't remember a time when he'd been happier. Gone was the stress of needing money, while food and drink were plentiful. He slept in late and went to bed late, normally completely loaded. He'd even managed to get talking to Karl Blockwell, a guy two apartments down who'd managed to smuggle in some primo weed. He had lots of it and was happy to share, so many of the hours between getting up and collapsing back into his bed would be spent get stoned with Karl, either watching old movies or playing Grand Theft Auto. It was all he'd ever wanted in life, but there was still that little nagging problem, the grit in the oyster, the one person who knew that Greg wasn't actually Walter Krezneg: Danny. He'd been putting off dealing with the problem, but he didn't think he could keep it on the back burner for much longer.

When Greg wasn't getting toasted, he would walk around the Sanctuary, exploring. He'd found a monitor room on the top level. He knew there were cameras dotted around the place and had made a note of the locations, just in case. He had paid special attention to the ground level. Beside the communal area of bars and cafes, there was a spider's web of tunnels and mini caves. No one bothered going into them. If a body was placed deep enough in, it would probably never be found. Greg had seen Danny go running. He knew his route. He knew what had to be done.

CHAPTER 13

M anning didn't need to look around the coffee shop. He recognized Rodchenko's bald head from the back, a few white hairs combed across it. Manning sat across from him. Rodchenko had a glass of water in front of him.

"Do you…" Manning began.

"What was their decision?" said Rodchenko.

"I think it's going through."

Rodchenko stared at his water. "You *think* or you *know*?"

"I know. That contact you gave from the venture capitalists came through."

"Brighter Futures Group?" asked Rodchenko. Manning nodded. "What did they say?" said Rodchenko, tapping the side of his glass.

"They want to turn the Sanctuary into an exclusive resort for the rich. It's a little bonus that it's also a nuclear bunker.

It provides an extra level of security."

Rodchenko smiled. "That's good."

*

MAY 2020

Stanley Miller looked at the cave painting in the communications room. They hadn't even bothered to replace the plasterboard wall this time. Stan didn't know who "they" were, but he'd noticed that they'd begun to break in about two years ago. They'd been subtle at first, but Stan had noticed some things had moved or hadn't been put back in their proper place. The plasterboard wall that covered the cave painting hadn't been put back correctly; there was a gap where you could see the rock face. There must have been a few of them. Stan didn't know why this particular cave painting was the only one to have been covered up; the others around the cavern were out in the open. Maybe the people who broke into the comms room knew. Stan certainly didn't.

As the months progressed following the lockdown and Stan became used to the sound of static, the mystery visitors became more blatant—it was as if they didn't really care if they were caught. Stan had brought it to Sarah Turner's attention, but she hadn't really been listening. He knew that she held him in disdain—a blind man could see that—but it was important that she knew these things.

He stood blinking at the image on the cave wall, a crudely painted black creature with some stick figures around it. He'd heard that when Joseph Jennings had occupied this room, he'd become obsessed by the picture. Stan looked at the cave painting and blinked. He couldn't see what all the fuss was about. No, Stan just didn't get it. He sighed and tried to move the plasterboard wall back the best he could.

*

Danny looked at the yellow pill between his thumb and forefinger. It could conceivably be the last Vicodin in the entire world.

The stark answer to his problem dawned on him. He was going to have to kick it. He'd been promising himself that he would quit for years. He told Connie and the doctor he had flu and was going to sweat it out. Danny brought in pints of orange juice, painkillers, and some Twinkies for old times' sake.

Cold turkey hit him on the second day. He woke up at 2:30 a.m. with crippling stomach pains, which made him curl up into a fetal ball. He crawled out of bed and dragged himself to the toilet just in time as painful diarrhea racked his body. He sat on the toilet with his pounding head in his hands. It felt like the worse hangover he'd ever had.

"Oh, man… oh, man…" Danny sat on the toilet sobbing, tears rolling down his face, praying for it to stop. He managed to drag himself back to his bed, drained of all energy. Once there, he took some painkillers with a large glug of water in an effort to stop the pounding in his head and to try and get some sleep, but he couldn't keep anything down.

"Oh, God… oh, God, please make it stop," he whimpered

as a bout of the shakes tore through his body. He must have passed out at some point; the next thing he knew he was awake and groaning again. He rolled out of bed and dragged himself to the bathroom to clean himself up. He took off his dirty, sweat-soaked Boston Red Sox T-shirt and boxer shorts and threw them in a corner as he got into the shower.

Hot water had never felt so good, and after toweling off and getting into a warm, clean dressing gown, he found temporary respite from his misery. He lay down on the bed and curled up, shivering with the towel over him.

When he woke he found, to his relief, that apart from some foul-smelling sweat, he was clean. He actually felt a little better, as if he were coming out the other end of a bad bout of flu. He swung his legs over the edge of the bed and decided to try to take some of the painkillers with a sip of the orange juice. When he found that he was able to keep that down, he nibbled at the corner of the Twinkie; his face crinkled at its sweetness and his stomach made an ominous growling noise. He swung his legs back onto the bed and was able to lie flat for the first time in he didn't know how long. He slept once more and, on waking, took some more painkillers—then remembered that he'd already had some.

Wouldn't it be ironic if I overdosed on painkillers from the Sanctuary hospital in an effort to kick Vicodin? Danny even managed a grim smile.

He spent what felt like hours on his back looking up at the ceiling as spasms rattled through his body. His sweat felt like pure toxic evil as it squirmed its way out of his pores. Having thought he was getting better, here was a fever that sapped all his energy and had him backed up against a wall, slipping in and out of consciousness, as he saw witches flying around the room on broomsticks, looking down at him and cackling with glee at his predicament. Danny giggled at the absurdity of it, but still tried to push himself back farther into the wall.

Witches are real? Well, ain't that a kicker, Toto.

He continued to watch, still giggling, as they pitched and swooped.

Gradually, Danny became aware of some whispering… but what did the whispers say? Danny thought he could hear something about a totem.

Then he noticed a shadow on the wall. At first, he thought it was a stain, maybe a patch of mold, but as the witches began to fade, their cackles hanging in the air like the Cheshire cat's grin, the shadow began to get bigger. As it expanded, Danny heard a soft tearing sound, which seemed to be getting louder in proportion to its size. As it grew, it very, very gradually began to form a shape: a head, two arms, two legs, but it wasn't human. *Oh, no, not human.*

Danny knew what it was. He knew with an instinctual certainty that seemed to come from some dark place in his subconscious.

Oblivion Black.

The shadow took over the entire length of the wall—over seven feet—and there seemed to be no obstacle preventing it from growing even larger. It began to solidify, becoming three-dimensional as it did so, and now obscured the wall behind it.

"No! Oh, no, no, no!" Danny sobbed.

The shadow began to move towards him. For such a large figure, it had terribly thin twig-like fingers, which, as he watched, slowly began to rustle. The ripping noise was now almost deafening. Oblivion Black began to descend on Danny. Deep in the cavernous darkness of the shadow, two red eyes glowed like coals, and Danny began to whimper.

I've got to get out.

He tried to stand, but his legs were like paper, buckling and collapsing under his weight. He fell heavily and passed out.

*

The first few seconds after Danny came around were filled with relief. He finally felt human again—weak, but human. Using a wall as support, he wobbled and lurched over to the bathroom. He checked his reflection in the mirror.

"Oh, Danny Boy, you look like shit." His skin had a horrible yellow pallor to it, his hair was stuck to his head, and patchy stubble dotted his face. However, despite being rimmed with red, the eyes that stared back from the mirror were clear for the first time in years. He stretched and had to use the wall to steady himself. He put the shower on and allowed the jets of hot water to pummel his skin as he scrubbed himself the best he could. The hateful stench of his own body began to fade.

Once he'd dressed and zipped up his jeans, which hung looser on his hips than the last time he'd put them on, his stomach gave a warning grumble, and with some relief he realized that he was starving. He looked around the apartment, wondering what there was to eat.

Yeah, the Twinkie ain't gonna cut it.

He would have to leave the apartment and find something. He would have to leave the apartment and find something. As he went to leave, Danny's guts lurched at the memory of a shadow detaching itself form the wall to reach for him...

He walked over to the wall and ran his palm over it.

Same as usual, but...

He gave the wall a last wary glance and, with some relief, left the apartment.

CHAPTER 14

R odchenko creased the spine of *The Life and Death of Joseph Jennings* and continued to read. He smiled. It never failed to amaze him how people could connect the dots to come to highly improbable and incorrect conclusions. But if only they knew how close they'd got.

They had the nuclear bunker right, and partly how unhinged Jennings had been, yet they hadn't even touched the surface of his illness. Rodchenko would love to know the identities of the "insiders" the book's author claimed to have spoken with. He suspected that they were figments of the author's imagination.

The phone rang. He let it ring six times before picking it up.

"Yes?"

"It's Martin."

"Martin?"

Rodchenko been expecting the call, but still wanted to put him on his wrong foot.

"O'Shea, Chief Financial and—"

"Of course. Hello, Martin. What can I do for you?"

"The TV show."

"Which TV show?"

Rodchenko already knew what he was talking about, he just wanted to hear O'Shea squirm.

There was a pause at the other end of the line. "There's an episode of a TV show about the Sanctuary and Jennings. The show is called *Mysterious Stories* and—"

"I'm aware of *Mysterious Stories*." Rodchenko thought he could hear O'Shea grinding his teeth.

"What are we going to do about it?"

"We're not going to do anything."

"What do you-"

"I've seen the episode in question and it's just conjecture and hearsay with no solid evidence."

"But-"

"They manage to hit a few targets, but for the most part, it's just trying to cash in on the popularity of the book."

"We've got to stop it! If it airs, it's going to cause a huge embarrassment to-"

"Yes, because that worked so well when you tried to block the book, against my advice."

"We can't do… nothing!"

"That's precisely what we *are* going to do. If we make a move, it'll shine a spotlight on the episode and legitimatize it. We're going to deny everything and let it burn itself out."

The line went quiet again for a moment. "Well, your neck is on the block if this goes wrong."

"Both of ours are. Trust me."

The line went dead.

*

Rodchenko waited a few months after the refit before visiting the Sanctuary. *Mysterious Stories* played out as he said it would and now had been forgotten. He knew he could have gone there at any time, and his decision to delay the visit felt like an itch he couldn't scratch. When he did finally enter the Sanctuary, it was like coming home. Without drawing attention to himself, he visited as many of the places described in the journals as he could. He even stood before the Bridge of Souls. He wanted to go in, but felt an uncharacteristic twinge of fear as he looked into the darkness. Were there shapes moving in the darkness? Were there whispers in the wind?

Find the Totem.

It dawned on Rodchenko that he'd need allies in the Sanctuary in his search for the Totem. He preferred to keep a safe distance from most of his business dealings, but soon realized that this was one job he'd have to do himself. As subtly as he could, he researched professionals who had made their own discreet inquiries about Jennings and the conspiracy surrounding his disappearance. Gradually, he recruited like-minded people. Once he was sure of their character, knew that they were interested, and that they could be trusted, he would casually say, "I think I have something you may be interested in reading." Then he'd pass to them a watermarked copy of some of the pages of Jennings's journal. A self-satisfied smile would settle on Rodchenko's lips as he watched their reaction. It was always the same: "Where did you get this from? Is this real? It can't be!" But the most important reaction was always: "Is there any more?" This was always said with a mixture of fear and expectation. His response was always the same: a measured "perhaps." He controlled the supply. Gradually, Rodchenko built his cabal.

CHAPTER 15

There was only one light burning in Jennings's apartment. It was a spotlight highlighting the cave painting. Jennings sat in an armchair before it, a glass of skimmed milk hanging limply in his right hand. His beard was now touching his chest, and his hair lapped over his shrunken shoulders. His skin was gray-hued and tightly wrapped around his skull. Was it days, weeks, or months since he'd last left the Sanctuary? He didn't know and, honestly, he didn't care.

His eyes burned, buried deep in hooded eye sockets. His ribs protruded from his emaciated torso. He wore only a pair of filthy, tattered shorts, but he didn't care how he looked. He hadn't seen another person for… a week, a month, a year? He didn't care about that either.

What did the painting mean? At first Jennings had thought that Oblivion Black was a trespasser on his property. Now he realized that it was the other way around. Oblivion Black had been around a long time before humanity's ancestors had managed to drag themselves from the primeval mud. Oblivion Black was the Queen of Shadows and the Sanctuary was her domain. Oblivion Black had been talking to him ever since those first few moments when he'd stepped into the cavern. He realized that now; he just hadn't been listening. Slowly, as the weeks and months had gone by, the voice had grown stronger. Jennings had to sacrificed much, but that's what Oblivion Black demanded: sacrifice.

A calm, easy euphoria unexpectedly enveloped Jennings as he sat in his chair and looked at the painting. Time seemed to stop for a moment, and it felt as if a fresh breeze had blown the fog from his mind. He had a moment of clarity. He heard an echo in his head.

Find the Totem.

Jennings's head drooped and his watery eyes fixed on the notes in his journal. He flipped the pages, staring with incomprehension at the spidery writing crammed onto the paper. The writing became more fractured as he turned the pages. He took up his pen and began to scratch out an entry.

I have cut out distractions. Cut them out like a tumor. I have had to make sacrifices. The Queen of Shadows demands sacrifice. I have to find the Totem. The more that falls away from me, the stronger her voice becomes. The longer I spend in the Sanctuary, the louder the voice becomes. The leaner I become, the stronger I become. Will I fade away and just become another shadow on the walls of the Sanctuary? Gradually, I've shed my responsibilities like a skin to become… to become something new. The message has become clear, as though it was written into the stones. It sings out to me, and the song it sings is "Find it!"

Find it. Find what?

"Yes!" Jennings croaked. "Find it!" He smoothed a page out in his journal and continued to write.

Find the Totem.

Oblivion Black has given me a mission. She whispers to me in the night. I have to find the Totem. That which was stolen and shown in the cave paintings shall be returned. The Totem. I must go to the Bridge of Souls. I must meet with Oblivion Black.

Jennings put the journal down and pushed it under his chair. He walked out of his apartment and blinked as he emerged onto the platform. He looked around for a moment before remembering about the elevator, but decided to take the stairs instead. It had been a long time since he'd walked this far, but it felt good to be moving. He could feel the rough concrete of the stairs through the thin material of his slippers. As he walked down the stairs, which spiraled the cavern, he got a good look at the work that had been done. It didn't look pretty, but that wasn't what he'd asked for. Thick, red, metal girders pierced the rock walls to provide support. They bolstered up the platform on which his apartment had been built. The pipes and wires snaked around the rocks to provide electricity, light, and water. A railing had been placed around the steps. Jennings coolly considered the eight-hundred-foot drop as he descended the stairs.

The Sanctuary was now self-sufficient when it came to energy. The lights had been rigged so that they dimmed at night. He could still see most of the details of the ground level—the farms and the fish farm. Light reflected off the water and caused ripples of light to shimmer across the nearby rock. Jennings's eyes had become accustomed to the low level of light in the Sanctuary.

When he finally got to the ground level, he craned his neck and looked up. The sheer scale of the place made him dizzy for a moment, and he fell backwards a few steps. It was a cathedral of stone and darkness swirling around him. He closed his eyes and took three deep breaths.

Find it. Find the Totem.

Jennings began to circle the vast ground level. He stopped at one of the storage spaces built into the rock and brought out a heavy-duty flashlight.

"Where are you?" It came out in a rasping whisper. The movement of the fish was the only thing that answered him.

He heard a noise. Shadows from the lights decorated the

walls of the Sanctuary, wind whispered in the tunnels, and the rocks loomed over Jennings. There were no other humans in the whole cavern. Jennings slowly circled, straining to hear.

"Where are you? Where are you?"

Then came a low growling and a sound like a chicken leg being torn from a carcass. It was coming from Tunnel Sixteen. The Bridge of Souls. It called to him. It sang to him. Jennings hesitated. There was something about Tunnel Sixteen. What was it? What had happened? Hobson had said something about it a long time ago. Jennings took a tentative step into the tunnel and shone his flashlight into the tar-like blackness, which swallowed up the illumination. The sickly-sweet stench of decay wafted past him, almost making Jennings turn back, but he carried on.

"Where are you? Where are you?"

He edged forward slowly. After a few steps the temperature dropped, and Jennings's breath curled into vapor in front of him—not that he noticed or cared. In the distance was the occasional drip-drip of water. The flashlight picked out the gnarled breaks of the rock tunnel. He shone the light around this part of the maze beneath the mountain and stared at the untamed granite jutting out. He remembered seeing the Cave of Diamonds with Hobson all those years ago when he'd first entered the cavern. The walls had looked like rows of teeth.

Again, a sound like meat being ripped apart echoed through the chamber, and Jennings felt an ice-cold stab of doubt and fear. But he continued to walk on.

After four more steps, his flashlight began to flicker. In a panic, he hit the flashlight against his palm, but it didn't help. The light continued to struggle for life.

All my choices, all the roads, they've all brought me here to this dark, cold, wet tunnel, hiding from the bombs, looking for safety, looking for sanctuary. Do I find the totem in the Bridge of Souls? Or...

"Where are you?"

The flashlight fizzled and strobed, making the rocks look like the backdrop to an old silent movie, and then died, leaving Jennings alone in the blackness. He could hear his breathing, heavy in his ears, and the sound of rending flesh echoing down the tunnel again. But this time it seemed closer. He was frozen to the spot and felt the urgent need to piss. The Bridge of Souls stripped away all his past achievements, all the successful years, and left Joseph Jennings a lost little boy in the dark. He wanted to turn around and flee, but he couldn't move. His eyes got used to the darkness and he saw something in it, something approaching. As it got closer, he thought he recognized it.

"Mother?" he choked, and then Joseph Jennings walked into the darkness.

CHAPTER 16

16TH FEBRUARY 2020

B eth Osgood walked around the Sanctuary and tried to
keep calm. Since they'd gone into lockdown she'd been
struggling with the confinement. More than once,
she'd felt the walls of the cavern closing in on her. Up top, she
had liked to spend what spare time she'd had hiking, going out,
and losing herself in the majestic expanse of nature. Now, she
regretted all the missed opportunities to get out when she'd
been too busy in meetings and building up her business. Now
here she was in this gilded cage. She tried to rationalize it by
telling herself that they were only here temporarily, but when
she awoke at three in the morning, unable to get back to sleep,
the voices in her head said something different. A big part of
her wished she'd taken her chances and stayed outside.

She spent as little time as possible in her apartment, and
then merely to sleep—not that she was doing much of that—or
to do some cooking, although most of the time she ate in one

of the restaurants around the Sanctuary. The one relief she'd found in the Sanctuary was in exploration; there were so many little tunnels and offshoots that sometimes, when she'd been exploring for a few blissful moments, she would forget where she was and often struggled to find her way out.

Beth liked to walk deep into the tunnels and get as far away as possible from the others. The deeper you got, the cooler it got. You could escape the air conditioning and the too-perfect temperature. She would frequently run her hands over the stone, enjoying the coolness against her skin. Her favorite place was the Cave of Diamonds. She never grew tired of the cave, of the serenity it instilled in her, but she forced herself to ration the number of times she visited. She didn't want over-familiarity to breed contempt.

This particular evening, she found herself wandering around the outskirts of the ground floor. She was trying to tire herself out, trying to delay the point where she had to return to her apartment. The lights in the Sanctuary had already begun to dim, and she felt a sickening dread at the prospect of lying in bed alone with her thoughts.

She heard something.

"Hello?" she called.

Beth gasped as blood shot from her chest. Her hands went to the wound to try and stem the flow of blood, but it ran between her fingers. Her chin hit the top of her chest. Beth tried to breathe in, but a blood bubble blew out. It popped, sending blood cascading down her body to join the viscera oozing out of her chest. She heard a ripping noise as a knife was pulled down through her and felt a tearing pain as the wound opened up and she was slowly gutted. Her hands flailed out trying to grab her attacker. She managed to grasp an arm, but it was quickly pulled away.

Beth's head was pulled back, her throat was slit. She saw a stream of blood shoot out in front of her, she gasped and tried to breathe in again but heard a rattling noise. The knife was pulled out and she was left to stand on her own. Beth's legs buckled and she collapsed, pitching forward into a pool of her own blood.

Why? Hurt, hurt why why why me red red black …

Her fingers scratched against the floor and a shudder rattled through her body as Beth breathed her last.

*

16TH FEBRUARY 2020

Greg was sitting in front of a console with Karl, getting stoned. He checked his watch. *Time to get a-rockin'.*

"Ah, man. I'm getting wasted. I'm going to go and get some air. Clear my head."

"I know what you mean. I think I'll join you."

Fuck.

"You don't have to do that, Karl. It's getting late. I'll probably just walk around the ground level and then head back to my apartment."

"That sounds perfect—unless you don't want me to join you?"

Fuck, fuck. "Nah, come along."

They made sure the joints were out. Greg put his shoes on while Karl sprayed some air freshener to get rid of the smell of weed.

"Why're you doing that? No one gives a shit anymore!"

"Force of habit. Jesus, the smell of the air freshener is making me want to puke. Come on, let's get out of here."

They took the steps down to the ground level.

"What time is it?" Karl asked.

Quarter past no one gives a shit. "Uh, it's ten past one. You finding it hard to keep track of time?"

"Yeah, but that's no bad thing. Up top, I had all kinds of stuff barking time at me. I was in here a week before the lockdown. I was taking some time out. First thing I did when I got here—"

"Was get stoned?"

Karl laughed. "Okay, the second thing I did when I got here was take my watch off and put it in a drawer. Then I turned off my cell phone and took the battery out. I'm just enjoying not having to be anywhere for the time being."

"Do you think we'll ever get back up top?"

"Yeah, at some point," he made air quotes, "'order' will be restored, and we'll go back to the same old shit."

Greg felt a twinge of angst at this and realized that he never wanted to leave the Sanctuary again.

As they walked, a pair of eyes in the darkness watched Greg

and Karl, waiting for them to get closer to the Bridge of Souls.

"But hell, what do I know? None of us know for certain how bad it's gotten up top. For all I know, they could be getting on a lot better than us bunch of over-entitled assholes, locked up safe and sound down here."

"Well, fuck, I'm enjoying it down here," said Greg, then instantly regretted saying it. He didn't want to do or say anything that would mark him as unique.

"I know what you mean, buddy. Life's a lot less complicated, that's for sure. I don't doubt I'll get bored with it soon, but for now it's nice to have the time to-"

Karl never finished the sentence. A thin, steel wire sliced into the skin of his throat. He was able to get his fingers under the wire, which sliced through the skin to the bone, sending out an eruption of thick blood. Karl's eyes bulged as his hands clawed desperately at his eviscerated throat. He staggered back and his arms were pulled back up his back by a strong assailant.

Greg ran at Karl's attacker, but before he could help, someone smacked him hard on the back of his head.

"Fuck!"

Greg's vision was filled with red, and he fell to one knee. Looking up, Greg could see Karl get his mutilated hands free and try to wrap a hand around his throat in a vain attempt to stifle the blood pouring from the gaping wound. His arms were pulled back again sharply behind his back. Greg blacked out.

*

Karl's vision began to cloud, and he could feel his consciousness slipping away. He ground his teeth and tried to fight back.

He managed to work his arms free and used all his strength to force his elbow back into the person behind him. He felt his elbow connect with someone, and Karl was beginning to pull away when he felt a sharp pain in his abdomen. He looked down and saw a hand holding a knife in his lower body. With some effort, the hand began moving the knife up Karl's body. He tried to scream but only blood bubbled from his lips.

The knife ripped up to Karl's chest, and his eyes rolled up into his head. Karl gave a last agonized breath and then went limp.

The assailant withdrew the knife and let the body fall to the floor. The figure, dressed head-to-toe in black, their face covered in sheer fabric adorned with a crude drawing of an animal face, looked between the two bodies on the floor and then went to work on the corpse.

*

17TH FEBRUARY 2020

Stan had just been talking to Sarah, and she'd begun to zone out. He'd been saying something about the comms room being broken into and the mysterious attempts to get access to Jennings's old cave paintings. She'd nodded in the right places, pretended to write some notes, and said she'd look into it.

He's been spending too much time on his own.

Stan left, and the crackle of her walkie-talkie broke Sarah out of her contemplation.

"Sarah, we have a critical situation. Please respond." It was Michael Dunning, the deputy administrator. The panic in his voice was unmistakable.

With a sigh, she picked it up. "This is Sarah. What's the situation?"

"Uh, it's better that you come down here. We're on the outskirts."

"I'll be right there." Sarah put down the walkie-talkie. *Fucking great.*

Sarah was grateful to see that Michael Dunning had retained enough presence of mind to make a temporary screen out of some plastic sheeting. Dave, one of the farmers, was standing around, but the expression on his face betrayed nothing.

"It was Dave who found her and came to find me," said Michael Dunning.

Sarah went to the other side of the screen and saw Beth's mangled body.

Oh, sweet fucking Jesus …

She looked around. A thousand thoughts scrambled for ascendancy in her head. "You did the right thing, Michael." She ran a hand through her hair and fought hard to retain her superficial gloss of composure. "Who else has seen this?"

"No one. As soon as I found her, I got him," Dave inclined his head toward Michael.

"Right, well, that's something." *Calm, Sarah. Whatever you do, just keep your fucking head.*

"OK, here's what we do. We keep this *strictly* between ourselves until I can think of our next move, right? Good. Now, you two help me wrap up her body and we'll take her to the hospital. I'm sure we can rely on the doctor to keep quiet …"

Sarah had expected Theresa to be shocked, but she just looked at the body with a numb weariness.

"How did this happen?" asked Theresa.

"We don't know. We're in the process of investigating. And with that in mind, I'd appreciate it if we could just keep this between ourselves."

"You want me to hush it up?"

Yes, that's exactly what I want, bitch… "Discretion, doctor. That's all I'm asking. Only until we can work out what's happened. We don't want to panic the residents, do we?"

With a hefty sigh, Theresa said, "Fine. I'll need some help moving the body onto a gurney."

Michael and Dave obliged and Beth's body was wheeled away.

Sarah had just settled back into her office and was in the process of working out her next move when her walkie-talkie crackled to life.

"Boss?" It was Michael Dunning.

This isn't going to be good news, is it…

"We've found another body."

Sarah closed her eyes and rubbed a hand over her face. "Great. Just great."

"There's more. Looks like there's been a struggle and there's someone else here."

"Jesus! Another body?"

There was a pause. "Yes, this person is unconscious but still alive."

*

"You can't do this! Fuck! Fuck! Please, I'm begging you, please! It wasn't me! It wasn't *me!*"

Greg had hoped it was a nightmare and that he'd wake up in his apartment in the Sanctuary—or even in his apartment in Arrow's Reach—but as the fingers dug into his arms and dragged him towards the door, he knew that it was all-too-real. He tried to make sense of what had happened as he wrestled to get away. He pleaded again, repeating that he hadn't done it. For once in his life, he was telling the truth.

He'd come to in a dark, silent room with three people staring at him. He was sitting behind a table. The three of them were sitting on the other side, against the wall. Greg knew an interrogation when he saw one.

"Is that him?" asked one of the people from the shadows. Greg recognized the voice: It was the female senior administrator.

"Yes, that's him." A cough, a pause, and then, "Can I go now?"

I recognize that voice, too.

A nod, a door opened, and the person who'd just spoken left.

"We know who you are and what you've done." The sentence chilled his blood. He'd been found out, but what did they mean by *and what you've done*? Then it dawned on him: They thought he'd killed Karl. And no matter how much he pleaded his innocence, they kept repeating their accusations.

"We suspect you forced your way in using extreme violence."

"Yes, yes, okay, I did force my way in, but I didn't-"

"So, you admit to being violent!"

"No! You don't understand. Karl was my friend! I'd never-"

"Did he know your secret? Is that why you murdered him?"

"I didn't murder him! It wasn't me! The person who did it knocked me out. I-"

"We know you did it."

"You can't *know* I did it because *I didn't do it!*" he shouted, slamming his fist on the table.

Silence.

"There is only one punishment for a crime of-"

"But I-"

"There is only one punishment for a crime of this severity and that's expulsion from the Sanctuary."

"What do you mean? You're throwing me out? You can't do that! You can't do that!" he screamed. He kept screaming for a long time after he'd been left alone in the room.

*

Danny was waiting outside. "What are you going to do with him?" he asked.

"Expel him. What else?"

"Hold on, hold on. You don't know he killed that guy."

"Even if he didn't, the result would be the same. At the very least, he forced his way in here under false pretenses—and you should want him expelled anyway for the number he did on you."

"I don't deny that he needs to pay for what he did, but aren't we being too hasty? Shouldn't we investigate? Find out what happened? Look at the surveillance footage?"

Sarah ran a hand through her hair.

"Don't you think we haven't done that already? We checked the video footage. We only saw the two of them. I'm going to announce that, for the greater good of the Sanctuary, he's to be expelled today."

"No, wait! Wait!" But Sarah and her assistant were already walking off.

*

"I didn't fucking do it!" Greg screamed. He was being restrained and, when he wouldn't stop shouting his innocence, Sarah ordered that he be gagged. She had already read out the charges.

Danny and Connie watched from above, looking down from the railing outside Danny's apartment.

"There's no doubt about how he got in here and what he did to you, but the other thing with Karl?" said Connie.

"I tried talking to them, but no one's listening," said Danny.

"Yeah, me too. I might as well have been talking to a locked door. I don't like what's happening here one bit. He's far from an innocent man, but is he guilty of what he's been accused of, and does he deserve what's happening to him?" Connie left the question hanging in the air.

"Greg Wysneck, you've been found guilty of the listed crimes." Sarah's voice was measured, authoritative.

Found guilty by whom? thought Danny.

"We only have one punishment fit for your crimes and that is to expel you from the Sanctuary. We will show you more mercy than you showed your victim. We will give you a week's supplies, but after that, you're on your own. Take him away."

He was dragged away.

Somehow, he had managed to work free of the gag, and he began to shout, "I didn't do it! I'm fucking innocent! *I'm fucking innocent!*" His screams echoed around the Sanctuary until he was dragged to the elevator. Only the closing doors silenced him.

"I need a drink," said Connie.

"I'll join you," Danny replied.

*

In her office, Sarah sat back in her chair and tried not to think about her daughter. It was at times like this that thoughts of Alice crept up on her—the few quiet moments. Overall, Sarah was relieved now that Greg had been expelled from the Sanctuary—tired, but relieved. She threw her head back, closed her eyes, and breathed deeply. She checked that no one was around and reached for her cigarettes.

Only three left in this pack.

She lit one, watched the smoke curl in the air, and felt a little more in control. She thought how she might even allow herself a glass of wine.

Fuck it. I'm going to get hammered tonight.

*

Dave was working on the farm when one of the residents walked past, finished a can of Coke, and threw it to his left, just where Dave was weeding. Dave shouted after the resident, a short, stocky, bald man in jogging bottoms. "Pick that up!"

"What?"

"You heard me! Pick that up!"

"Why don't you pick it up?"

"'Cause I didn't drop it."

"Well, I'm paying you, so you pick it up."

"You're not paying anyone anything anymore, so pick the fucking soda can up, you ignorant fuck."

"How dare you speak to me like that. I'll get Sarah Turner to kick you out of here."

Rodger had seen the argument out the corner of his eye. As the volume began to increase, he stood up and ran over just in time: Both men were eye-to-eye and looked as if they were about to trade blows. Rodger stepped in between them.

"Lads, lads! Calm down! What's going on?"

"Tell your man to do his job."

"Calm down, Dave!" Rodger had to push him back. "Right, so what's this about?"

"He-"

Rodger stopped him and looked at the resident. "Do you want to tell me?"

The resident pointed to the Coke can. "I dropped that, and your man started attacking me."

"Dropped it?" exclaimed Dave.

Rodger put his palms up. "Now, we don't know what happened. I'm sure …"

"Miles."

Of course that's your name. "I'm sure Miles would be happy to pick the soda can up."

Miles smiled, which made Rodger want to punch his teeth in. "Well, you'd be wrong. I'm not picking it up because that's not what I do."

"Just one punch, Rodge. That's all I'm asking."

Rodger was tempted to let Dave thump him. *No, it's not worth it,* he thought. Instead, he clapped Dave on the back and smiled. Then he went over and picked the Cola can up. Miles walked off muttering to himself.

"You shouldn't have done that. You should've made that pig pick it up."

"Hey, don't insult our lovely porkers," Rodger laughed, but Dave didn't join in.

"It's not always going to be like this. They think they're better than us, but they'll get what they deserve."

"What do mean by that?"

"You'll find out."

"Meaning?"

"Nothing." Dave looked over at the farm. "Down here none of us are any different. We're all just surviving. The sooner they learn that the better."

"Right."

Rodger walked back to the cup of tea he'd made before he'd had to get involved in that argument. *It's probably cold now.*

He rolled a cigarette as he walked and watched Dave out the corner of his eye.

*

When the shit finally hit the fan between India and Pakistan, Rodchenko had already been living in the Sanctuary for six months. When he'd first arrived at the Sanctuary, he had assumed that finding the Totem would be straight forward, but it had proved to be frustratingly elusive. He had approached this task as he approached everything in his professional life: quietly and behind the scenes. He had spent a week walking around the place, listening in on conversations, and getting a feel for the dynamics at work. He whispered in the right ears to make sure that the committee knew the part he had played in financing the Sanctuary and that he would be an observant but non-interfering partner — well, that's what he told them.

On Sarah Turner's first day, he made sure he was one of the first people to speak to her. "Welcome to the Sanctuary!" He put his hand out and plastered on his most charming smile.

"Thanks." She shook his hand. Did he see her go to wipe it on her pants?

"We hope you have a long and happy career with Brighter Futures Group. You'll see me around, and if there's anything I can do for you… *anything*… don't be afraid to ask."

She just nodded and thanked him again.

"Well, I'll leave you to it." Rodchenko had moved to walk away, then turned back in a manner designed to look casual and said, "Oh, it would be useful if in the next few days, you could check if there are any artifacts from the original inhabitants that haven't been declared. It's not a big thing, just an interest of mine." He looked her straight in the eyes. "I'd appreciate it if you could look into it." He smiled. "So… I'll leave that with you."

*

It was only after the man had walked off that Sarah had realized that he hadn't given her his name or even what he did in the Sanctuary.

The following few weeks had gone by in a blur. Sarah was introduced to Michael Dunning, the deputy administrator, an easy-going, blond-haired, bearded man, who looked as if he'd be more comfortable on a beach somewhere than helping to run *the* go-to luxury hideaway. He'd quickly become her indispensable right-hand man. Sarah also met the eight people who made up the committee—effectively her team—and was shown the workings of the Sanctuary. The cavern was a warren of tunnels and corridors leading off the main piazza on the ground level. Corridors led off from corridors. More than once, Sarah found herself completely lost in a white corridor with a silver foil ventilation pipe snaking across the ceiling, which looked identical to a dozen others she'd been in.

It was in one of these identical corridors that Michael showed her the generously stocked armory. He tapped in a number and a heavy metal door opened to reveal rows of guns and hand grenades.

For a moment she was speechless.

"How and why?" Sarah asked with a nervous laugh.

"During the early stages of the refurb, they were still going for the bunker vibe, so one of your predecessors who was... uh... particularly twitchy put in a request for the armory. Amazingly, he got it. After that it was too much of a pain in the ass to get rid of it, so it's been under lock and key down here ever since. Only three people know about this and have the code. It's not written down."

He told her the code twice and got her to repeat it back to him. She typed it in to open the door and it swung open. She had become number four.

Sarah was walking back to her office, mentally repeating the six-digit code, when she bumped into the man she'd met on her first day. By asking around, she'd discovered his name was Rodchenko, but nothing else.

"Settling in?" he asked.

"Yes, lots to learn, but everything is great."

"Good, good. I was wondering if you've had any time to

look into the matter I asked you about? About the artifacts?"

As well as learning about the corridors and the armory, she had also found time to ask about what had been found when the Sanctuary had first been scoped out.

"Yes, I did some searching, and we've got a full list of what was uncovered. If you've got a moment, I'll get it from my office."

He nodded and clasped his hands behind his back. Five minutes later, when she came back, he didn't seem to have moved an inch; he was eerily still. She handed him a printout. He scanned it.

"And that's it?"

"Yep, that's everything that was found."

"Really?"

"Yes, I even went and checked what they had. Most of it is set up in the original locations on the ground level, and the more fragile pieces are in storage. They're the ones with the red stars next to them."

"Really?"

"Uh, yes."

He smiled and turned his head slightly to the left. When Sarah didn't say anything else, he nodded and walked off into the Sanctuary as though he was taking a stroll in the park.

*

She was lying. He knew it. She *had* to be lying. The committee had the Totem and they were keeping it from *him*.

He knew the truth.

They knew it was a thing of great power and whoever controlled it controlled Oblivion Black. *They* were keeping it from him. Hiding it from him. He knew. They didn't know its importance, the power it had. He would have to be more forceful in his efforts to acquire it, and that would mean using the network of true believers he'd set up, Rodchenko's cabal. By the time of the lockdown, the fifth column numbered over fifty, with a hardcore of six. He'd learned that Jennings's old apartment had been converted into the comms room and that the paintings he mentioned in his journals had been covered over. The answer could be there.

The cabal had gained entry to the comms room and had torn away the plasterboard wall that hid the first cave painting Jennings had seen, as described in his journal. Being hidden for decades hadn't diminished their impact. They had to clean away layers of dust, but there it was. In the center stood a long-dead artist's depiction of Oblivion Black, towering magnificently over her cowering followers, who held up tributes to the fiery creature with red eyes. At first the cabal had just stared at the paintings, then one or two of them had broken out of their reverie to take photos of the paintings. They remembered to put the plasterboard wall back to cover the paintings, but they did so reluctantly.

At first, the group had only moved covertly through the Sanctuary, noting any reference to or mention of Oblivion Black and reporting back to Rodchenko. In the weeks and months following the lockdown, Rodchenko had reasserted his control over the cabal. One night, he ordered them to meet at the Bridge of Souls.

"We are just tourists in our own domain," he said to the group. "We are just passively observing what's gone before and living in the past."

"What else can we do?"

"We can be Oblivion Black's chosen ones. She's biding her time. We have to find the Totem. She was here long before us. She lived alongside and outlasted the Athabastara. We have to learn from the Athabastara."

"Oh, fuck, you can't mean…"

"Oblivion Black demands tribute. We shall resurrect Oblivion Black and she shall reward her servants. We shall be the select few."

"But at what price? What will we have to give to be one of the select few?" asked a female voice.

"How long do you think the supplies are going to last? How long do you think the food is going to last?"

"They said that…"

"'They said.'" Rodchenko laughed. "They are cattle that we must cull to survive. They aren't worthy of life. We're the chosen ones and Oblivion Black demands sacrifice."

He looked at the follower who had voiced concerns about the price to be paid.

"Are you with us?" A dozen eyes turned to her. She looked around and could feel sweat prickle on her skin.

"I didn't mean to… yes, I'm in. I'll do whatever needs to be done." She dry-swallowed. "They are cattle."

"We are the cabal. We are the select few. We shall move in the shadows and choose our tributes to Oblivion Black. By the time they know anything is happening, it will be too late."

He could almost hear the voices echoing down the years. Now Oblivion Black had new followers.

"Oblivion Black demands sacrifice," repeated Rodchenko, and he looked around the group. There was no further dissent.

CHAPTER 17

During his time on the farm, Danny began to chat with Rodger. After about a month of working there, he began to trade insults with him. "Hey, Hollywood," Rodger would ask, "do you want to get your hands dirty?" Danny felt as if he'd passed some unspoken test, even more so when he felt he was able to tell Rodger that he didn't share his passion for prog rock, which Rodger accepted with a shrug. He even began to learn the names of some of the other gardeners, but so far, he had only managed to get a grunt and a nod from one of them called Dave.

Part of what Danny loved about volunteering was getting up early. It spoke to the exclusive side of him that he was experiencing something that few others did. On one of his early mornings, he thought he'd seen something out the corner of his eye and had heard a faint growl. Danny told Rodger this, fully prepared to "have the piss ripped out of him"—a phrase, he had been relieved to learn from the Englishman, was more affectionate than painful.

"That'll be Oblivion Black," said Rodger, munching on a sandwich.

"Oblivion Black?" laughed Danny.

"Yeah, mad old Jennings was the first person to see it. He named it. It was mentioned in some book or another a few years ago."

"Are you serious?"

Rodger nodded.

"What is it?"

Rodger shrugged. "Who knows? One thing's certain, Oblivion Black was here long before we were, and it'll be here long after we're gone."

"Have you actually seen it? Have you seen Oblivion Black?"

Rodger smoked the last of his roll-up, drained his tea, and thought for a moment. "Yeah, well, I think so. A few years ago, I got into the farm at stupid o'clock in the morning and found that one of the sheep had been torn to pieces." Rodger put his cup down, his hand shaking slightly. "The blood was soaking into the earth. I looked around but I couldn't see what could have done it. I saw something though. A huge… presence. There was something there." Rodger pointed at one of the tunnels. "Over there, I'm sure. We have to let it have one now and again, when it wants one: an offering. I've often wondered what'll happen when we run out of sheep."

"People?"

Rodger shrugged. "I've thought about that—I think most of

us have. It's a fact of life, but for now it leaves us alone and we leave it alone."

"It didn't leave the sheep alone."

"Yeah, well." Rodger shifted. "It's a price that has to be paid, just a fact of life. We still herd sheep into one of the tunnels occasionally."

"That's horrible."

"That's just the way it is. We have to get back to work."

"Do you really believe that, Rodge? Do you *really* believe that there's something in here that demands sacrifice?"

Demands sacrifice. The words echoed in Danny's head.

"I don't know, what do you want me to say? I've told you all I know. You make up your own mind. Let's get back to work."

The rest of the digging, weeding, fetching, and carrying was done in silence. Danny went back to his apartment exhausted. He managed two mouthfuls of a sandwich before falling into bed.

Next morning, he woke up with a pleasant muscle ache. He stretched and then got up and made himself a cup of coffee.

It's a price that has to be paid.

The deadpan phrase "That's just the way it is" echoed around his head.

What'll happen when there are no more animals for Oblivion Black's tribute? What or who will get served up to the dinner table? He didn't know what to make of what Rodger had said. Could he be joking? Would Danny go into work that morning and them all laughing at how gullible he had been? Then he remembered the tremble in Rodger's hand. Danny eventually convinced himself that what Rodger had said was a prank. It had to be.

He dealt with it by ignoring it. He really wanted to talk to Connie about it, but she was nowhere to be found. He was sure she'd turn up eventually.

As well as seeing Theresa and volunteering on the farm, Danny had recently taken up running. One day, he'd come across a pair of dusty old sneakers at the back of his closet, and they'd gotten him thinking about exercising again. He'd been feeling a bit flabby lately—plus he hadn't really explored the Sanctuary and he thought running would be a good way to do so.

Once he started running, he realized just how out-of-shape he was. Ten minutes in and he was bathed in sweat, out of breath, and aching—and that was before he'd tackled any of the inclines. He hadn't taken any particular notice of his surroundings, but he did enjoy the endorphin rush afterwards. He found that his fitness quickly improved. He enjoyed the ache in his muscles, and the waves of pure endorphins made him wish he'd taken it up years ago. It felt good to be working the parts of his body that he didn't use on the farm. Every day he went a little farther and a little faster, and he was taking in more of his surroundings. He hadn't appreciated just how much work had gone into building the place. He thought he could see the fit between the old work and the refurb. It was very subtle, but it was there—a barely healed-over surgery scar. The rocks jutted out, and all the work that had been done couldn't quite tame the gnarled primeval surroundings.

Unexpectedly, Danny found he even enjoyed seeing other people on the same route—some walking, some running. He'd taken to nodding and smiling at some of his fellow residents. Sometimes his smiles would get returned and his day would become a little bit better. One of the runners he saw quite often actually called out "Danny!" when they passed each other. Although he had no idea who the guy was, Danny always smiled and raised his hand. He had tried to find out the runner's name. Was it Neil or Nigel? He couldn't remember—something beginning with N, anyway.

*

On the outside, Nick Goldsmith had been a real estate developer. He was probably one of the few people in the Sanctuary who had welcomed the apocalypse and the lockdown. He'd managed to get an apartment in the Sanctuary for a steal when he'd done a business deal with Brighter Futures Group over some beach property one of their directors wanted. He'd gotten himself trapped in the outside world. Caught between eighteen-hour days at his office and an impending divorce at home, Nick had found himself backed into a corner and he couldn't see an escape. The escalation of hostilities between India and Pakistan had come as a relief to him. He'd actually missed the coverage of the missiles being launched as he'd checked into the

Sanctuary on that day, gone straight to his apartment, kicked off his trainers, and slept for thirty-six hours straight. As a result, Nick didn't fully realize how serious the situation was. He had assumed it would blow over, so he was treating his stay as an extended rest and an opportunity to detox. During his stay, he got to spend time with a lot of books he'd been putting off reading and had reignited his passion for running. He couldn't remember being this happy or healthy since he'd been in college. He was enjoying the rest and assumed that everyone else was too. He couldn't help but smile and nod at people when he saw them.

Nick had been shocked and pleased to see Danny Keins run past him one morning. But later, when he thought about it, he wasn't too surprised to see Danny in the Sanctuary. Nick only dealt with the higher-end real estate. He'd sold Danny a Malibu beach house. He hadn't actually expected the deal to go through as Danny had had a glazed, disinterested air about him while he was viewing the property. So, when he saw Danny out running, Nick had called out his name, but it was clear from Danny's reaction that he didn't remember him—which didn't bother Nick.

Nick was running and enjoying the recycled air pumping through his lungs. As he ran downhill past some outcrops, he thought about his post-run routine. He was going to have a long hot bath, with a book in one hand and a glass of red wine in the other. The prospect put a massive smile on Nick's face. Suddenly, his foot caught something and he fell forward.

He swung his arms around to try to regain his balance, but he pitched forward, and nothing could save him from falling over. He landed heavily and had just enough time to see his bleeding knees and the wire that had tripped him strung between two rocks before a bag was put over his head. He struggled, but two pairs of strong arms were restraining him. He felt a sharp blade pierce his abdomen and rip through his chest. He coughed up blood into the bag. His assailants took off the bag. They had no intention of killing Nick quite yet. As he lay on the ground, a blood angel was pooling around him and blood bubbles were slowly blooming and bursting from his mouth.

"You're not dying yet," a voice whispered to him. "We've got work to do on you."

*

Danny was feeling a contentment that he hadn't felt in years—perhaps one he had never known. Connie had reappeared. She said she'd been on a trip around the outer rim of the Sanctuary.

"Much to be seen there?"

"Not much… some rocks," she said, looking down at her coffee.

"You know, this is not what I expected the end of the world to be like."

"Yeah? You enjoying it?"

Danny shifted in his seat. "Well, I wouldn't say that. It's just that all this has made me focus on things I never had time for before. Now I seem to be able to concentrate more. The stuff

I used to spend time worrying about doesn't really seem so important now."

"Yeah, I know what you mean."

Yes, Danny was enjoying the new routine he'd eased into. Right up until the point when he found the body.

CHAPTER 18

25TH AUGUST 1975

"Well, then, when can I speak to him?"

The smartly dressed, smiling, dead-eyed assistant stared back at Hobson. "No one meets Mr. Jennings," he said.

"Jesus, I know that. I don't want to *meet* him; I just want to speak to him… what about the board meeting?"

The assistant flinched. It had been years since Hobson had seen Jennings in the Sanctuary. Jennings hadn't been seen in public for over two years and dark rumors had begun to circulate about his underground bunker. Hobson suspected that Jennings hadn't actually left the Sanctuary during this period of time, a time when six assistants acting on Jennings's behalf had appeared in the office. They seemed to have formed a barrier which was almost impossible to penetrate. Hobson had dealt with all of them in turn. He found it hard to tell them apart, and they all insisted on calling him Mr. Hobson, which creeped him out.

"I know he chairs a monthly meeting with the board on a via an intercom. I just need ten minutes after the meeting. Is that possible?" asked Hobson.

The assistant put on a pained expression, which Hobson knew was pure show. They were veering towards a solid "no," so it was time for some Washington diplomacy.

"If you could use your influence to get me some time with Jennings," said Hobson.

"I'll see what I can do. I'm not promising."

"Any help you could provide would be gratefully received." Hobson put his hand out to shake, but Jennings's assistants seemed to have inherited his aversion to physical contact. However, once the assistant saw Hobson's fifty-dollar note, he reached for his hand and grabbed it.

"I'll see what I can do," he repeated.

After twenty minutes, the assistants were looking flustered, and for once Hobson didn't think they were being obstinate. They genuinely didn't seem to know what was happening.

"Mr. Jennings isn't speaking to anyone!" the assistant barked.

Something was happening, that much was sure. Hobson had been in the Manhattan head office for the last three hours and people were walking back-and-forth, looking agitated. He'd seen a number of senior board members going in and out of rooms, their brows furrowed and worried looks on their faces. Hobson knew for sure that there was a "situation" occurring when, in the maelstrom, he saw the tall, slender figure of

Rodchenko. Even in the chaos, Rodchenko still retained the look of detached amusement. He scanned the room with his green, catlike eyes. At some time in the past, Rodchenko's nose had been broken and it had set with a slight kink. He had high Slavic cheekbones, and his thinning black hair was slicked back. Hobson had heard somewhere that Rodchenko was younger than he looked, that he was actually only in his late twenties.

What must he have seen and done to age him?

There were quite a few members of the Jennings Tool and Bit Co. board who owed Rodchenko a debt of gratitude. He was a fixer. He cleaned up messes, both business and personal, and helped problems disappear. It was rare to see him out in the open. Hobson had probably seen him twice in the five years— both times had been during a tsunami of shit.

He probably doesn't know who I am.

Rodchenko walked up to him, thrust out his hand, and said, "Mr. Hobson."

Hobson shook it and let himself be guided to a corner.

"Mr. Hobson, we have a proposition for you." Despite his name, Rodchenko had a slight Boston burr, which came out occasionally when he said Hobson's name.

"Would it have anything to do with Jennings, by any chance?"

"You don't have to be Einstein to work that out."

"What can I tell you? You know as much as I do—probably more. I haven't seen him in years."

"We want you to go back into the Sanctuary and find

Jennings—or at least find out what happened to him," said Rodchenko.

"Why would I possibly want to go back into that place? I like the sun, air, and being able to buy snow cones."

"Because if you go in with a team on a search-and-recovery mission for us, we'll make it worth your while."

"How much?"

"You'll never have to work again. You'll be able to buy all the snow cones you want."

Hobson thought about it for a moment. "Right… and I'll have a full team behind me?"

"Whoever you want and however many you need. You can pick anyone from this organization or go external, but obviously keep it as discreet as possible."

What the fuck am I thinking? Don't go back in there, no matter how much he offers you!

"You'll never have to work again," repeated Rodchenko.

"When do I go?"

The answer to that question was, predictably, as soon as possible. And so, late the next day, having assembled a team of six people—two medics, two highly skilled security guards, and two of the original engineers who had helped put the Sanctuary together—Hobson found himself once again on a private jet touching down on a remote landing strip.

He had just enough time to get chilled by the wind before getting behind the wheel of a truck. The rest of the team loaded the equipment into the back. Hobson watched the familiar terrain go by as he drove them to the cavern and felt a heart-clutching dread growing in him. He wished that something, *anything*, would happen to delay or stop them getting to the entrance.

Maybe the truck will turn over. Maybe we'll drive over the cliff. All it would take is one sharp turn of my wrist, pushing the steering wheel right, and then… He pushed the thoughts aside and looked out of the window. Rain was falling.

The team was mostly quiet for the journey, but as they got closer to the cavern one of the medics, who was sitting in the passenger seat next to Hobson, asked him what he was expecting to find.

What am I expecting to find? Jennings, mad and emaciated.

Hobson remembered the sounds he'd heard in the cavern. "I don't know," he replied. "Maybe nothing. We won't know till we get there."

When the truck finally reached their destination, there was an initial relief to be out in the open. They'd been driving for nearly four hours. Hobson was pleased to get some fresh air and stretch his aching legs. But his relief was replaced almost immediately by a familiar dread.

"Get the kit and follow me," he said. The six-strong team took their equipment from the truck: lights, medical supplies, walkie-talkies, food, and drink. Hobson glanced at the wind turbines standing guard on the outcrop, circling slowly.

They walked for fifteen minutes until they got to the familiar clearing, and Hobson descended to the cavern entrance. The stream, which he and Jennings had once waded through, had been redirected. It still ran into the cavern, but it had been dammed, so you no longer had to get wet entering the cavern. Hobson tried not to think too much about what he was doing as he tapped the code into the steel door. It opened up with a sigh of air. They were in. The lights were still on.

"Right, we'll split into two teams," said Hobson. He took one of the security men and one of the medics with him. "You start scouting the lower level. We'll check out Jennings's apartment. Stay in regular contact." Hobson looked over the railing. Spotlights picked out details, but it was as quiet as a mausoleum.

The room had an unkempt, musty smell, like a long-abandoned library. The lights here had been turned off. Hobson turned his flashlight on and swept it in a long arc. The beam glinted off a tall glass with the remains of something inside that had been left for so long it had turned black. Hobson turned the lights on and looked around. The glass was next to a chair that was facing the paintings.

"What are we looking for, boss?" asked the medic.

"Just any clues as to what's happened to Jennings… where he might have gone. I've also been asked to return some items to the office."

"Like what?"

"Well, any personal items of Jennings. They obviously don't know him well; he was never in the habit of keeping much personal stuff. Other than that, there might be some schematics that were left behind, and they've asked me to make sure that all security matters are taken care of."

"Eh?"

"They want me to lock the doors behind me, and also change the door codes where possible."

It didn't seem that the apartment had been lived in for a while. There was no sign that anything unusual had happened. Aside from the musty smell, everything was pretty much the same as it looked the last time he'd been in here—apart from the absence of Jennings, of course. The only part of the room that seemed to have been used recently was the chair facing the cave paintings. Hobson walked towards the chair and stared at the paintings. He ran his hand over the top of the chair, wiping off a thin layer of dust. His foot hit something under the chair. He leaned down to find a battered book with a red leather cover. He picked it up. Written on it was "The Private Journal of Joseph Jennings." Hobson went to the last page and read the entry.

"Holy shit! The Bridge of Souls," he mumbled to himself.

"Have you found something, boss?" one of the others called.

"No. Still looking." Without really knowing why, Hobson put the journal in his bag and out of sight. After looking around the apartment for another twenty minutes, he told the team to move down to the ground floor. "There's nothing to be found here." He could feel the weight of the journal in his bag. It had been light when he'd picked up, but now it felt like a breeze block. They made their way down to the ground level and met up with the other team. Hobson looked around at the cavern.

Never thought I'd be back here. Never wanted to be back here.

"What have you found?" Hobson asked the others.

"Not much of anything, to be honest. Certainly no clue as to what happened to Jennings."

"Okay, fine. Let's all do another sweep of the floor… see if anything turns up."

Hobson directed each member of the team on where to search. He took the outer rim and found himself in front of the Tunnel Sixteen. Subconsciously, his hand patted the shape of the journal in his bag. He knew he had to check the Bridge of Souls out, but his mouth ran dry and his shoulders hunched at the prospect.

Come on, for Christ's sake.

He took three deep breaths and turned his flashlight back on.

Sam Hobson stepped into Tunnel Sixteen. He swept the flashlight beam around, and for that moment, he felt some relief. All that was in front of him was a dark, damp tunnel. He shone the light down at the ground. There was a very faint outline of what looked like footprints.

Hobson looked behind him. He could see the lights and comparative safety of the ground floor of the cavern. He decided to press on, but not too far. He pointed the flashlight down at the floor. The possible footprints had become fainter, but his flashlight beam traced the outline of something partly hidden in the dirt. Hobson bent down to pick it up. He brought it up to his eyes. It was a flashlight almost identical to his own. He turned it around in his hand and tried to switch it on. The battery had long-since died. There were no markings on it to make it distinctive from any other flashlight. He dropped it and carried on walking.

The flashlight didn't penetrate the darkness, which seemed to swallow up the light. Hobson got the feeling he wasn't alone. He turned around slowly. No one there. Suddenly the lights of the ground level seemed very distant. A breath of air rustled through the tunnel.

The smell of peppermint brushed past his nostrils.

"Jennings?"

Hobson looked around and felt a chill run down his spine. He moved on down the tunnel. He shone his flashlight to the right, and a gaunt, worried face stared back, making Hobson stagger back. He smiled when he realized it was his reflection, and the face smiled back.

"Get out!"

Hobson was in danger of making himself giddy as he spun round. The voice had been faint, but distinctive. It sounded gruff, as if whoever had spoken had a sore throat, but there was no mistaking what had been said.

"Who said that?"

The smell of peppermint was replaced by the stinging smell of rotting meat. He heard a roaring wave, which sounded like something being torn apart. He was frozen to the spot with fear. His legs would not move. He seemed to be enveloped in complete darkness.

Hobson felt a thin, cold hand on his shoulder.

"Get out now," a voice whispered in his ear.

His eyes picked up the light of the ground floor again, as though a curtain had just been pulled open. Hobson pushed himself forward, his legs leaden. He felt as if he were walking in calipers, but gradually, the stiffness began to loosen as he hobbled along the tunnel. The tearing sound receded.

Hobson stopped a few yards outside Tunnel Sixteen and took a deep breath. He wiped his arm across his forehead; it came away wet. By the time the rest of the team came back to him, he'd calmed down.

"Find anything down there, boss?"

"No, nothing. Except," he smiled, "maybe bats. Let's get the requested items and get the hell out of here."

Hobson and the team gathered up their equipment and prepared to leave. As the elevator shuddered up to the top level, Hobson looked down at the floor and tried not to think of what he had seen in Tunnel Sixteen. Some of the team chatted, but the conversation petered out long before the elevator lurched to a stop at the top floor. Hobson led the team out of the cavern. He reset the entrance codes to the ones requested on the sheet of paper he'd been given. When the last door closed behind him, he strode to the truck and didn't look back.

*

"So… no clues at all as to what happened to him?"

Hobson and Rodchenko were in a small room in the basement of the Jennings Tool and Bit Co. building. It wasn't quite the janitor's closet, but that was only because there wasn't a mop and bucket in sight.

"You've seen the report."

"Yes, I have it with me now." He thumbed through it. "I'vc read the report, Mr. Hobson—and very detailed it is, too—but I'm asking you… no signs at all? Nothing?"

What's he accusing me of? Hobson looked Rodchenko straight in the eyes. "No, nothing."

"You went into Tunnel Sixteen?"

"Yes," replied Hobson.

"You, yourself?"

Hobson nodded.

"What did you see in there?" asked Rodchenko.

Hobson hesitated for a moment and his gaze flicked off to the side. "Nothing."

"Nothing? Didn't I read that you saw *tracks*? Could they have been footprints? Maybe belonging to Jennings?"

Hobson began to sweat. "No. As I said in the report, I saw some faint tracks, but they could have been made at any time."

"What about the discarded flashlight?"

"Again, that could have been left at any point by anyone."

Rodchenko nodded as he skim-read the report again. "And you found no… written material? Nothing to suggest what state of mind Jennings might have been in?" Rodchenko looked up from the report, smiled, and fixed Hobson with a steely gimlet stare.

How does he know? Hobson had to stop himself from gulping. "No, I didn't find anything."

"Very well." Rodchenko looked up at the ceiling as though he were getting instructions. "We'll start the legal procedures to have Jennings declared dead."

"That's very cold."

Rodchenko shrugged. "What other options do we have? He's been missing for over eight weeks now. I've been working with the board to put a plan in place should Jennings become… unavailable. We just didn't expect to put it into play so soon. The company can't be seen as rudderless, so we're filling the vacuum. The official story is that Jennings is ill, and he will remain so for the next six weeks until we can shore things up. Then… he will sadly pass away."

"What about the death certificate?"

"That can be arranged."

"What about a body?"

"Jennings hasn't been seen in public for years. There won't be any requirement."

"But what if there is?"

"That can be arranged."

Hobson felt sick. "What's going to happen to the Sanctuary?"

"We've already salvaged everything of value. We haven't found Jennings, so the Sanctuary will be mothballed until the board can think of something to do with it."

"So that's it?"

Rodchenko shrugged his shoulders. He was already looking past Hobson at the door.

"Why are you telling me all of this?"

"You're one of the few people who knows the truth, and, as a result, the board has authorized a very generous severance package, as I promised. You'll never have to work again. I hardly need to mention that comes with a gagging clause. There are certain forms the board will be expecting you to sign." Rodchenko stared into Hobson's eyes. He continued to stare as he grabbed Hobson's hand and shook it vigorously. "I presume you can find your own way out?" Hobson nodded and Rodchenko left the room.

When Hobson pressed the button for the elevator, he realized that his involvement with Jennings and the Sanctuary was over. It had happened so suddenly that he couldn't quite believe it. He didn't know what to do with himself.

Where is Jennings?

Hobson thought back to the time when the two of them had looked over the railing into the abyss. He also remembered the first time he'd seen Jennings, striding into the office, full of youthful energy and a twinkle in his eyes. All those years, all that energy, all those people—and what did it get them?

He took a deep breath and smiled at the elevator music. "I'm going to a bar and I'm going to get wasted," he said quietly to himself.

Hobson found a small Irish bar around the corner from the

office. He found the farthest, darkest booth and took his drink over. He looked around and, when he was sure no one was looking, he reached into his bag and brought out a battered, red, leatherbound book. He took a sip of his drink and began to read.

"He dies in the end."

Hobson jumped. Sitting across from him, as if he'd appeared from thin air, was Rodchenko.

Fuck! Hobson slammed the book shut.

"I'm sorry if I spoiled the story for you." Rodchenko smiled, but the smile didn't touch his eyes. It reminded Hobson of a great white shark.

"I was…"

Rodchenko looked down and raised his palm as if amused by what Hobson was about to say. "Oh, come on, Sam. We've both been 'round the block. You're insulting both of us."

Hobson felt violated by Rodchenko's use of his first name, but he was also aware of his shoulders relaxing a little, knowing he no longer had to spin out a tale of deception. "How did you know?" he asked.

"Jennings was a lifelong diary keeper, and if there's one thing we both know about him it's that he was a creature of habit. It would have been highly unusual for him not to have kept a journal while in the Sanctuary."

Rodchenko held his right hand out, as if just extending his hand would bring the journal into his possession. Hobson clutched the journal tighter. A flash of annoyance appeared on

Rodchenko's face, which was quickly replaced by a smile.

There's that smile again—a smile just before he stabs me in the eye.

"The way I see it, the only person this belongs to is Joseph Jennings," said Hobson.

"So, we agree that it doesn't belong to you?"

"Or you… so we seem to have a bit of a standoff."

Rodchenko didn't put his hand down, but the smile faltered. "I would hate your relationship with the company to end on a *sour* note. Let's be sure it doesn't. Give me the book."

Hobson hesitated and then handed the journal to Rodchenko.

"I just remembered…" Hobson didn't finish the sentence. He got up and left the bar.

*

The smile reappeared on Rodchenko's lips. He looked around the bar.

The rest of the denizens were oblivious to him and the exchange he'd just had with Hobson. Rodchenko had never seen the appeal of bars. He'd had a few drinks over the years, mostly to lubricate some business social event that he would have preferred not to be at. Alcohol had never been something that held any allure for him. Why poison yourself just so you can lose control? Rodchenko was certainly keen to put as much distance as he could between himself and the bar and its boorish patrons. There didn't seem to be any part of the table that wasn't sticky. He propped the journal up against the wall and the least-sticky part of the table he could find and ran his hand over the cracked leather cover.

One of the requests from the board was to return any material found at "Jennings' Folly," as the Sanctuary had begun to be known. Only two people knew of the existence of the journal, and one of those was certainly not going to mention it to another living soul. Rodchenko looked at the cover and traced the letters with his index finger.

CHAPTER 19

T he lighting system in the Sanctuary followed the rhythm of the seasons. Now that it was late spring, Danny was enjoying the lighter mornings. The rational part of him knew it was insane because they could put the last arc light on whenever they wanted. He remembered a particularly messy week in Las Vegas, where, having spent hour upon hour in constant artificial sunlight, he had been left feeling totally jaded, as if he'd been locked in a brightly lit elevator for hours. But Danny didn't feel that way in the Sanctuary, so the artificial light must be working. He had a coffee and a bagel before leaving for the farm.

"Morning, Rodge," he said, but Rodger just grunted at him. *Possibly hungover, the miserable bastard.*

Rodger could be a mercurial SOB: chatty one minute, monosyllabic the next. Danny got his tools and wheeled them over to the plot he was working on.

He noticed the hand first. He felt his blood run cold.

Danny looked around, hoping he'd made a mistake, but he saw the body strung out like a scarecrow. The eyes had been sewn shut. The mouth had been slashed open at either side. The throat had been cut and was caked in dried blood. The torso, also streaked in blood, had been slashed and gutted. Despite the mutilations, Danny knew it was the runner he passed all the time. He looked down at the ground. The blood had pooled around his feet and had begun to soak into the ground, just like…

Jesus, is that it? Is this the answer to the question of what happens when Oblivion Black wants more than livestock as a tribute?

"Rodger!" It came out like a strangled cry. "Rodger!"

Rodger came running. "Fucking hell!" he said when he saw the human scarecrow. "What have you done?"

Danny was sitting at the same table where he'd been interviewed when he'd first applied to enter the Sanctuary.

"But you'd met this person before?" asked Sarah.

"Yes," he said, running his fingers over his face. "How many times do I have to repeat the same thing? He was a runner. We'd pass each other occasionally and nod at each other."

"When was the last time you saw him?"

Alive? The killer's still in the Sanctuary. We threw Greg out for nothing. "I can't remember. Oh, for fuck's sake!" He slammed his fist down on the table. "You do realize what's going on here, don't you? Eh? The killer's still in here with us."

"I… we don't know that." Sarah looked away.

Danny took a sideways glance at Rodger, who was looking down at the mud on his boot. His hands shook as he tried to roll a cigarette. He swore under his breath as he spilled some of his tobacco.

"What about the video footage?" asked Danny.

"We checked, and that's one of the few blank spots not covered by the cameras."

"Very, very unfortunate. What about the rest of the cameras around the place? Did they pick up any activity?" said Danny. He looked around the table. No one would look him in the eye.

"But the footage didn't show you at any point, Danny—which is why we're still talking."

"What are you trying to get at?"

"You seem to be connected to a lot of people who are turning up dead."

"Fuck you! You're not going to make me a scapegoat like Greg! I have nothing to do with these murders!"

"I'm not saying you have. It just seems to be a huge coincidence that-"

"I'll stop you there, Sarah." Danny stabbed a finger in her direction. "You say one more word that even hints that I'm in any way connected to this and I'll shout about this from the highest roof top and blow the fucking whistle on this whole situation."

Silence.

"So, what *are* you going to do?" asked Danny.

210

"We'll be… continuing our investigations. But for the time being, Danny, we'd be grateful if you kept this to yourself."

"Right!" Danny got up and left without looking at any of them.

For the first time in a long time, Danny felt like getting falling-down drunk. He headed back to his apartment to find Connie at his door.

"Fancy a drink, hombre?"

"Fuuuuuuck, do I!"

It was noticeable that the bar wasn't quite as sparkly and pristine as it once had been. Danny noticed that some of the slate was missing from the walls and that the bare bricks and cavern walls were poking through. When he took the first sip of his beer, Danny knew they'd run out of the good stuff. The bar staff weren't wearing their uniforms and Danny was sure he'd seen one or two of them working on the farm. They weren't as quick to serve—or smile—and the drinks didn't flow so readily.

"How're you doing?" asked Connie.

"Fine, yeah, fine. There's some knockdown freaky shit happening,"

"Like what?" she replied.

Danny took a deep gulp of his drink and wiped his mouth.

"I found a body."

"Oh, fuck, Danny. I'm sorry. What…"

"He'd been murdered. He was a runner I'd seen all the time. I think his name was Nigel. He'd been eviscerated. I don't know what's going on."

"Nasty shit for nasty times. We've got to do something about it, Danny. We can't just sit back and hope it doesn't happen to us."

"Agreed, but… but not tonight, yeah?"

*

Danny didn't go back to the farm for a while. One day melted into another and the only difference in routine was the length of the course he ran. Two weeks had gone by when, on his way to see Theresa, something caught his eye. The door to the apartment four doors up from him was open.

Nothing odd about that, but…

Despite himself, he looked around and pushed the door open with his foot.

I'm not really doing anything wrong.

The apartment was pretty much the same as his, except it had a blue color scheme.

Danny looked around. He didn't know what he was expecting but there was nothing odd. He noticed a driver's license on the bedside cabinet and picked it up.

He stared at the photo showing a ginger-haired guy wearing glasses. Danny vaguely recognized him. He'd seen him about, although he'd never spoke to him. But he couldn't remember the last time he'd seen the guy. He put the license down and took another look around the apartment. It didn't look like anyone had slept here for a while. The room had a stale smell, partly coming from a heap of dirty clothes that hadn't been washed, a half-eaten apple that was going moldy, and a long-cold cup of tea.

Of course, he might have hooked up with someone else. He might be sleeping in someone else's bed…

Danny gave an involuntary shiver and left the empty apartment.

*

They were in Hobson's Bar and Danny was coming back with their drinks.

"Busy tonight," he said.

"It's busy every night. Remember what I was saying about people struggling with the confinement?" She waved her glass of double vodka and Coke around at the crowd in the bar. "This is how the others are coping. Self-medicating. How are you coping with the whole situation, Danny?"

He smiled and clinked glasses with her. She smiled back.

"Hmmm, self-medicating, yeah. I know I'm drinking a bit too much, but I'm still running."

"Ah, lovely, lovely endorphins. The body's own anti-depressants." Theresa raised her glass.

"Yeah, it's been great. I run every other day. It's a great way to explore the Sanctuary, but the gradients," he blew out his cheeks, "yeah, they can really knock the stuffing out of you. But I've been timing myself and I'm getting quicker, going farther. It's a great way to level out your mood."

What about the little yellow pills? Man, wouldn't they *be good?*

Danny ignored the voice.

"How are you coping with everything? It can't be easy for

213

you. You never signed up to be the primary physician, after Doctor Schriver didn't make it back from leave at Arrow's Reach. That must be a lot of pressure."

"No more pressure than when I was working sixteen-hour shifts in ER. Do you know why this bar's called Hobson's Bar?"

Danny was a little surprised by the swift change of subject.

"Uh, no, I've never really thought about it before."

"It's named after Sam Hobson. He was Jennings's main man when this was built. He was the guy who originally came out to Black Cove and found the cavern. He's not given the credit he deserves."

"Well, he does have this bar named after him." Danny smiled, but Theresa was looking down at her drink.

"He should have more. His name is barely mentioned in any of the books."

"The books?"

Theresa laughed and smiled at Danny.

"Oh, right, you're not joking. Yeah, there's two or three books about this place; the best one is *The Life and Death of Joseph Jennings*. And there's dozens of websites. Do you know that, when this place was being built, a work crew went missing in one of the tunnels and they were never found? It was all hushed up."

Danny laughed out loud.

Theresa looked taken aback.

"All hushed up?" he said. "So, what, like a conspiracy?"

Theresa paused, laughed, and finished her drink. "Yeah, I

know it sounds a little mad. I dunno, this place, it's… weird." She looked around the bar and up at the ceiling. "We've done our best to try and tame this place: We cover the rock, we put in lights, but it's never truly been tamed. The real cavern is just waiting. You can see parts of it are already beginning to poke through. It'll win in the end."

"You're a regular ray of sunshine."

She laughed again at this, and it did seem like a ray of sunshine had found its way into the bar. "Sorry. I've been in the hospital all day and I just get caught up in my own thoughts. I could do with another drink."

"Your wish is my command."

Danny turned towards the bar. He didn't see the smile disappear from her face or the blank stare that replaced it.

*

When Danny woke up the next morning, Theresa had already left to start work in the infirmary. He put his hands behind his head and looked up at the ceiling of his apartment. He had nothing to do and nowhere to go. He looked at his clock. 7:45 a.m. Way too early to be calling on Connie. She'd be getting over her hangover and wouldn't surface for breakfast until 10 a.m. at the earliest. His muscles still ached from yesterday's run, but even if he did go for a run, the rest of the day stretched out ahead of him. He wanted to feel useful.

Danny stared at the ceiling for a few more seconds. He had to get back to working on the farm.

*

Rodger was doing what he always seemed to be doing—rolling a cigarette and looking for his Harley-Davidson lighter—when Danny turned up. He looked at Danny and nodded. Danny nodded back.

"I was wondering if you could do with any help?"

Having found his lighter Rodger lit his roll-up. "I might," he said. "But why would you want to come back?"

"I'm bored."

"You're bored. Yeah, that's a really great reason to turn up for work."

"Uh… how about, I miss being called 'Hollywood'?"

"How do I know you won't quit again?"

"I promise I won't."

Rodger took a long, deep, thoughtful drag of his roll-up.

"Welcome back."

CHAPTER 20

She could still remember when she had been young, even after all this time.

She could still remember the smell of the hairless apes that chased her and her kind across the swamplands and grass plains. She could remember the warmth of her mother and fighting with her siblings. After the many, many years, she could still remember the smell of grass on a hot day after the rain.

It had been a day like any other, the day she had fallen into the darkness. Running for survival with the rest of her kind, the hairless apes throwing rocks and sticks at her brethren.

That day had been her day to die. She remembered feeling the whoosh of air as one of the hairless apes threw a spear, ruffling her fur but not hitting her as she veered sharply off to the right. Instead of the feeling of the hairless ape's hot breath on the back of her neck, she fell, and then darkness. Small plants and weeds cushioned her fall, but she still landed at the bottom of the cavern with a thump, momentarily stunned.

Gradually, she managed to pull herself up onto her hind legs to look around. She sniffed the damp air. The place smelled like nowhere she'd been before. It was dark but there was some light from algae on the walls. Despite her fall, she felt stronger. There was something in the cavern that made her feel different, made her feel more than she had been. She gave the air another sniff and began to explore her surroundings. There was a plentiful supply of water for her to drink and to occasionally bathe in. The only part of the cavern that she couldn't venture into was the cave with the sharp and shiny green teeth; simply getting near it sent a shard of pain through her head. She roared at it, her echo cascading around the cavern, but couldn't get too close. Even the sight of the teeth scattered around caused her pain. Not that it was a problem for her; there was more than enough of the cavern for her domain.

As she padded around the cavern she began to change. It was giving her abilities beyond anything her species had ever had before. She found that she was able to move her thoughts into the tiny skulls of the other creatures who shared her new home. She was able to influence their behavior and their actions to snare them. But there was another change happening to her that had nothing to do with the cavern.

Some of the hairless apes discovered a way into the cavern, which many years later would be closed off by a rock fall. They set up a dwelling in the cavern. She found that she could enter their minds, and slowly, she began to influence their actions to a small degree. Some of them misinterpreted her thoughts and made blood sacrifices as though she were a god. Yet they seemed to understand that if they left sacrifices of food, she would leave them alone. She tried to stay as far away from them as she could. Their thoughts were like worms squirming in mud.

She had seen others of her herd give birth before, and she knew instinctively what to do when her stomach began to swell. She explored the tunnels branching off the main cavern and found the most suitable location; it had a ring of fiery red around its entrance. Then she found an enclave, which was warm and dry, and began collecting twigs and branches, dragging them back to make a birthing nest for itself. When she felt the time approaching, she retreated to her nest to wait. But when the time did come it wasn't right. The pup was born underweight and sickly. She did her best, but normally, the herd would have helped feed and tend the newborn. Her pup died.

She let out a mournful cry. As was the custom of her kind, she wrapped the body of her dead pup in a cocoon of sticks, leaves, and mud until it was covered.

She picked the cocoon up softly in her jaws and padded out of the tunnel. Her thoughts were consumed by the bundle, so much so that she didn't see the ambush. The hairless apes caught her in a net made of vines, hit her with rocks and clubs, and took the cocoon away. They held it aloft, triumphant. She got free of the net and tried to swipe the apes with her claws, but they held the green teeth in front of them, causing a stabbing pain in her head. She was driven back into the tunnel, bloodied and bruised. Before sleep dragged her down, she searched the minds of the apes that attacked her. They had put the cocoon at the heart of their worship. The body of her dead pup had become their Totem.

As her breathing became shallow and her eyes closed, she vowed to retrieve the body of her child and give it the burial it deserved. She'd tear the cavern—and the apes —apart if she had to...

The decades drifted away like leaves in the wind until the hairless apes forgot about her and the cave, and she became the stuff of myth and legend. She awoke from the hibernation after they'd left, and she took back her domain until the thing which called itself "Jennings"—a creature with a mind like a hornet's nest—decided to try and make the cave its home. And then a new dance began.

CHAPTER 21

E ven after a relatively brief absence from the day-to-day routine of the Sanctuary, something became apparent to Danny: Food wasn't as varied as it once had been. Rationing hadn't yet become necessary—the produce from the farm was making up more and more of what was eaten in the Sanctuary, allowing them to keep up with demand—but he remembered Connie questioning what "self-sufficient" actually meant. They could keep up with demand now, sure, but "now" didn't mean "indefinitely."

Danny and Theresa met up for what had become their regular evening meal in the piazza. They'd managed to schedule their work so that they both finished at the same time. The choice of food was getting more limited, and it caught him by surprise to see one of his fellow residents working in one of the kitchens. *A life of constant leisure gets boring—that's why I work on the farm, I guess.*

Danny had been the first to arrive. He settled back into his chair and enjoyed the afterburn of endorphins from a day of weeding and digging.

"Hey, there, handsome!" Danny did a mock look over his shoulder to see whom Theresa was talking to.

"How you doing?" he asked her as she slumped into the chair opposite. "You look tired."

"For that, you're buying dinner."

"Which is only fair. Sorry. Hard day?"

Theresa shrugged. "Not particularly. Just trying to make a finite set of resources stretch into infinity."

"We're running low on supplies?"

"Not really. It's just we don't know how long we're going to be down here, and what with the specific needs of some of the residents—diabetics, asthmatics, a few who are HIV positive—we have to start planning for the longer term." She stared at the menu.

"What happens when we run out?"

"That'll be a few years down the line. I suppose we'll have to look at producing drugs ourselves. Look, can we eat? I'm famished."

"Yeah, sure, you ready to order?"

"I am, and afterwards, I've got a treat back at my apartment."

He leered at her. "Oh, yes?"

Theresa laughed. "You're an utter pervert, you realize that? Mind you, if you play your cards right… no, I've got a bottle of wine that I don't feel like drinking alone."

"A bottle of wine? I thought you'd used up all your drink allowance?"

"You're a bit naive for a businessman, Danny. I may have given a patient some extra drugs in exchange for a little sweetener. You don't have a problem with that, do you?"

"No, not at all." The surprise must have been obvious on his face, however, because she leaned into him and spoke in a low voice.

"There's quite a black market operating here, Danny. Has been for a while. Let me know if there's anything you want. I could probably hook you up."

Vicodin.

He instantly dismissed the thought from his mind, but he was disconcerted by Theresa's offer. However, this didn't stop him sharing the bottle of red wine with her—and much else besides.

Later, in bed, basking in the afterglow of sex, Danny was settling into sleep.

"Do you ever wonder what happened to Joseph Jennings?" Theresa asked.

"I can't say it's been something that's ever crossed my mind," said Danny, trying hard not to sound annoyed at being kept awake.

"Really? Not even a little?"

Jesus. "No, not even a little."

"One of the most famous and wealthy men in history walked into this cavern one day and never came back out again and you don't find that fascinating?"

Danny tried to spoon her, partly in an effort to make her stop talking, but he just ended up against her side. "I dunno, aren't there lots of conspiracy theories about what happened to him? Wasn't the official story that he died of a heart attack in a hotel in Las Vegas?"

"Everyone knows that's bullshit. He found the Sanctuary and maybe discovered something else. He never left."

"I'll look into it in the morning," Danny muttered. Seconds later, he was snoring, leaving Theresa sitting up in bed and staring into the dark.

*

The next day on the farm, during their break, Danny was chatting with Rodger.

"Hey, Hollywood! You want to get your hands dirty?"

"I don't mind getting dirty," said Danny, "as long as it doesn't mean I'm cultivating some of your cash crop."

Danny had instantly recognized the sweet smell that wafted his way occasionally when Rodger decided he wanted a "herbal" cigarette.

"It's purely medicinal, for my arthritis."

"Yeah, sure."

*

After his shift on the farm, Danny met up with Connie at the piazza.

"Have you noticed that there's more space around here?" Danny asked her.

"Not really. But it is a bit more pleasant than normal."

"Jesus! The reason there's more space is because there's less people here."

"Are you sure?"

"Yeah, I'm certain. I noticed a few weeks ago. Some of the faces just aren't around anymore. You know Andy, ginger hair, big city banker on the outside?"

"Yeah."

"He's gone."

"What do you mean?"

Danny put on a hillbilly accent. "He ain't around here no more." He continued, "I checked his apartment, and it doesn't look as though the bed's been slept in for a while. I've been asking about, and no one's seen him in at least two weeks. And his isn't the only empty apartment I've found recently."

"Where do you think they've gone?"

"Well, I'm as sure as shit that it's not some mystic fucking creature spiriting them away. Something's going on."

*

Miles yawned, stretched, and scratched. It was 2:45 a.m. and he couldn't sleep. He decided to get up and go for a walk. He descended to the piazza on the ground level and was thinking of walking around the outskirts. As he walked down, he noticed that the stairs were chipped and mold had started to grow on the walls.

This place is a fucking dump.

It certainly wasn't as plush as when he'd first bought his apartment. The booze in Hobson's Bar had taken a turn for the worse and now the staff were starting to get surly. There was that incident recently with the farm worker who spoke back to him. Standards had slipped since the lockdown.

It had been fun for a while—drinking, watching films, and generally not giving a shit—but now he was getting the itch. He needed to get back to it; he needed to get out. He was pretty sure it wasn't nearly as bad as they pretended it to be.

I'll give it another week or so and then I'll see how I can get out. I just hope Glen hasn't fucked the business up too much. I'll nail his balls to the wall.

In fact, the idea of eviscerating Glen put Miles in a good mood. *Regardless of what he's done, I'm going to destroy the little prick when I get out of here.*

The thought put a smile on his face and Miles decided not to walk around the outskirts of the cavern, but instead to walk across to the Cave of Diamonds that he'd heard so much about.

He felt out-of-breath walking across the piazza.

Shit, maybe I should use however long I've got left in this dump to hit the gym.

After shifting down to a slower pace, he got to the entrance of the cave. He could see a dim green light coming from deep inside. Looking in, his eyes could just detect the faint outline of what looked like an altar.

I wonder if the bar will be open.

From the green-tinged darkness of the cave, three veiled shadows emerged and marched towards him. He saw that they had animal faces painted in white across the sheer fabric of their masks.

"What the fu-"

Two of his assailants grabbed him by his arms and dragged him into the Cave of Diamonds. They laid him by the altar and held him down.

"What the fuck is this?" Miles yelled as he struggled to free himself.

He saw the tallest of the figures pull a large knife out from his belt and hold it up. Green light picked out its razor-sharp edge. His eyes bulged as he struggled harder against his assailants.

"No!" he tried to scream, but his throat was dry.

With a swift movement, the knife was plunged into Miles's heart. Blood erupted out of his mouth and chest as his body convulsed violently. The other two black-clad figures struggled to keep him down. Miles let out a series of death rattles, and his eyes rolled up into his skull as the life shuddered out of him, his blood spilling onto the stone of the altar.

*

From behind the sheer fabric of his mask, Rodchenko breathed deeply. His breath made the fabric wet. He liked the sensation.

Other black-clad members of the cabal bled out of the darkness and gathered around the sacrifice. Rodchenko pulled off his mask to talk to the group.

"The reckoning is here. They know we're here; the blood we've spilled has been noticed. We have to make our move. We're going to slaughter those who stand against us."

The members of the cabal readied themselves. They put their decoys and barriers in place. They sharpened knives and machetes, preparing them to be wet with blood, and spread out into the Sanctuary like a disease.

CHAPTER 22

The light sparked in the darkness.

From somewhere in the distance came the slow drip-drip of water. Sarah looked around not knowing which way to go, but knowing that she had to move. Something was coming. Something was coming to get her. She traced her hands down the metal of the corridor wall and moved forward—but was she moving away from her pursuer, or towards it?

She knew where she was.

She'd been here before.

Sarah had been here during Greg's last seconds in the Sanctuary. It had been her decision, so she'd taken the responsibility and made sure that her order was carried out. She had watched as Greg's fingers had been prised off the final door as he was expelled.

She'd watched as he'd been dragged, kicking and screaming and pleading, out of the Sanctuary. His screams echoed around Sarah's skull and now they echoed around the corridor in which she found herself.

A horrible realization hit her as she stumbled in the flickering darkness. *Somehow, some way, Greg has found his way back in.*

He'd managed to trap her here, in this corridor. Except he wasn't just Greg anymore: Something had happened to him on the outside. He'd returned as something strange and terrible. He was coming for Sarah, and all she could do was stumble up the corridor hoping that she was moving away from him.

The sparking light made shadows dance on the walls in a kaleidoscope of shapes.

Sarah was sure that Greg was behind her and was catching her up. She tried to move quicker but her legs felt as if they were made of lead. From up ahead came a tearing sound. She knew what that meant.

Oblivion Black.

She spun around. There was nowhere to run. In the steel mirror of the wall was the image of a man with long white hair, blue eyes, and gaunt cheeks. He was saying something, but Sarah couldn't hear what it was.

The tearing sound was getting louder.

She was powerless to move, and from behind her, surfacing from the darkness, came a grinning Greg Wysneck. She was right, though: It wasn't the Greg she remembered. He was much taller, the back of his neck scraping against the roof of the corridor. The right side of his face was a red spider's web of weeping cuts and gouges. A baleful, bloodshot eye stared out from the crimson mush. His arms were freakishly long, nearly dragging on the floor. Instead of hands, he had talons that ended in three sharp, serrated claws. His lip was torn away on the right, revealing his lower jaw and leaving a trail of drool hanging.

"Sarah Turner!" he howled in a wet voice as he got closer.

Sarah still couldn't move and, as Greg moved closer, she could smell his fetid breath. When he was within feet of Sarah, he brought his hands up to strike her with his claws.

"There's a reckoning coming!"

The claws swept down…

As Sarah woke, she clutched the sweat-drenched bedsheets. She ran a hand down her face, then propped herself up in bed and reached for a glass of water. She took a deep gulp and looked at her clock.

4 a.m. She sighed and resigned herself to the fact that she wouldn't be getting any more sleep that night. There would be a thousand thoughts galloping around her head. These days, if she managed to sleep until four, she considered it a blessing.

In the stodgy, endless minutes of the early morning, she started to plan out things to do to stave off the panic. She reached into the top drawer of her bedside cabinet. There, right at the back, was a crumbled packed of Camels. Only six remained. She fished one out, lit it, and took a deep drag of the smoke. She was already shaking off the vestiges of the nightmare, but some parts of it still clung to her. She had glimpses of the talons and the sputtering light, but what remained crystal-clear was the warning.

A reckoning is coming.

For now, she watched the tendrils of smoke twist and weave in the air of her apartment.

*

"What do you think is going on around here?"

"What do you mean?"

"My mom said never answer a question with a question, but you know I've been around this cavern and…"

Danny was too ashamed to admit that he hadn't explored much farther than the refitted part of the Sanctuary.

"Shit, Daniel, you really need to pull your head out of your ass and take a look around this place."

Danny put his hands up. "Whoa! Whoa! I will ask the senator for Delaware to refrain from using such language!"

Connie laughed. "Okay. Yeah, sorry. It's still very early, and it's been a bit of an odd night."

"You can say that again," added Danny.

"The original inhabitants of the cavern were Native Americans—I think I read somewhere that they were the Athabastara tribe. There are some pretty grisly cave paintings here. You must have seen the stick figures: They sort of look like scarecrows. That's what happened to poor Nick. He'd been trussed-up like those."

"So, what are you saying? That the ghosts of the Athabastara have come to wreak their terrible revenge on us?"

"No, I think what's happening here is much more flesh-and-blood in nature. What do you know about the diary of Joseph Jennings?"

The mellowing effect of the booze was beginning to kick in, despite the macabre turn of the conversation.

"Ah, now *that* I've heard of. But I thought it was a fake?"

"It was never proved conclusively to be a fake. I suppose it depends on who you listen to. A lot of the time it doesn't matter if these things are fake or not. The Nazis didn't care if that *Elders of Zion* pamphlet was bullshit or not when they clutched it to their hateful hearts. These things have a habit of hanging around like a bad smell."

"So, you're saying what?"

"Myths can be powerful things—just ask anyone who's chased after the Holy Grail. And that's without factoring in the cabin fever that's setting in down here… who's to say that some of us in here haven't read some conspiracy theories and had some latent pagan belief system reinforced? It would certainly be a credible explanation for at least some of what we've seen."

"I hope you're wrong."

"So do I, but do you have a better explanation?"

They sat in silence. Danny could feel the walls closing in on him. He shot up from his chair.

"I'm going to take a look at these cave paintings that all the critics have been raving about."

"Hold on, I'll come with you," said Connie.

The cave paintings had a rail around them and were dimly lit. Danny moved to read a nearby plaque explaining the paintings' significance and suggesting possible origins. They looked at the images of stick figures standing—either in fear or in reverence—before an ominous black figure.

"You're seriously telling me you've never been here before?"

"I'm ashamed to say that I haven't," said Danny, but at the same time, there was a nagging feeling that he'd seen something very similar, while he'd been drenched in sweat and coming off Vicodin. Before he could make more of a connection Connie spoke:

"You've been to the Cave of Diamonds, though?"

"Umm…"

"Daniel! It's the most stunning natural feature of the cavern! Right, come on, I'm taking you there now."

As they walked, they carried on talking.

"I know this is going to make me sound paranoid," Danny began.

"Just because you're paranoid doesn't mean that they're not out to get you."

Danny shook his head as though trying to clear his thoughts. "It's just that… well, some things aren't sitting right."

"Such as?"

"Stuff that Theresa's been asking. And our Nosferatu man."

"Yeah, Nosferatu man worries me. Normally, I can pretty much get any information I want, about anything—usually by buying the right people a couple of drinks and asking a few well-targeted questions—but either no one knows who he is, or no one's talking. That's not right."

"We should do some more digging."

Connie shrugged. "I haven't got anything better to do."

*

"Right, here we are, Daniel, the Cave of-"

Splayed out in front of them was the eviscerated body of Miles, his blood congealing on the stone of the altar, his sightless eyes staring at the roof of the cave.

They were struck dumb for a moment.

"Oh, Christ, I think I'm going to…" Danny's eyes watered. He felt an acidic taste at the back of his throat. "Oh, Christ!" With one hand, he clutched the wall and put the other one over his stomach.

Connie couldn't look at the corpse. She turned her back to the horrific sight as a blinding headache washed over her. She sat down and cradled her head in her hands.

Danny's nausea faded. He wiped his eyes and tried not to look at Miles. He pulled Connie to her feet.

"We've got to let Sarah know."

He dragged her to the main stairwell, passing a large group of people assembling in the piazza.

"What…?" Danny slowed down to ask what was happening.

Connie pulled him on. "We haven't got time!"

They took the staircase two steps at a time. When they got to the third level, they nearly bumped into Rodger.

"What's going on?"

"Didn't you see that message from Sarah Turner to meet in the piazza at ten?" He held a flyer.

Danny checked his watch: it was 9:55 a.m. "I must have missed it. Are you on your way down?"

"It looks legit, but I don't know… something doesn't feel right. I was coming up here to ask Sarah what it was all about."

Danny looked over the rail and saw that most of the Sanctuary's inhabitants were milling around the piazza. He looked back up to see Sarah—clutching her walkie-talkie in one hand—and Michael Dunning walking towards them.

"Do you know about this?" Connie asked, handing her Rodger's flier.

Sarah read it. "First I've heard of it. I've normally had a dozen calls by now, but it's been dead. I was coming out to see what's up. Loads of the stairwells have been closed off and shut. I was trying to get hold of maintenance, but no one's answering." She pressed a red button on the side of her walkie-talkie and got static as a reply.

Danny looked around at the ringed level. At this time of the morning, it would usually be busy with people, but there were only the five of them.

"We've got to get down to the piazza," said Rodger.

"Agreed."

They walked to the stairs and found themselves and another eight stragglers blocked off with a hastily nailed-up chipboard barrier.

"It looks like someone's trying to keep us out," said Connie.

The realization of what was happening hit Danny like a slap.

"We're not being kept out… *they're* being locked *in*! They're being kettled, driven down to the piazza! It's an ambush!"

*

"What are you doing here?"

Stue laughed when he bumped into Stan the comms guy in the piazza. Stue had gotten bored and decided to investigate more of the Sanctuary, taking a particular interest in the comms side of things. He had made his money in IT and wanted to find out what their setup was in an attempt to stave off the endless boredom. His first encounter with Stan had been in the comms room and, on that occasion, he'd gotten the distinct impression that Stan didn't want to talk to him. Stue had told him of his background, but this had been received with barely contained irritation and the occasional "hm, yes" while Stan had fiddled with a desktop motherboard. He had sensed the irritation ramping up when he decided to try to help Stan out. Despite this—or maybe because if it—he liked Stan, and over the last few months, they'd cultivated an awkward friendship, especially when he had helped sort out a networking issue.

Stan blinked and shrugged. "I tried to get up to the comms room, but all the walkways up are closed off. It's very annoying."

"And a little weird. You didn't get the note, then?"

"I did, but I ignored it. I'm really not happy, not happy at all. I hope, whatever this is, it's over soon. I need to get back to my work."

Stan nodded at Amanda as she walked past with her hands thrust into her pockets. As always, Amanda ignored him.

*

It wasn't simple contempt that caused Amanda to ignore Stan this time. She'd received a summons from Sarah Turner, the same Sarah Turner who had turned her down for a place on the committee. It was a disgrace: She knew the Sanctuary like the back of her hand, yet all she was deemed suitable for was basic admin. That decision meant less food. The residents still got free food and free booze, while the support staff—from the farmers right up to admin—had to sing for their supper. It wasn't fair. She could just about stomach being treated like shit by the residents when she was getting paid well and when she could get out, but since the lockdown things had gotten worse. Danny Keins hadn't said a word to her since they'd stopped sleeping together. He'd dropped her like a stone when he'd taken up with the doctor. He'd walked right past her in the piazza a number of times.

Things had to change.

*

They appeared from the shadows and drifted into position around the piazza. There were five exits, including the elevators and the staircases that had been blocked off. The cabal had been moving through the Sanctuary closing off walkways and doorways to funnel people onto the piazza. People were milling about, laughing and talking, completely oblivious to the threat, when the cabal struck.

A cabal member crept behind a Sanctuary resident and pulled a thin piece of wire around the resident's neck, then pulled tight. The victim grabbed at the steel, vainly trying to prevent it cutting through his flesh and into their windpipe.

The rest of the cabal fell on the residents like a pack of wolves.

Blood sprayed and ran down their bodies, leaving tracks across the piazza floor as the cabal dragged their struggling victims off to the side and into the shadows. Soon they were trussed up like the original stick figure scarecrows, a tribute to Oblivion Black.

Wet screams filled the space of the piazza as the second wave of the cabal waded into the other residents with knives.

*

Finally!

Amanda ran towards the ring of black-clad—but now crimson-stained—assassins.

"I'm on your side! I want to jo-"

One of them spun around and embedded a machete into her throat, removing it in one fluid movement before turning his back on her.

Amanda's hands went to the gaping wound as she frantically tried to stem the torrent of blood. Her eyes opened wide as blood spurted out of her mouth in place of the intended scream. She collapsed to the floor and lied twitching as her blood pooled around her and her life ebbed away.

Some of the residents tried to run; some of them tried to fight back with anything that they could get their hands on—chairs, bottles—but their assailants were better-prepared and merciless. Gradually, a dozen members of the cabal penned the residents in around the fish farm. But like animals aware that they were being led into a slaughterhouse, some of the residents threw themselves against the barriers blocking the exits.

Danny looked on helplessly at what was unfolding in the piazza. He saw one thickset man helping four others to clamber through a broken barrier before the cabal caught up and dragged back the rest and cut them down. He yelled down, "Get to the elevator! We're on level two," and saw the man look up, nod, and begin to usher the four along.

In the center of the piazza a tall figure, clothed in black like his comrades, stepped up to the podium where, at the start of lockdown, Sarah Turner had addressed the residents of the Sanctuary. Painted in white across the sheer black material of his mask was a perfect copy of the cave painting of Oblivion Black. He pulled the mask off and smiled. Rodchenko patted his few hairs back into place before looking up at Danny and the others huddled on level two.

Connie turned to Danny. "You know what? That doesn't surprise me."

"There may be some of my lot from the farms with them," said Rodger.

Rodchenko began to speak. "I now control the Sanctuary." His words were slow, carefully enunciated. "I am holding the remainder of the residents. I will kill one of these hostages every thirty minutes until you hand the Totem over to me."

"I don't know what the Totem is," replied Sarah.

"Don't fuck with me!" Rodchenko screamed. Then, with a big show of regaining his composure, he patted down some stray hairs and smoothed his trousers. "You made me shout," he said with a humorless chuckle.

"He doesn't control the Sanctuary," Sarah said to Connie. "We still have control of all the infrastructure."

"Even so, he's got those hostages. And do you suppose he'll think twice about killing them?"

Sarah considered this for a moment, then leaned over the barrier.

"Right, we'll get you the Totem, but you have to give us time."

"You've got half an hour," Rodchenko shouted back, "then people will start to die."

Sarah turned back to the small group. "I have no idea what he's talking about. What the fuck is this *Totem*?"

"You genuinely don't know?" said Danny.

"Not a clue. But something's beginning to make sense. When I first started working here, he was needling me for information and I didn't know what he was talking about,"

"So, he doesn't know what he's looking for? He doesn't *actually* know what the Totem is, either?" asked Danny.

Sarah shrugged. "I guess not."

"Why don't we give him what he wants? Let's make up a totem to give him. We've got a rough reference point for it from the cave paintings."

"Jesus, Danny, that's lame," said Connie.

"You got a better idea?"

"What do we do after that?" asked Stue.

"We're going to have to try and rush them, get them off-guard somehow."

"There's an entrance to the piazza that Rodchenko doesn't

know about. It leads to a service corridor for the restaurants," said Sarah.

"How do you know he doesn't know about that entrance?" asked Danny.

"I had a fake wall put across it; it's still in place. There was some repair work to be done—nothing major, but it never got done. If you look closely, you can see it's a different color." She pointed it out to Danny.

He squinted and could see a faint difference where the shade changed slightly. He nodded. "We'll split in two. The second group can rush them from the back while we keep Rodchenko talking. We'll only have one chance at this; the element of surprise is about the only thing we've got going for us. Let's get moving."

Sarah led them to a storage room where some of the artifacts found in the Sanctuary had been kept. "Who wants to be our totem maker?"

"I'll do it," said Danny. He remembered the time in his apartment when he was going cold turkey—the shadows and the glowing eyes.

"Great," said Sarah.

"Have you got any reference pictures?"

"Wait, I think we've got some photos of the cave paintings around."

Sarah went searching and brought back a dogeared photo of the cave painting showing figures holding up the Totem. Danny squinted. It didn't give him much to go on. The Totem as depicted in the painting was barely more than four brown, scratched lines.

"Do we have any idea what the Totem's supposed to be?" asked Danny.

"None at all—probably just a collection of things in the cavern that the Athabastara found."

"No, it's got to be something more than that. It's got to be something important to Oblivion Black, something that want from it."

"Danny! We're running out of time!" yelled Sarah.

Danny found a bundle of twigs, some old animal skins, and vines. He wrapped the skins around the twigs and fastened them with the vines. He showed his totem to Sarah.

She looked less-than-impressed. "It's going to have to do. Quick, we're running out of time," she said, and turned to Connie. "I'm going to lead Danny and the others. Connie, take the Totem. This is what I need you to do…"

*

"I have the Totem!"

From the piazza, it was difficult to make out anything but a vague shape. Rodchenko strained his eyes to see it.

"Okay…" He was unconvinced. "This had better not be a trick, because-"

"It's no trick. What will happen to us after you get it?"

"That's for me to know and you to find out."

For the first time, Rodchenko had to consider just what *would* happen when he got the Totem. He'd spent so much time—and money—chasing it that he hadn't given much thought to what would happen when it was actually in his hands. He knew in his heart that he'd finally come face-to-face with the Queen of Shadows, the deity of the Sanctuary, but what might happen after that, he really couldn't imagine. He hoped that she would show him her secrets and show him a way to live in this new reality. A feeling of uncertainty stabbed at his heart.

"Okay, I'm coming down."

"Go to the main stairwell; we'll have it unblocked." He pointed up at the woman and smiled. "No tricks."

Rodchenko watched her walk towards the stairs. He could hear the sound of his heart beating rapidly.

*

Danny, Rodger, Stue, and the others followed Sarah through the corridors, picking up whatever makeshift weapons they could find along the way. Danny couldn't help but feel underprepared. They came to an intersection and Sarah squinted at the three dimly lit and virtually identical corridors leading off in different directions.

"I think it's this one off to the right," she said.

They began to run down the corridor.

"This doesn't feel right," said Stue, coming to an abrupt halt. "It feels like we're moving away from the piazza. Look! There's some of the waste disposal units. Aren't they at the back of the Sanctuary?"

"I know where we've gone wrong," said Rodger. "We should've taken the left turn."

"Are you sure?" asked Danny.

Rodger nodded.

The group stopped, spun around, and ran back in the direction they'd come.

Danny had begun to sweat. *Rodger had better be right. The Totem's not going to stand up to close scrutiny. We've got minutes to get there. Connie will be walking into a massacre.*

*

Connie got to the bottom of the stairs to face a dead-end of chipboard blocking off the entrance to the piazza.

Maybe Danny and the others have managed to take back the piazza. Maybe I don't have to…

With a groan of nails being torn free, the barrier was removed by two of the cabal members. Connie steadied herself and walked through holding the fake Totem close to her chest, determined to keep her arms wrapped tightly around it until the very last moment. She walked past the hostages who'd been rounded up in one of the pens normally used for the animals. Some of the hostages were sobbing; others looked into the middle distance, as though trying to prepare themselves for whatever lay in store. Connie wanted to nod to them, give them some kind of reassurance, but she was every bit as terrified as them, if not more so.

She was conscious of Rodchenko watching her approach, as though she were an interesting specimen he'd just discovered. She walked as slowly as she could, trying not to glance at the entrance that Danny and his group would be using. Rodchenko put his right hand out and made a beckoning gesture. She stopped in front of him and handed over the "Totem."

He looked down at the loose collection of twigs and animal skins. He laughed, looked up at Connie, and then back down at the bundle in his hands, which had already begun to unravel.

Rodchenko slapped Connie hard across her face, sending her sprawling to the floor. Her head came down hard and she passed out as he threw the fake Totem after her.

*

Danny burst through into the piazza.

"Kill them all!" Rodchenko yelled, spit flying, his face crimson. "Kill all the fucking cattle!" he screamed, with his fists clenched so tight that the knuckles had turned white.

Danny and Sarah led the charge. Sarah fought dirty: She scratched, bit, and kicked hard. A childhood in Spanish Harlem had taught her to take no prisoners. Others fought hard, taking members of the cabal out by sweeping garden tools at their feet or just using bare fists.

Stue steamed into two of the cabal, knocking them flat and kicking them hard in the head before they could get up. He caught another with a lucky right hook before four more began to advance on him.

Rodger landed heavily on the ground, knocking the wind out him. He recovered in time to roll out of the way of a knife being plunged down. He kicked the legs out from under his attacker and scrambled to get back up.

Sheer numbers of the cabal flooded over the opposition,

cutting down any resistance they encountered. Screams echoed around the cavern.

Rodchenko laughed and, smelling blood, jumped off the podium and waded into the fight.

Danny was backed into a corner and was being pummeled by a member of the cabal when Sarah kicked the back of the assassin's legs hard. Danny punched him for good measure as he collapsed to the ground.

"Danny! Come with me! We've got a chance."

Still groggy from several blows to the head, Danny lurched along behind her. He tried to keep up as she weaved her way down different offshoots and side corridors until they stood, breathless, before a large steel door that resembled a bank vault. To the right of the door were a large handle and a keypad. Sarah closed her eyes, tapped the side of her head, and mumbled under her breath.

"Codes, codes, codes…"

She typed in six numbers, but was met with an angry beep and a red flashing light. She closed her eyes, ground her teeth, then took a deep breath.

"Right."

She typed another six numbers into the keypad, and this time, there was a high-pitched beep and a green light. Sarah clutched the handle and hauled the door open. Inside was row upon row of metal shelves stacked with handguns, assault rifles, explosives, and even more fearsome items of hardware.

"Fuck," said Danny.

"You'd better believe it. Here, get your jaw back in place and give me a hand."

Danny didn't stop to question how or why. He and Sarah grabbed as many arms and as much ammunition as they could reasonably carry and made their exit, pausing only to secure the arms vault door against the enemy. They slung weaponry about their shoulders and waists as they ran, while fitting clips into their rifles.

Sarah reentered the piazza like a Valkyrie, shooting at any figure in black that moved. The cabal had forced Danny's group back into a corner. Sarah's shots hit home with some of the cabal members, striking them in the lower back and legs.

Danny fired into the air.

"Get the fuck off them!" he yelled.

Three ran towards him. He fired a shot that chipped the floor just inches from one of the running cabal. Danny slipped in some blood and fumbled his next shot, sending it high above their heads, while the cabal members were only feet away. He pulled the trigger again as he hit the floor, and this time it flew true, hitting the nearest cabal member in the side, sending him spinning and shrieking into a corner. Then, getting to one knee and leveling his weapon at the remaining attackers, he growled at them, "The next one gets a bullet in the balls—if any of you motherfuckin' freaks have got any."

They stopped. The hostages who had broken free ran over to Danny and Sarah, who handed them their excess guns.

"Don't kill them if you can help it!" Sarah shouted.

The sound of gunshots cracked around the piazza, and soon Danny saw the remnants of the cabal either in flight or falling to the floor under fire. More weapons were handed out, the rest of the hostages were freed from the pens, and the cabal was pushed into them.

*

Rodchenko fought until the end, but at length, he found himself in front of Sarah. She pressed the muzzle of her automatic against his forehead.

"Give me a reason why I shouldn't put a bullet through your skull!"

"I can't think of one, to be honest," he said with an aggravating smirk on his face. "But it really doesn't matter one way or the other. Whatever you do, it isn't going to delay the inevitable. You're just animals, you see. Animals who deserve only to die—pigs whose only destiny is to be slaughtered in your own filth. You're all going to die squealing in the dark. What did humanity do up there when it had the choice between survival and destruction? You tore yourselves apart. You made a sincere and conscious choice *for* death and annihilation. What makes you think that hiding down here somehow exempts you from extinction? The human race now consists of a bunch of pampered billionaires and their servile flunkies. You don't deserve to survive."

"What do you mean?"

Rodchenko lunged towards her. In her surprise, Sarah fumbled with the gun and just managed to get a shot off. The bullet nicked the side of his ear, but it didn't slow him down. He ran past her, nearly knocking her to the floor. She spun around and fired the gun at Rodchenko's retreating form. The bullet passed him by a wide margin as he disappeared into one of the tunnels.

Sarah ground her teeth in frustration, but quickly returned to her immediate priorities. "Right, let's round the rest of them up!"

*

The remaining cabal members numbered thirty-five. Danny and Rodger went amongst them, pulling off their black masks. They unmasked three farmers. The penultimate was Dave.

"I always knew you were a wrong 'un."

Dave avoided looking Rodger in the eye.

Danny walked up to the smallest, slightest figure, sick with the near-certainty that he would recognize the face behind the mask. He took hold of the mask along the jaw area and hesitated for a moment before pulling it off, wanting to live just one moment longer with that small spark of hope that he might be wrong. Finally, he pulled the fabric away and a wave of red hair tumbled out.

"I wanted to be wrong," he croaked.

"You don't know what it's like," she said, looking down at the ground.

"Well, why don't you explain it to me."

"You don't understand what's going on here, Danny. It's bigger than any of us…"

A burning rage flashed through him and he pulled his

hand back to slap her. Theresa closed her eyes, bracing for the impact. Instead, Danny ground his teeth and took a couple of deep breaths before letting his hand drop loosely to his side. "You make me sick."

She looked up at him. But instead of remorse or surrender, what Danny saw in her eyes was a look of pity. For a fleeting moment, the urge to strike her, to strike *what she had become,* returned.

"What are we doing down here?" she asked him softly. "Just drinking and fucking until the light goes out? Whatever is in here with us isn't Oblivion Black; *we're* Oblivion Black. The people are Oblivion Black. Trust me, I've seen it: all the suffering, decay, and sickness. We're the darkest and most evil creature down here. We don't deserve to survive."

"You don't have the right to make that judgment!" he screamed at her, his frustration and rage seeping through once more.

She stared back at him dispassionately.

How could I not have known? Did I know?

"A reckoning is coming," she said quietly, but he had already turned away.

Danny wasn't there to see Theresa ejected from the Sanctuary. She went calmly, someone told him later, without any resistance. Some of her party had been sobbing, but she had looked out at the storm-lashed horizon with not a trace of emotion. "I take my punishment," she said. Tight lipped and staring straight ahead, she stepped out.

CHAPTER 23

Rodchenko didn't know anymore where he ended and Oblivion Black began. He hadn't for a while. He thought of himself as Oblivion Black wearing the skin-mask of Rodchenko. He'd felt the tendrils of Oblivion Black spread into him as she'd found the crack in his mind and prised it open. Oblivion Black grew within him slowly, like a malignant tumor. As the horror of the apocalypse grew, he'd felt Oblivion Black's skin grow over him, and welcomed it. He realized that, now, he was Oblivion Rodchenko. He heard her whispers echo around the cavern, and he knew he had to complete the act of suicide that humanity had started. Oblivion Black demanded tribute, and Rodchenko proved his loyalty by carving up the spoiled meat. Oblivion Rodchenko knew that he wouldn't have much time in which to complete his work before the survivors tried to stop him. He would have to work fast…

*

Danny was nursing a drink from Connie's stash while she nursed her bruised face. They looked out across the ocean from the rain-lashed viewing deck, the window of which now had a spiderweb of cracks in it. He looked across at her.

"How you feeling?"

She lifted up a glass of whisky and pressed it against the side of her face that Rodchenko had slapped. "Getting better. It's still sore and will be for a while." The swelling caused her to speak with a slight lisp.

They watched the Arctic Ocean crashing onto the shore.

Michael ran up to them. "You've got to help us out. There's been a break-in."

"What's been taken?"

"Some explosives and detonators left over from when Jennings had the Sanctuary fitted out."

"Rodchenko," said Connie.

"Yeah. And you don't have to be a genius to figure out what he's up to."

*

Oblivion Rodchenko made sure he was completely covered in black. On his face, he wore the balaclava he'd recovered from the fight before he'd made his escape. The only other color that could be seen were the whites of his eyes and teeth. The creature that was Oblivion Black had found the cracks in his mind, slowly crawled in, and taken up residency.

He moved in the shadows and set the explosives.

*

Sarah called the group together.

"He's got to be stopped. He's taken enough for six bombs,

and we've identified six key structural areas we think he'll attack. The explosives he's taken aren't sophisticated, and it should be a relatively simple matter to defuse the bombs. It's just a matter of cutting the wires; they're too simple to booby-trap. Let's get to work! Connie, you come with me."

*

Oblivion Rodchenko knew to keep to the shadows, and he knew that they were looking for him. He had to move quickly.

"We've found and neutralized one set of explosives," Michael's voice crackled over the walkie-talkie.

"We've got one," said Danny. "We've checked the other locations you mentioned, and they came up clean."

"Right, right," Sarah whipped the sweat off her forehead, "that leaves another four to find. We've gotta move quicker, people! Danny, Michael, you split the groups again. Cover more ground. He must have targeted more. Danny, sweep those sites again."

"Right," crackled Danny.

*

The survivors were closing in. Oblivion Rodchenko found himself in the red-ringed entrance to the Bridge of Souls. Part of him had always known that he'd find himself back here eventually.

The small sliver of Rodchenko that remained remembered another time, another darkness—a secret darkness in his childhood. The dark crimson as he closed his eyes tight, the door to his bedroom opening again...

He would send himself to another place to escape the horrors of what was happening in the real world: the comforting darkness of the old cupboard in the corner of his room where he could curl up and hide, and now the beckoning darkness of the Bridge of Souls.

Angry, frightened voices drew closer. Oblivion Rodchenko walked on towards the Bridge of Souls. He had walked only a few steps when his flashlight began to flicker—and for the first time a knife of doubt stabbed at his heart. A few more steps forward and the flashlight continued to splutter. He turned around and, despite having only gone in a straight line, he couldn't tell which way to go. He was startled by the sound of frantic human laughter. He couldn't tell where the laughter was coming from. He spun around, making himself sick, before he realized that *she* was making the noise.

He looked deep into Oblivion Black's eyes and it was then he realized that he'd been wrong. All the scheming, all the betrayals, all the bloodshed had been for nothing. Nothing. The creature towering in front of him, drooling, didn't give a shit about him or any of his plans. He was just a wrinkled hairless ape.

Rodchenko felt a deep, dark despair before Oblivion Black tore him apart.

*

Sarah was sweating as she prepared to snip the wire on the device. She breathed in deeply and gently squeezed the handle on the clippers. Then she breathed out.

"How many is that?" asked Connie.

"That leaves three to find."

Sarah pressed the red button on the walkie-talkie.

"Michael, any update? Any more found?"

She listened intently until a crackle of "No, nothing yet," came through the airwaves.

"Connie, can I ask you to make me a promise?"

"This isn't really…"

"Please."

"Okay."

"I left my daughter, Alice, outside… I didn't… none of us knew…" Sarah sighed. "If you ever manage to get outside—I mean *outside* outside—I want you to find her. Make sure she's okay, make sure she's safe. There's a former government nuclear bunker in San Francisco; it was owned by Brighter Futures Group. If Alice is anywhere, she's there—her grandmother had instructions to take her there. Look in my top desk draw there's a picture of Alice, and instructions on how to get there, it's called The Retreat."

"I…"

"Just promise."

"Okay, I promise."

"Thank you." Sarah took a deep breath. "Let's try and keep calm. Where have we got left to look? Where would he have placed the explosives to cause maximum damage?"

"We've looked at all the key strategic points. We must have missed some. He's got to have placed something by the water pumps. They were installed in the refit to help draw the water up from the spring, and there's a filter system installed, which is essential for it to work. Without the pumps, the Sanctuary would die of thirst. Come on! Let's go take a look."

Sarah ran off and Connie followed her.

They entered the pump room and began a frantic search, running their fingers along the walls and under shelves. The sweat dropped into Sarah's eyes and stung them.

Where the fuck is it? There's got to be another one here...

Sarah's hands ran down some pipes and found something soft: the explosive device. With a sigh of relief, she stooped to look at it. The setup was different from the others: more complicated and with a timing mechanism. Only two minutes left. Her fingers hovered over the wires.

"Have you found anything?" Connie shouted from across the room.

Sarah dry-swallowed and stared at the explosives.

"No, nothing. You go and join the others. I'll keep looking around here."

"Okay!"

Sarah wiped her palms against her trousers and took the device into a side room away from the water pumps, closed the door behind her, then picked up as much movable furniture as she could and piled it up against the door to soften any explosion.

"Now, come on, Sarah, you can work this out..."

She looked at the explosives and the ticking clock. Fifty seconds left.

"Here goes nothing," she whispered, and yanked the wires out. A red light flashed, and Sarah closed her eyes and wrapped herself around the device.

"Alice!"

*

Danny was sweating as he pressed the button on the walkie-talkie.

"How many more have we got left?"

There was the crackle of static.

"We've just got three to find. There-"

The first of the explosions came from the direction of the water pumps. A second ripped through the north side apartments two seconds later, followed by the third and final explosion from the direction of one of the farms. Danny stumbled out of a white cloud not knowing where or who he was. There was a ringing in his ears and everything seemed to be moving at a slow, underwater pace. Someone was trying to talk to him, but he couldn't hear them.

"Where's Connie?" he heard himself say. "Where's Connie?" His voice sounded dull in his ears. "Where's Connie?" The dust began to settle, and through the din he could hear screams. He grabbed the arm of someone passing and yelled, "What's happening?"

The man just stared at him and then slapped Danny hard across the face, which suddenly brought everything into focus.

"Rodger, you fucker, you didn't need to slap me."

"I think I did, pal. You need to help me put fires out."

The two men staggered through the burning debris, found fire extinguishers in a corner of the Sanctuary, and put them to work. Other survivors helped the injured. Time sped up as the dazed, dust-covered survivors tried to pull together.

Danny stood and stared at the battered and bleeding remnants of humanity. He couldn't quite focus on the person walking towards him. She was covered in dust and smeared with blood. It wasn't until she was a foot away from him that Danny realized it was Connie. He broke down in great wracking sobs of relief.

"Sarah sent me away. She knew there were explosives there and she sent me away. She must have tried to handle it herself. She saved my life."

*

Danny was so tired that he'd begun to hallucinate; he saw shadows out of the corner of his eyes.

Is this how it starts? Will I see Oblivion Black again?

There was still a ringing in his ears, too. Michael Dunning, now the acting senior administrator, was chairing the meeting in the very room in which Danny had first been interviewed for his place. Danny slowly scanned the room. Everything was covered in a patina of dust. Some people still had blood on their faces. They all looked dazed, uncomprehending. Some were staring into the middle distance, devoid of expression, and Danny understood truly for the first time the real meaning of "shell-shocked." As soon as the fires had been extinguished, Danny had gone straight to help stretcher the injured and the dying into the hospital.

Michael coughed, pointed to a sheet of paper stuck to the wall, and began.

"Those are the people currently unaccounted-for."

Danny blinked at the list.

"The bombs have wiped out about a quarter of the remaining population of the Sanctuary. They also took out Farm One and damaged Farm Two."

"What about the water supply?"

"It's fine. No damage to the pumps. Sarah must have…" His voice trailed off.

"How are the power cells?" Connie asked, breaking the silence.

"We've yet to find out. It could be pretty bad. Rodchenko was strategic in what he hit. It's just a case of survival for us now; we've taken care of the immediate problems. There's nothing more we can do today."

Danny staggered to his apartment, collapsed into his bed, and slept a dreamless sleep.

*

The first thing Danny noticed when he woke up was the stink. It smelled as though something had corrupted, putrefied. He looked around the apartment before he realized the stench was coming from him. He stumbled to the bathroom while trying to make sense of what had happened the previous day. He stood in the shower and let his forehead drop onto the tiled wall. As he straightened, he noticed for the first time the black mold creeping around the seal. He twisted the faucet. When the water didn't flow, he looked up at the shower head. Sudden jets of ice-cold water hit him like needles, and he yelped. The water continued to splutter out but didn't get any hotter. Danny washed the best he could, ate some stale bread, and left the apartment. His stomach growled.

He was instantly called into a meeting with many of the same people who had been around the previous night. They looked scrubbed, red-raw in places, but they didn't look *clean*— the dust seemed to have ingrained itself into their very pores. They all looked exhausted.

Michael looked at the assembly, cleared his throat, and spoke. "We face an altered reality. We have to accept that we are the sole survivors of humanity, and now we number under two hundred. Because of what happened yesterday, our sanctuary has been compromised. Everyone will have to work to reinforce the infrastructure and ensure we all survive. Daily rosters will be posted. People will get food when they've undertaken work. There's a lot of cleaning-up and fixing to do, and there are no free rides anymore. We have to deal with the situation in which we find ourselves."

*

She knew. Oblivion Black kept to the dark, but she was biding her time. She needed to rest; her time of long sleep was coming up. She was starting to feel the lethargy and the comforting downward pull of sleep. She had made a nest in her favorite tunnel and had gained the necessary fat and fur.

Oblivion Black was ready to sleep, but she knew. She knew she had to resist the urge to sleep. The game was nearly finished. They were hurt; she could smell the salt of the blood coating the cavern floor. She could feel their terror, but also their sheer weariness, the sweat, and exhaustion. Oblivion Black gathered her strength, ready for the final battle. She would find her pup, the Totem, even if she had to tear the cavern and everyone in it apart with her bare claws.

CHAPTER 24

D anny led one of the teams in clearing the rubble.
They found a tunnel that had been partly excavated
during the refit but, for reasons unknown, had been
abandoned. Danny and his team shifted as much of the debris
as they could into the tunnel.

All-too-often Danny would move some rubble to be
confronted with the sight of a mangled gray limb. He thought
he'd never get used to it, but after he'd uncovered the third body,
he greeted it with numb acceptance. Some of the bodies he
recognized; some were mutilated to the extent that he couldn't
even tell what sex they were. He made sure that every recovered
body was afforded the greatest amount of dignity they could
muster. The body would be put on a stretcher and covered with
the cleanest sheet they had. Danny took it as his personal duty
to take the bodies to the infirmary and attempt to get them
identified. One of the nurses, Nadine Jurgens, having earned
herself a promotion she didn't want, was now the acting locum
doctor. Her left eye had recently developed a nervous tic and

the dark lines underneath it were a testament to how little sleep everyone was getting.

At the end of every shift Danny would go back to his apartment and resist the urge to collapse straight into bed. He'd drag himself into the shower and let the faltering spray spit and cough over him. He wanted the water to be scalding-hot, but it remained tepid at best. Regardless of how hard he scrubbed, he never felt clean anymore; the dirt and dust seemed to have soaked into the very marrow of his bones. Danny didn't even have the pleasure of the gradual drift into sleep: it seemed as if he just had to shut his eyes and his alarm clock would go off. He'd groan and force himself to tumble out of bed, then go to greet the rest of his team with a weary smile, taking some small comfort in the fact that they were all feeling the same.

Danny was walking to work to start one of his shifts when something hit him on the forehead. His hand went to his head, and he found a flake of blue paint. Craning his neck, he looked up at the metal roof. The blue of the painted sky was slowly being obscured by the rust that was spreading throughout the Sanctuary like the tendrils of some monstrous weed. Entropy would not be denied. The main elevator had developed a worrying shudder over the last few days and had begun to make a groaning sound between floors. One of the walkways was completely out of use after the explosion, as was the secondary set of stairs that connected the levels. Yes, Connie had said that one hydroponic farm was up and running, but the food was tasteless, gritty, and—whichever way you spun it—there wasn't enough of it to go around. The water supply hadn't been affected, but hot water was sporadic, and the long hours needed to put the Sanctuary back together meant that people weren't having time to wash themselves or their clothes. A musty smell followed everyone and people began to look grimy. An explosion had taken out one of the food storage facilities, so supplies were limited. The eateries in the piazza had, bar one—a former Tex-Mex place called El-Niño—all closed down.

In the rubble and the dust of the Sanctuary, the days bled into one another. Danny often had trouble remembering a time when he hadn't been clearing rubble.

This is the price I have to pay.

Eventually, he cleared some rubble away and saw the scratched concrete Sanctuary floor. He stared at it, then realized that no one had found a body for over a week.

He jumped when he felt someone put a hand on his shoulder. It was Connie.

"Enough, Danny," she said gently. "All the bodies have been accounted for. We're reassigning the teams, and you've got a more important job. We need you to get back to working on the farms."

Danny nodded, but it didn't really sink in that he wouldn't have to do this again.

"First, though, I need you to come to an important committee meeting."

"No problem." He followed behind her.

In the boardroom, Connie stood in front of what was left of the committee.

"I'd like to nominate myself for the role of senior administrator. All those in favor?"

The remaining committee members, including a relieved-looking Michael, all lifted their arms limply.

"Carried."

Way to carry out that palace revolution, Connie, Danny thought.

"Effective immediately, we are on stricter rations: The more work you do, the more rations you get, but there will be a cap. We're going to operate three mealtimes out of El-Niño, on a ticketed system."

The news was announced in a mass gathering of the survivors in the piazza.

Danny looked around at the remaining, ragged human beings.

Jesus, is this all we are?

The news was accepted dumbly, and they stumbled off.

Danny tried to take less of the food rations than he was entitled to, hungrily scoffing down potatoes and cabbage. They'd never tasted so good. He got sick of continuously hitching up his pants, so he punched an extra hole in his belt to keep them up.

The livestock had been decimated by the explosion. The fish farm was still viable, but the stock was getting dangerously low. They'd manage to cull some meat from the dead animals but that didn't go far. They'd just been left with an underfed bull and two heifers, and everyone in the Sanctuary was pinning their hopes on one of the heifers getting pregnant. Danny had never thought that his hopes and dreams would boil down to the reproductive habits of cattle.

One evening, before he collapsed into his bed, he splashed some water on his face and didn't recognize the reflection in the mirror. His skin was pulled tight over his sharp cheekbones, and his brown eyes stared out from deep, gray, sunken sockets. His sandy hair was no longer so much expertly tousled as plain straggly.

Fuck, I look like the other lost souls stumbling around here. Shadows slowly fading into the rock walls.

Thirty seconds after that thought, he was sound asleep.

*

Danny woke up with a gnawing hunger in the pit of his stomach and feeling like he'd only just closed his eyes. He checked his wristwatch; he'd actually overslept by half an hour. He looked at his alarm clock and the digital display flashed 12:00. Sometime in the night, the electricity had gone off.

The apartment had a moldy, damp smell to it despite looking dusty. A pile of discarded dirty clothes in the corner of the room contributed to the musty smell. There wasn't a ration on water yet, but Danny hadn't found the time or energy to do any washing. There were chunks out of the wall, and the kitchen worktop was scratched and dull; Danny didn't know why, as he'd never cooked there.

He groaned as he swung his legs over the side of the bed, and his weariness lay on his shoulders like a wooden yoke, every part of him aching. He dressed, hiked up his pants, and left his apartment.

The lights were dim, and his head felt muddy.

What am I doing today? Oh, yes… more weeding.

He was suddenly seized with a desire to run, to run away from all the dust, the smell, the despair, but there was nowhere to run to.

Something was wrong.

It took a moment for Danny to realize what it was. The lights were flickering. It made the survivors look like actors in a silent movie, but they looked animated for the first time in weeks.

"What's wrong?" Danny asked the man next to him. When Danny looked him in the eyes, he saw fear.

"It's the power. It's only been back on for the last hour. It's failing."

CHAPTER 25

"We estimate that at the current rate, we have around two weeks of energy left until the lights go out. The wind farm on the outcrop is the main problem—the feed is failing; we think that one of the cables may have been damaged in the explosion."

"Why am I thinking you're going to tell me it's not a simple case of repairing it?"

"The feed in the Sanctuary is fine. It's… it's the external feed."

"Outside?" A stab of terror.

"Yes."

"How does that work? The explosions were in here. How does that affect anything that's been going on out there?"

Connie shrugged. "We don't know. Maybe a shockwave affected it. There's only one way to find out. We're going to have to go outside and repair it."

"By 'us,' I presume you mean me," said Danny.

"You're the man who made millions out of renewable

energy, and wasn't it you who fitted the wind turbines and the hydroelectric plant?"

"It was my company. The problem could be anywhere. Are you sure it's the wind farm? Could it be the hydroelectric plant?"

"Your guess is as good as mine. In fact, your guess is probably better than mine."

"Jesus! Okay, well… if it is the hydroelectric plant, we're fucked. It'll be using at least four Archimedean screws. Each screw is four yards in diameter and nine yards in length. Up to two thousand gallons of seawater will be passing through each screw per second. Those screws are connected to a gear box, which turns a generator." Danny rubbed his palm over his eyes as he spoke.

"Thanks for the lesson."

"You don't understand. If just one of those Archimedean screws is gone, that's it, game over."

"We have to do something. The Sanctuary's dying. We've done a survey," said Connie, "and the explosions made all but one of the exits impassable. The only way out of the Sanctuary now is via the original entrance that Jennings and Hobson first used to get into the cavern… we think."

"You think?" he took a deep breath. "Does anyone have the specifications of the wind turbines?"

*

"Part of the entrance is flooded. One of the first bits of work Jennings had done was to redirect a stream, but that work was undone with the explosions. The water shouldn't get any higher than your midriff."

Shouldn't?

"You'll be in the water for around eighteen feet, then you'll see some steps that'll take you to the antechamber. In there, you should find a few radiation suits hanging up."

"Should? That's a lot of gray areas you're talking about."

The committee man—whose name Danny had forgotten—shrugged.

"Here's a two-way radio." Connie handed Danny a device that was about the size of a matchbox. "Attach it to the inside of your helmet when you suit up. There's a volume control on the outside of the helmet. Stan told me that the transmitter is pretty powerful and should be fine for the range. He told me a few technical details, but I zoned out."

"Great."

The committee man coughed.

"That entrance hasn't been used in twenty years, so we're going on records. It was serviced around five years ago, so you shouldn't have any problem getting out."

Yeah.

"The helmet can fog up quickly, but with the air filter, you'll be fine. As long as you breathe slowly, it should clear. You'll need the two sets of security numbers." The committee man passed Danny a laminated piece of card.

"You okay, Danny?" Connie asked.

He gave Connie a shaky thumbs-up.

"You won't be alone. We'll be with you every step of the way. Any trouble—which of course there won't be—let us know."

And you'll do what, precisely?

He picked up his toolbox and put on his backpack.

Danny had never been so nervous about anything in his life. Ever since he'd looked at the schematics, he'd had a phrase on repeat in his head: *Really, it's a two-man job. Really, it's a two-man job. Really…* It had become a comforting kind of mantra to him.

"Oh, God! Oh, God!" he muttered under his breath as the first metal door groaned open after so many years of being shut. He stepped through.

Right! I can do this. I can do this.

On the other side was a sloping floor, which descended into a stretch of water. In the distance, he could hear water flowing. There were cracks in the wall, and it looked as if one wall had given way completely. The light in the room flickered on, making patterns on the water.

Danny stepped into the water.

"Fuck!" he gasped as the frigid water nearly took his breath away. Danny walked farther into the water, which rose from his thighs up to his waist. He moved carefully, as there was some debris, under the water and he found it hard to retain his balance; twice, he wobbled but managed to right himself.

He stumbled on farther—it was getting deeper and the water crept farther up his body until it was just past his chest. He could smell the fetid, oily whiff of the stagnant water.

Shit, shit, what if it's deeper?

Danny pulled the toolbox up to his chest and continued to move forwards, trying his best not to slip. He waded and wobbled through the water but still couldn't see the steps. Part of the roof had collapsed, causing him to duck, which brought his face closer to the water than he would have liked. Finally, when he got to the other end of the collapse, he saw the steps and had to restrain himself from rushing toward them.

Really, it's a two-man job. Really, it's a two-man job.

Danny put his arms out to steady himself as his feet found the first underwater step, and he gradually began to rise out of the water, his feet slipping on the rocks. He half-staggered up the steps and found himself in front of two metal doors. The security codes he'd been given were in his pocket; even though the card had been laminated, the numbers were smudged, but they were at least readable. He tapped the first set of numbers into the keypad, and the doors wheezed open.

Danny found himself in a small room, an antechamber, which acted as an airlock to the outside. There was a scratched porthole through which the world outside looked gray and overcast. To the left of it was the final door to be opened. There were four hooks on the right-hand-side wall, and on two of them hung radiation suits. Danny put down the toolbox and rucksack and tried on the first of the suits, but there was a sizable tear in the left leg. He took it off, threw it to the ground, and tried on the second one. There was a tear in this one, too, on the left arm, but it was relatively minor. He repaired it quickly with some duct tape after he'd put the suit on, zipped it up, put the radio transmitter inside the helmet, and clamped it in place. The visor instantly fogged up. He clicked on the filter and slowed his breathing. As promised, it cleared.

He steadied his hand to type the second release code into the outer door. A weak green light winked in affirmation, the door gave a short grinding noise, and then… nothing.

Danny gave a short yell of frustration and did the only thing left to him.

He kicked the door and called it "Bastard."

The door shuddered open.

Danny had to prize the door open the last few inches, but there he was: outside for the first time in years—the first time anyone had voluntarily been outside the Sanctuary since the war. He felt the panic rise in him briefly, and he had to resist the urge to turn and just flee back inside.

He slung the toolbox over his shoulder and began to walk toward the outcrop.

"Danny?" Connie's voice shrieked into the helmet followed by feedback.

"Shit!" Danny fumbled turning the volume down.

"You okay?" she crackled.

"Yeah, I'm fine and out of the doors and heading towards the outcrop."

After just a few steps, he was sweating profusely, and he found he could walk no more than four minutes without having to stop and take a rest. Leaning against a large boulder, Danny surveyed the landscape. He didn't know what he'd expected, but he hadn't thought it would be so... bland. He'd thought that the sky would be red, or some other "interesting" shade; instead, it was cloudy and not particularly dramatic—except for the ocean, which violently smashed itself against the rocks as though it were an invader intent on breaking down the doors of the Sanctuary.

"What's it like out there?"

"Bleak."

Having caught his breath, Danny continued the long slog over to the outcrop. He felt like one of the Apollo astronauts lumbering across the moon's surface. As part of the refit, a metal gantry bridge had been built across to the outcrop. It didn't look too stable to Danny, but he didn't have any other choice. His feet squelched in the sweat puddling in his boots.

There were six points he needed to check before he even got to the bridge. To Danny's disappointment, the first connection—hidden under a green plastic cover—was fine, which meant that it was farther up. The next two connections were also fine.

As he finished checking the fourth, there was a sound like thunder rolling across the plains. Danny stood up and looked in the direction of the noise. A second boom shuddered through the air and a plume of smoke bellowed on the horizon. Danny picked his toolbox up and his first step onto the gantry made it shudder and groan alarmingly.

"Fuck! Fuck!"

"What's happening?" Connie crackled.

"Nothing. I'm fine."

He took another step and, although the bridge still shook, he managed to negotiate his way across, all the while trying, largely unsuccessfully, to ignore the rampaging ocean below.

"What the hell was that?"

"You okay?"

"Yeah, I just thought I saw something."

He tried to turn his head to the right, but the helmet restricted his movement. Shrugging, he took a deep breath and pulled out the schematics from his backpack to check again where he should be looking. Before he had time to unfold the diagram, however, he saw something dart to his left. As he swiveled his head to look around, he lost his footing and felt himself tipping backwards. He was close to the edge where the hungry ocean waited. With effort, he managed to right himself. He looked around the outcrop, searching for what had darted across his vision.

He looked up at the eight towers of the wind turbines, craning his neck and reflexively shielding his eyes against an anticipated sunlight that wasn't there. The blades of the turbines stood still and silent. He looked back at the schematics, traced his fingers over the powerline, and then looked down to the ground where the next point should be. He checked it out with his voltmeter; it was fine, so that just left one. Danny checked the schematics for where the main power-in cable would be. He found the earth box that the thick, insulated cable ran into and found where it should come out.

It was cut clean-through: not ragged, not damaged; it had been deliberately severed. Danny looked around.

"Can you see what the problem is?"

"Yeah, uh, it's general wear-and-tear. I should be able to fix it."

Danny replaced the severed cable, paused, and then stripped away the insulation. As he approached the first tower, Danny smiled with recognition at what he saw: In his old life, his company had installed many of these. He pulled the ratchet lever down to shut it off. It would take around an hour to fully power down. Having repeated the operation on the other towers, Danny was left with nothing to do other than wait, but his eyes kept being drawn to the clouds of dark gray smoke on the horizon.

"*Really, it's a two-man job.*"

"What was that?"

"Nothing."

Danny pulled the lever on the last of the towers and waited to see if his repair had worked and the blades would turn again. Behind him, the gantry made a prolonged creaking and groaning noise. Danny turned around to look at the gantry. It was swaying even more fearsomely in the wind.

His foot crunched on something. Looking down, he saw the scattered bones of an animal—maybe a small bird—and the charred remains of a fire.

He looked around for anything else.

Hearing a tearing and growling noise, Danny spun around.

The blades began to rotate, but slowly. He checked the power with his voltmeter. Nothing.

Anxiety over his failure to restart the turbines mingled with a more immediate, more *primal* fear. He felt exposed, like a goat tethered to a post to appease or ensnare a predator. The urge to run across the gantry back to the Sanctuary was almost overwhelming.

Danny thought he saw something, whipped his head to the left, and found that he couldn't breathe. He grabbed and strained at his helmet and then fell to his knees as, with a "pop," the visor sprang up and he sucked in deep lungfuls of air. The air seemed to coat the roof of his mouth with a chalky lining. It had an unpleasant chemical odor, which burned the inside of his nostrils and made his eyes water, as though he were close, *too* close, to a refinery. Danny put the visor back down, but couldn't get it to click into place quite right; he could still smell the acrid, chemical air. He looked at the towers; the blades were close to their original speed. He leaned down with the voltmeter.

"Come on, come on," Danny muttered. The dial didn't move. "Come on, you little fuck…"

Then, almost as though he had *willed* it to happen, the little arrow swung across until it showed the full wattage.

"Oh, thank God for that!" Relief washed over him as he quickly packed his backpack and made for the gantry. On Danny's second step, it swayed to the right. As his hand reached out to grab the rails, the backpack slipped down his arm. He let go of the rail to try to pull the bag back up, but the gantry got hit by another gust of wind and the backpack slipped off his arm and into the waiting, churning ocean below.

Danny waited as long as he dared for the swinging of the gantry to subside, and then, when he judged the time to be right, he sprinted across the gantry, his eyes tight shut, his stomach in knots.

"How's it going?" crackled Connie.

"Yeah, it's fine, I'm just…"

Just before he reached the end, he tripped and fell forward in a huddle onto the stable, unwavering ground. Having once more attempted to vent his fury with a kick to the gantry rail, Danny looked across at the outcrop with the towers and their revolving blades.

"What was that noise?"

"Me being clumsy."

The image of the neatly cut cable scared him, and so he gave the gantry another kick. And another. It rattled and shuddered.

Danny suddenly felt very tired, and walking back towards the entrance to the Sanctuary felt like wading through molasses. He'd been on the outside for a total of six hours. Over the mountain rolled the sound of thunder.

He looked around, once more struck by the feeling that he was being watched. He twisted around, but there was no one there. He looked to his left and saw something dash to hide. He caught only a glimpse of it, but it looked like a large rabbit, its fur caked with blood.

The visor misted up again. His breathed deeply, counting for his in-breath.

One.

Breath.

Two.

Breath.

The visor cleared except for a small black smudge on the horizon in his eye-line. Danny instinctively put a finger up to wipe out the smudge. He laughed to himself.

"What's so funny?" crackled Connie.

"Oh, it's nothing… except…"

Except the smudge became larger.

"I… uh…"

Oh, God.

"What's wrong?"

I've been here before.

The visor began to mist up again.

Oh, God, what is that?

The smudge came into sharper view. It was a figure lurching rapidly towards him.

"There's something chasing me."

"What? I thought you said…"

Danny broke out of his paralysis and began to run away.

"There's something coming towards me!"

Danny could hear his own breath heavy in his ears, the visor fogging up so all he could see in front of him were indistinct shapes.

The Sanctuary door seemed miles away. Interference crackled in his helmet. Connie's voice was faint, but the panic cut through the noise.

"What's happening?"

"There's something…" Danny turned to look behind him and stumbled. He felt himself falling forwards, his legs tangled in themselves. Somehow, he managed to regain his balance.

"Danny are you okay?"

"No, I'm not okay. There's something, some*one* chasing me!"

Interference.

"Connie! Connie! Can you hear me?"

Interference.

He turned to look again, his own breath deafening and misting up the visor. Whoever was chasing him was getting closer.

Oh, God! Oh, God! This is it. This is where I've always been.

"Connie! Connie! Help me!"

Interference.

Wake up! Wake up! Oh, God! Oh, God! It really is a two-man job. It really is a two-man job. One, breath. Two, breath.

The visor cleared enough for him to get a clearer view. There were now around six other figures close behind the first, and they were gaining.

Danny looked ahead to the Sanctuary.

I'm never going to get there in time.

"Connie?"

Wake up! Wake up!

He clenched his teeth and dug in.

All the running must have done me some good. I've got to get there.

Danny tried to look to each side, but he couldn't see anything; his peripheral vision was completely obscured by condensation. The Sanctuary was only eight hundred yards away.

Fuck! I'm going to make it!

He put in a last-effort sprint.

A cloaked figure stepped in front of the door. Danny skidded to a halt. The figure was covered in a rough mismatch of clothes, but the face was uncovered. Open sores leaked pus down skin the color of oatmeal. The rest of the skin was a patchwork of cuts and bruises, pockmarked with sores and ulcers. Despite the scarred face, Danny recognized Greg, who smiled, revealing blood-red, bleeding gums.

"This is becoming a habit. People are going to start to talk."

Danny put his arms up. "Look, I…"

"Shut the fuck up!" Greg yelled. "Did you really think we were going to let you get away with it?"

Get away with what?

Two figures came up behind Danny, grabbed him, and turned him around so he had his back to the Sanctuary door. He felt pressure on either side of the helmet and his head was battered around as the helmet was pulled off.

Including Greg there were eight bent and malformed figures. Danny recognized some of the former members of the cabal. They now shared similar facial abrasions to Greg. Ragged threadbare clothes hung off their unnatural twisted bodies.

"I-"

"I told you to shut the fuck up!" Greg nodded to the two cabal members holding Danny. They searched him and found the codes for the Sanctuary door. Greg held up the laminated card.

Danny flinched.

Greg licked his cracked lips. "I'm guessing that this is the key to the door?"

Danny shrugged. "You can guess."

"I thought this was going to be more difficult. We're going to get ourselves some reckoning."

Danny tried to break free, but the cabal members were stronger than they looked; their fingers dug into his shoulder.

Greg held up the card with the numbers and laughed. "If we've got this, then what's the point of you?"

Danny's vision exploded in red, and he felt the cold, tough grass on his cheek. The other side of his face throbbed. He was pulled back up to his feet. Danny's vision cleared long enough to see another punch come his way. He collapsed and received a kick to his side. Every breath was labored with pain as he was pulled up to face Greg.

"You think you're *so* much better than us, don't you? Well, it's our time now! You're finally gonna pay, you rich fuck!"

From within the folds of his of his ragged clothes, Greg brought a battered and rusty machete. The blade was serrated, and recently dried blood clung to its teeth. Greg, teeth bared in an animal snarl, ran towards Danny, swinging the machete. Whether by plan or in panic, the two cabal members let go of Danny as Greg rained down on him.

There was a loud crack and Greg flew back in a geyser of blood. Two further loud cracks sent the two cabal members spinning.

"Danny!"

Standing in the open doorway to the Sanctuary was Connie, holding aloft a pistol with vapor trails whispering into the air.

"Oh, Jesus! Am I—"

"Shut up and get inside!"

Danny stumped forward as Connie let off a warning shot over his head, but the cabal members had left.

Greg's sightless eyes looked up at the dark gray clouds as the other two cooled in pools of their own blood.

CHAPTER 26

"Well, you can fuck off as well," Rodge whispered to Danny.

"Yeah, yeah, yeah."

He hadn't expected a hero's welcome when he got back in—which was just as well, because he didn't get one. Connie had congratulated him, and two others had asked how it had looked outside. Danny had shrugged and said that it looked very stormy and that they were all better for being inside the Sanctuary, which seemed to satisfy them. There was so much to do; it seemed that people didn't have time to ask many questions.

"At the last count, there were under two hundred of us left alive. The medical team did their work well, and the good news is that we've turned the corner. Thanks to Danny's efforts on the outside, we've got the juice back on."

Danny nodded, smiled, and was surprised to feel his cheeks redden when people turned to look at him.

"Also," continued Connie, "thanks to Rodge and the hard

work of the farm crew, the second farm is now able to produce food again and the first farm is at full capacity."

Rodge, at the back of the room, nodded, giving Connie a chance to look at her notes.

"Even with this and the… err… reduced number of mouths," Connie cringed at the phrase but, in the spur of the moment, couldn't think of a better way to put it, "rationing will stay in place for the foreseeable future. In addition to the farms being back up and running, the recovery team headed up by Stue has managed to salvage supplies from the store rooms, which will not only supplement the food we have but also provide us with some backup. So, people, the facts are that it was bad, it's still not great, but we're in a better state than we were. We can survive. We *will* survive."

There was a louder round of applause, and this time some cheers. Connie allowed herself a smile.

*

On the farm, Rodge was the first person to notice the lights flickering again. He put down his cup of strong tea," finished rolling his cigarette, and looked out across the Sanctuary. He'd called this place home, after being pushed from children's home to children's home and then temporary housing. The Sanctuary was the first place he'd felt secure, but deep down, he knew it wouldn't last. He'd been kidding himself to think it could.

The flickering was becoming more frequent, and others were noticing it, too.

*

At first, when the lights went off, there was stillness, and silence filled the space. Then people began to scream and shout.

Connie somehow managed to make herself heard about the chaos.

"People! People! Keep calm! This is just a temporary fault. We're getting the backup generators online. It'll be a matter of minutes." Her voice echoed around the cavern.

The lights intermittently flickered back on, sending elongated shadows out across the cavern walls. In the shadows, Rodge watched the survivors blink momentarily into view.

One of the shadows seemed to have detached itself and was getting closer to two of the survivors. It was like watching a silent black-and-white horror film. As the shadow loomed, the two people stood completely unaware of what was behind them. Rodge began to run towards them as the lights failed. They plunged back into inky darkness. Rodge stopped.

Another flicker of light revealed the black shadows to be over the mouths of the two survivors. Their eyes bulged with terror, and Rodge could see their legs kicking. They were digging their heels in to try to stop themselves being dragged off. But it wasn't working. Rodge could see the drag marks on the ground. He hesitated. They'd been dragged into the Bridge of Souls. The red maw of the tunnel opened out in front of him.

He sighed.

"Bollocks to it!" He ran to where he knew some garden tools were stored, picked up a trowel and a pitchfork, and ran into the darkness after the disappearing figures as the shadow enveloped them. He followed them along the tunnel as the lights continued to flicker wildly. Brandishing the trowel in front of him, he put the pitchfork down so he could use his battle-scarred Harley-Davidson lighter to illuminate the way. He inched deeper into the tunnel. From deep within came a high-pitched scream. Rodge ran towards the noise and looked down at the drag marks to guide him.

Wind whistled down the tunnel and sounded eerily like a person calling out.

"Shit!" Rodge stumbled over a rock.

"Hello!" he called, raising the lighter high like a flashlight. "Shout if you can hear me! I'm here to help you!"

For a moment there was silence, but this was punctured by someone yelling. It sounded like a male voice, but he couldn't make out what was being said.

Well, he thought, *at least one of them is still alive.*

He ran in the general direction of the voice and tried to move as quickly as he could, although he stumbled as he went.

The path had changed to uneven ground. Rodge could feel a faint breeze, and he soon came to a junction where the tunnel split in two. He hesitated. Then a muffled sob made his decision for him: the tunnel on the far right.

Rodge could make out scratches on the tunnel walls, but couldn't tell if they were fresh or not. He stopped to inspect the drag marks and, turning around, he found he was surrounded in darkness, only the small flame of his lighter providing any guard against the black. He gripped the trowel tightly and tucked the trowel under his arm. For the first time, he was regretting his bravery.

Suddenly, there came a tearing noise, which within seconds became deafening. Rodge instinctively clamped his hands over his ears, and in the process his lighter slipped out of his hand.

Bollocks.

But Rodge was in too much pain from the noise to be overly concerned by the loss of his lighter.

As suddenly as it had begun, the noise just stopped.

With the trowel held out in front of him like a bizarre talisman.

It's bugger-all use as a weapon.

He shuffled around in a circle, trying to get his bearings.

"Hello! Anyone there? Shout if you can hear me!"

The tunnel swallowed up his words.

Rodge squinted into the darkness, trying to make out any signs of life, but he may as well have had his eyes clamped shut. Gradually, his eyes acclimatized to the gloom, and he could make out the direction from which he'd come.

From the darkness, a shadow coalesced and began to grow. The stench of rotting meat and something else—sulfur?—stung the inside of his nostrils.

Rodge could now sense the huge presence in front of him—could hear its slow, measured breathing. He heard it sniff the air, followed by what sounded like rope being wrung tight.

Rodge smiled. "Come on then, yer fucker... let's be having you!"

The entity's eyes glowed like red-hot coals, burning into Rodge's chest, tearing through his mind. The dark, damp tunnel seemed to melt away as the red eyes filled his vision and burned away his soul. Until those last few moments of his life, as he was lifted off his feet with a blissful euphoria, Rodge had never felt so high.

"It's *beautiful*!" he cried, almost in exultation, as the flesh-and-blood thing that had been Rodger was pulled apart, shredded into muscles, ligaments, marrow, and further, to molecules and atoms, which soaked into the earth of the Sanctuary.

*

"What's the problem?" Connie had to resist the urge to chew her nails.

"I don't know!" Danny said, a little too harshly. He'd been checking the connections by flashlight. Sweat had been dripping into his eyes from the moment he realized what was at stake. He had no idea what was wrong—only that this was a problem he couldn't fix and, as a result, the burned remnants of the human race were doomed to live the remainder of their troglodyte existence in a dark mausoleum. He tried again to get the backup working.

Danny checked the wiring.

Have all those years of abuse killed off a few too many brain cells?

He couldn't find anything wrong. It should be working, but it wasn't.

Then, without him doing anything more, the lights returned. He looked around as the Sanctuary released its collective breath. Danny sighed and smiled, but his relief was tempered by the realization that he didn't have any control over the Sanctuary's power source.

"Panic over, people!" Connie yelled.

"Wait, where's Michael?" someone called out.

Danny looked around and there were spaces where people should have been. Those who remained looked around to see who was missing.

Danny moved closer to Connie just as the lights began to flicker again.

"No! No!" someone began to scream, as the sound of tearing began to echo round the cavern.

The Sanctuary plunged into darkness again.

Some of the survivors elected to stand rooted to the spot, while others rushed to grab whatever they could find to defend themselves, and still others ran to lock themselves in their apartments.

The light returned—just for a moment—and showed the shocked and scared faces of those who remained.

When darkness fell again, it was greeted by the sound of sobbing.

Danny grabbed Connie, who was yelling at people to keep calm and stay together. He pulled her aside to stop her getting trampled in the panic. There was a brief flash from the lights before the Sanctuary went dark again. The tearing sound was getting louder… and was joined by screams.

Danny and Connie ran blindly, and the sound of chaos faded into the distance; for a moment, it was relief enough just to be away from the panic. They ducked into a tunnel entrance that was haloed in red—into the darkness of the Bridge of Souls.

CHAPTER 27

They made their way down the tunnel in the pitch black by running their hands across the cool, irregular surface of the walls. Danny didn't know how long they'd been walking before Connie stopped.

"We've got to go back," she said.

"Look, let's just-"

"We can't just abandon everyone! We've got to get back."

"Are you kidding! It's mayhem there, and… I don't know what's causing the lights to go out. None of this makes sense, Connie!"

"Calm… calm… calm…" repeated Connie. "Don't worry, we'll work something out. There's got to be a reason. We've just got to keep our heads. It's up to us to pull things together. Try and help as many as possible. Okay?" She put an arm on Danny's shoulder and smiled.

"Okay. Yeah, sure. Okay."

They turned around and began to make their way back.

"Did you have a plan?" asked Connie.

"A plan? Are you kidding? I was… I was… just trying to get away from the chaos." He shrugged. "I panicked, that's all. Just like everyone else, I guess."

They carried on walking.

"Shouldn't we have heard something by now?" Connie asked.

"Let's give it a little while longer. We're getting closer, sure of it."

After another few minutes, Connie looked around. "Are we going the right way?"

"We haven't veered off. We've only moved straight ahead. This has got to be the way. We've just got to keep going."

They walked for a further five, maybe ten minutes—neither of them was sure—before they heard a familiar sound like meat being torn apart.

Danny's panic returned. "We need to get away now."

The distant sound of screams echoed down the tunnel.

"This time, Daniel, I'm not arguing."

They ran blindly through the ink-black tunnel, stumbling and falling against each other, trying to put as much distance between themselves and that sound as they could. But the sound was increasing in volume.

Danny pulled Connie along, but nearly ran straight into a stone wall.

"Fuck!" he shouted.

"Calm! Calm! Calm!" Connie shouted back at Danny in a way that wasn't calm at all.

She took his face in her hands. "Daniel, come on! We've got to focus. If we give in to panic, that's the end of us!"

Danny took some deep breaths. "You're right, you're right. What now?" He had to shout to be heard over the noise.

Connie looked around. They were at a junction where the tunnel split into two.

"Right, right. So... look! The... noise is coming from that tunnel. Dunno what's down the other one, but," Connie squinted, "there's a weak light coming from that tunnel, so let's take that one."

More slowly than they really wanted to go, they eased their way down the tunnel towards the light.

The two of them were silent for a moment as they slowly but very deliberately tried to put as much distance between themselves and the tearing noise as they could. Danny could hear the pounding of his heart in his ears. Danny ran his fingers across the surface of the tunnel, trying to focus on the feeling of the cool rock under her fingertips.

We don't even know if we're going in the right direction! This could be a trap. We could be heading straight into... straight into whatever the fuck Oblivion Black is... Danny continued to breathe deeply and resisted the urge to give into blind animal panic. *And run, just run, just keep running until the lungs explode from my chest...*

"Look! Look! We must be heading in the right direction!" Connie was touching the tunnel wall to her right. For a moment Danny thought that she'd gone mad. In the gloom the wall looked no different to the rest of the rock stretching out, and Connie had to forcefully stop him from walking on. "Look!" she urged.

Danny stared at the wall. The fact that he could see anything at all was a good sign: the light was improving. Carved and painted on the wall were figures, not dissimilar to those found in the main cavern. "It's not exactly an arrow pointing 'this way,' is it?" he said.

"Isn't it? Which way are the figures looking?" She was right. All the figures were looking and gesturing in the direction they were heading.

But is it an instruction or a warning?

"We need to keep calm and keep moving," Connie said over the tearing noise.

Is it getting lighter?

"So how can we see a light if all the lights are off?" Danny asked.

Connie shrugged. "Maybe they've come back on?"

"I wouldn't have thought that the light from there could reach this deep."

"Look, I've done some exploring of these tunnels, and I found that some of them have a slight luminosity about them. Maybe there's an element of phosphorescence?"

They reached a fork in the tunnel and Danny's foot hit something. He looked down and noticed, scattered in the dirt, the gnarled fragments of human bones and what looked like the shattered husk of a skull. Danny took a deep breath, kicked dirt over the remains with his foot, and hoped Connie hadn't noticed.

"Which way now?" he asked. Both options seemed to have a faint low light in the distance.

"Uh, there seems to be a breeze coming from that direction." She pointed in the direction of the tunnel on the right.

The sound of the tearing became louder, and a nauseating smell of rotting meat wafted down the tunnel.

"It's Oblivion Black. She's coming for us," whispered Danny.

"She?"

Danny nodded. "I don't know how…"

"We've got to get away."

"We're never going to get away from Oblivion Black. She's never going to stop until she gets what she wants."

"And what's that?" Connie shouted over the noise.

A calm, easy euphoria unexpectedly enveloped Connie. She breathed in the earthy musk of the tunnel, and time seemed to stop for a moment. It felt as if a fresh breeze of air was blowing the fog from her mind.

Find the Totem.

"It's the Totem," she said.

"What?"

"We've got to find the Totem. That's the key to all of this. Why would Rodchenko be after it? Why would it be so important?"

"We don't know what it is, or even if it's in the Sanctuary."

"It must be in the Sanctuary. It must be here!"

"Jesus, Connie, but where? The Sanctuary's massive."

Connie chewed at her nails. "It's got to be in the Cave of Diamonds! Think about it! The cave paintings, and… and… it's there. It's the only place that's been untouched since the renovations. It's got to be there. We've got to get to the Cave of Diamonds."

They moved along the tunnel, and to their relief, the sound of the tearing was getting quieter; all they could hear was their own breathing.

"What's that?"

From ahead came the sound of shuffling. Something was coming towards them. Danny looked around for something to defend them with. There was nothing, so he crouched, ready to throw himself at whatever came round the corner.

Is this it? Is this how it ends? Crouched in a damp tunnel underground?

Two figures appeared. Danny felt a wave of relief when he recognized them, although his mind drew a blank when it came to the woman's name. Connie came to his rescue.

"Michella! Stue!" she yelled.

The two couples ran together and hugged.

"How did you get here?" asked Connie.

"After the lights went off, people went pretty much apeshit," said Michella.

"We basically went for the tunnels and got away from the panic," said Stue.

"That's pretty much what we did," said Danny. "Wait, which route did you take?"

"We headed into the Cave of Diamonds. We found a tunnel right at the back of that. We ran into it and we've been running blind since then," said Stue.

"So, these tunnels are connected? We can get to the Cave of Diamonds? Can you remember which way you came?" asked Danny.

Michella and Stue looked at each other.

"I guess so, but we were just trying to get away. We'll try our best."

"We've got to get back to the Cave of Diamonds. That's the key," said Connie.

"The key to what?" asked Stue.

"Let's not run before we can crawl," replied Connie. "Lead us back to the Cave of Diamonds."

Stue led them through the maze of dim tunnels. A few times, he said that it didn't look right, so they backtracked and took another tunnel.

"What happened to everyone else?" asked Danny.

"I dunno. You heard that noise… People panicked. It was everyone for themselves."

"I'm sorry we ran. We just… we didn't know what to do. I just had to get away."

"You and everyone else."

"Come on, we've got to keep moving," said Connie.

"But where are we going? What are we doing?" Danny asked, and took a deep breath.

They felt a slight breeze whistling down the tunnel.

"Go towards the breeze," said Connie.

The tearing sound was getting louder. They picked up the pace accordingly, only to come up against a rough blank wall.

"That's impossible!" Connie yelled, as the tearing sound grew.

"Calm, calm, calm. Isn't that what you taught me?" said Danny. He turned back to the others. "We must've taken a wrong turning."

"There was another tunnel back there a little," said Michella. "Stue?"

Stue nodded and led them back along the tunnel to a junction.

"Are you sure?" asked Connie.

"Yeah. Yeah, this is the way," said Stue, but he didn't sound entirely convinced.

*

As the four of them walked on, Connie brought her fingers up to her mouth and began to chew on the nails.

We're lost. We're lost deep in the mountain. Danny thought I hadn't seen those human remains, but I saw them. We're going to wander around and around in this mountain until our bones join those. No! No! I'm going to tell Stue to head back. We've taken a wrong turn somewhere. We'll keep calm and find our way…

She spat out some fingernails and cleared her throat.

"Stue, I think we-"

"Look!" Michella shouted, and pointed down the tunnel.

Connie strained her eyes. "I can't…"

But eventually, they all could see the dim, green-tinged light at the end of the tunnel, the same green light she'd associated with the Cave of Diamonds.

"Well done, Stue! Come on, we can move quicker!"

*

As he emerged from the constraints of the tunnel, Danny found himself at the back of the Cave of Diamonds and able to stand upright. He didn't know if it was because they'd come from the darkness of the tunnels, but the green light from the stalagmites seemed intense.

It feels as if we're in the mouth of a beast.

*

Connie looked around at the moss-covered walls and closed her eyes. "What was in the paintings?"

"Fucked if I know." Danny watched her run round the cave. In the distance came the sound of tearing meat off bone.

Calm... calm... calm...

She tried to bring the cave paintings to mind, hoping to map them over the cave.

The sound was deafening and seemed to envelope them.

Connie rushed over to the altar and tried to push it over, but it wasn't budging. "Danny, quick, help me."

He ran over and threw himself against it, the sweat pouring from him. Stue and Michella joined in, and gradually, they felt it first give, then eventually topple over. When the dust settled beneath the altar, they could see a discolored patch of earth.

Please, God, let me be right...

Connie began to scrabble at the dirt. The others, almost unthinkingly, followed her example. Now the sound seemed to be all around them. They dug deeper and deeper, but found nothing.

Danny leaned back. "Connie, we've got-"

"No, it's got to be here." She carried on digging.

Stue stopped. "Look! Look!"

Danny leaned over. "What? I can't …"

But then they saw it. In the dirt, they could make out a shape.

Connie and Michella pulled it out of the hole. It was roughly the size of large loaf of bread and it had a musty, earthy smell. Discolored animal skins, fastened tightly with sticks, leaves, and mud around the object.

"Is that it? Is that the Totem?" asked Danny. It didn't seem much different from the Totem that he'd put together.

"It's got to be. Come on."

They ran out of the Cave of Diamonds and made their way back to the ground level and the piazza.

*

The scene that confronted them caused Danny to stop in his tracks.

It was a vision of hell.

In the aural maelstrom of rending flesh, he could hear people screaming and sobbing. The light continued to flicker, and something was sparking red in the piazza, sending shadows swirling around the space. Debris still lay around from the explosions, but the blinking light twisted them into cruel and unfamiliar shapes.

Danny forced himself to run after the others, and then nearly ran into the back of them when they came to a halt.

The tearing sound had stopped.

"What …"

In the flickering hell, high above them, were two red glowing eyes.

Danny could hear heavy breathing, like a large dog at rest.

Oblivion Black towered over them. Danny thought she must have been at least fifteen feet tall. Her fur was thin in parts and missing completely in others, but what fur remained was matted, brown-and-gray, and tangled with twigs, leaves, small bright rocks, and the bleached bones of small animals. She had a long snout, a wet nose, and long-healed scars criss-crossed her face and body. She opened her mouth, revealing razor-sharp teeth, and let loose a roar that echoed around the cavern.

Her eyes, which turned upon them once more, were ringed with dark, pulled flaps of discolored skin, and the eyes themselves glowed red like twin furnaces. Muscles and sinews bulged like twisted rope on her long arms, her long fingers tipped with jagged claws like black daggers. She shifted her weight from one leg to the other as she surveyed them.

She looked coiled, ready to spring.

*

Calm… calm… calm…

Connie shuffled forward with her eyes closed, expecting to

feel the bulk of the creature crash against her at any second.

She was so close now that she could feel the rank breath. She opened her eyes and could see that the creature had a chipped tooth in the front of her mouth. Connie looked into the crimson eyes of Oblivion Black and, in what she assumed would be her final thought, the memory of her time in the hospital flooded back—even the smell of Lloyd's aftershave—and of everything she'd lost. The memory of the cold numbness she had felt came rushing back to her when she looked into the creature's eyes.

Something changed.

Oblivion Black let out a high-pitched whimper, and her eyes became heavy with moisture. Both Connie and Oblivion Black felt tugged downwards by the heavy sadness of stolen possibilities.

Oblivion Black padded up to the Totem, sniffed it, paused, sniffed it again. She made a plaintive mewling noise and gently clamped the Totem in her jaws, turned and padded away.

Connie realized that she'd been holding her breath and relaxed with deep relief.

"Holy shit." Connie ran a hand over her face and nearly collapsed.

*

Oblivion Black went deep into the mountain, back to parts which no human had ever reached. She retreated and found her nest. She took some of the whisper-thin fur she had saved from her pup and buried her nose in it for a moment before moving round in diminishing circles in the twigs and hay in dim remembrance of a burial rite from centuries ago.

Then she dug a deep hole and placed the remains of her pup inside. She stared at it with tired red eyes for a moment before covering it with dirt. When she had fully covered the pup, Oblivion Black patted down the earth and lied on top of it, finally providing a resting place, finally being able to protect her baby.

For the moment, Oblivion Black could rest.

*

Danny, Connie, and the survivors built a wall across the sides of the Bridge of Souls. They then dug two deep ridges either side and found two large planks of wood to embed in them, to crisscross the entrance, and used rubble left over from the explosion to shore up the wall. The mood amongst the survivors lifted when they'd finished building the defensive wall. After the work was done, everyone drifted away except Danny and Connie, who stood staring at the walled-off tunnel.

"What's next for us? Can we survive on what we've got?"

"We're going to have to. We have no other choice."

Danny still hoped that Rodger might turn up, but in his heart of hearts, he knew he wouldn't.

*

Connie looked around the boardroom. The paint on the walls was peeling badly, and was that mold in the corners? The room was beginning to smell very ripe, as if something had crawled behind a wall and died—then again, with water being rationed, everyone smelled bad.

Danny barreled into the room, dirt under his nails and streaked across his face. "How's life, Mr. Head Farmer?" asked Connie.

Danny gave her a tired smile. "Yeah, life's good." And he slumped in a chair, which gave an alarming creak. "So, you called me?"

Connie smiled as, from underneath the table, she brought up a bottle of Wild Turkey, which was three quarters full.

"Holy fuck! Where did you get that?"

"A final gift from Sarah."

Connie put two grubby glasses on the table and poured out generous measures. She held her glass up.

"Nasty shit for nasty times."

They both took big gulps. Danny felt the sting in the back of his nose and throat and it brought a tear to his eye.

Connie winced, then smiled. "Lordy lord, that hits the spot!"

"Connie, do you think…"

"Yes?"

"Do you think there might be something down here with us?"

"What, you mean bats?"

Danny started laughing and Connie joined him.

Eventually the laughter petered out and Connie wiped her face.

"Jesus, look at us!" she said. "What's going to become of us?"

Danny ran a hand over his face, smearing the dirt further. "You don't expect an answer, do you?" He sounded very tired.

Connie smiled and shook her head.

The door flew open. Stan, rushed in blinking rapidly. "Quick, you've got to come with me!"

Oh, shit, what now?

Stan had already left before they could give voice to that question, so they followed him into the communications room. Stan sat down in front of the radio, which crackled with static.

"What?" asked Danny.

"Wait! Listen!" Stan leaned towards the microphone and pressed a button.

"Can you hear us? Is there anyone there?"

From the static came a fragile "Hello?"

The End

COMING
DECEMBER 2023

Oblivion Black: Poisoned Kingdom

Visit:

www.atlasfloyd.com
www.stratospherebooks.com
www.oblivionblack.com

to sign up to the author's newsletters

ACKNOWLEDGEMENTS

In a rough alphabetical order:

Thanks to Karl Blockwell for a keen eye and laughs, Neil Davies for the brilliant illustrations.

Tim Lebbon for his kind words and encouragement, Chris Nurse for the amazing covers, Mark Thomas for the book interior design, Steve O'Brien, Miles Hamer and Paul Kirkley for frequent email fuckwittery.

To Brian Willis for an extra pair of eyes and suggestions.

Kate Mattacks, Helen Woodhouse and Chad Oakes at Nomadic Pictures

Lightning Source UK Ltd.
Milton Keynes UK
UKHW051550310822
408071UK00003B/98/J